STIGMATA

STIGMATA

Bill Reed

a novel

This reprint published independently by Reed Independent 2015
Melbourne, Australia

First published under ISBN 0908090358 in 1980 by
Hyland House Publishing Pty Limited

Printed by CreateSpace, an Amazon.com company

Available from Amazon.com, CreateSpace.com, and other retail outlets. Ebook
formats are available from all major online ebook retailers.
paperback: ISBN13-9780994280510
ebook: ISBN13-9780994239952

Cover: original by Jack Larkin; reprint redesign by Lahiru Sameera, Dart Lanka
Production, Colombo, Sri Lanka

National Library of Australia Cataloguing-in-Publication entry
Creator: Reed, Bill, 1939-author.
Title: Stigmata / Bill Reed.
ISBN: 9780994280510 (paperback)
Subjects: Brothers and sisters--Fiction.
Dewey Number: A823.3

National Library of Australia Cataloguing-in-Publication entry
Creator: Reed, Bill, 1939-author.
Title: Stigmata / Bill Reed.
ISBN: 9780994239952 (ebook)
Subjects: Brothers and sisters--Fiction.
Dewey Number: A823.3

For all the innocents toughing it out.

Chapter 1

The sex crimes of that north-eastern corner of the island were crimes against the region's own children.

Not one tourist child was known to have been touched during the ten years that the rapist kept the island in shock, in anger, in horror, in witch-hunt. The maniac was evidently a local, which made the crimes even more monstrous. He was someone who had to know the wetdark moors, the farm houses and the cottages. He was someone who knew where the children slept, who so knew the local terrain that, having taken the children from their beds and assaulted them, he could slip away across the seeping moors, in the dead of night and in any weather.

It was a reign of terror for ten years. For ten years the island rapist remained the alter ego of the north-easterners. That someone so satanic from among their own kind could so prey upon all human decencies finally became so shameful to every inhabitant that it was as if their very ineffectuality in catching him was in itself a show of perversion of not really *wanting* to catch him — of not even caring to root out an evil at the very core of their community.

It was all made worse by the mainland newspapers gaining mileage out of hinting that the island region was a dark and dripping and sinister and primordial place where satanic forces marauded and were harboured. A place, they hinted, not of any earthly location or of any human landscape but perhaps a fictional Gothic land of unspeakable bubblings out of an unspeakably evil community past.

The sins of the father visiting the children.

Except for one twelve-year-old girl, all of the raped children were under ten. Of the twenty-four victims, exactly half were boys. Each child had been woken up by a man wearing an old gabardine overcoat and a latex face mask, threatened with a carving knife,

1

carried out of the bedroom window usually to a place away from the home; there raped; there threatened to keep silent. Some were returned home. All had scratches (similar to claw marks) on the sides of their faces running from the temples, down the cheeks. Plough lines. Furrowings.

During those ten years a series of police manhunts took place, but each proved to be just as ineffective as the one before. At one time or another, practically every man in the region had been interviewed and had had a blood sample taken. The rapist, through the analysis of his semen, was known to have 0 Group blood, and this at least eliminated forty per cent of the 30,000 male population. Senior police officers from the mainland cities had at various times been called over to conduct the investigations; vigilante groups were formed to patrol the region's hedge-rowed roads on Friday and Saturday nights, the nights that the rapist generally struck.

But still the child rapist eluded capture. The community in the north-eastern corner of the island was beginning to turn in on itself out of fear and frustration.

At eleven-thirty on the Saturday night of 4 April 1958, police constables John Risdon and Tom Ginn were approaching the intersection of the St Helens and Ansons Bay roads when a 1954 Ford suddenly shot through the intersection, swerved just in time to avoid crashing into the police car, then sped off. It had no headlights on.

Risdon and Ginn gave chase just in time to pick up the car in their headlights before it swung off the road onto a side track. This track petered out into the garden of a farm house where the Ford careered into the field. The driver leapt out and began running. Risdon managed to pick out his form in the dark and went after him. He brought the man down with a rugby tackle. The man struggled violently and slipped Risdon's grip twice before Ginn caught up with them.

In the man's sports coat pocket they found a black wig, a pair of woollen gloves, a small torch, two pieces of sashcord and a pajama cord. More surprising were the rows of individually sharpened nails that had been sewn upright into the shoulder of the coat, along the lapels and around each wrist. The police naturally thought of the rows of scratches on the children's faces.

Back at the man's home, in the office abutment which doubled as a bed sitting room after the man and his wife had given up the marital pretence, the police found an alcove behind a black velvet curtain. It seemed to have the appearance of an altar. On the wall behind a central table hung a wooden dagger with its blade pointing upwards. To the left of that hung a communion plate; and to the right was a set of bathroom shelves containing a china toad, a chalice-shaped glass and two black candles.

On the table was a single book. It was Wyndham Lewis's *The Soul of Marshal Gilles de Rais,* the fifteenth century French nobleman who had kidnapped, raped, then murdered by decapitation an unknown number of children. Gilles de Rais was not only a mass children's murderer. He was, too, a Satanist.

Within twenty-four hours of the man's arrest the police had combed through the office abutment twice, yet they still had not found anything that could not be claimed to be circumstantial. They knew they had the right man; they equally knew that, if they didn't come up with something more concrete, they might only be able to hold him for minor driving offences and resisting arrest. It was Detective Ross Marsh who changed that.

A junior detective, Marsh had the nagging feeling that they had overlooked something in the two careful screenings of the office abutment. The next evening he decided to try again out of sheer bloody mindedness. Back at the farm house he concentrated again on the alcove and was examining the carpet felt with which it was lined when he noticed the cupboard next to the alcove move fractionally. He immediately reported the fact.

Behind that cupboard, which was finally forced from the wall, the police discovered a secret room — in fact it was another cupboard — and in there found semen-and mud-stained clothing, including an overcoat which, like the sports coat, was studded with lines of nails. They found, too, a latex face mask. But, most importantly, they found hair samples on the overcoat that matched the hair of the latest victim.

For years the people who lived in the north-eastern coastal town did not entertain the same doubts as the police seemed to have.

For them, the attacks were the work of only one man. The hermit Emile Gascoigne.

No one remembered exactly how Emile Gascoigne had arrived in the area. No one seemed to know how long he had been there. But stay, emerging from some suggestion of a French maritime past, he had, long ago.

Since the hermit evinced everything the police were looking for, the locals could not understand how he could be left alone to remain free. It was not only that he kept to himself and would only grunt when he wasn't talking fiercely and insanely to himself. It was that he was so basically *foreign* that he had just to be a sexual deviant. What more could be so pumpingly obvious?

The hermit lived in a filthy little shack along the cliffs; it was so derelict that he had a single sapling propping up the ceiling above his bed. He had a foreign accent — not the rustically strong Midlands accents of the locals, but something of a *patois* French inflexion when he spoke English. He was coarse and he had a coarse, hard-grating voice just right for rasping obscenities in the night. Moreover he wore an old gabardine coat, tied with string, which smelt of oil and musty damp. This was precisely the description given by the tenth, and oldest, girl of all the victims. They all knew, as well, that the hermit wandered about that dark and twisted countryside at night, talking fiercely to himself, emerging and receding, appearing and disappearing, mostly frighteningly, sometimes annoyingly. Putrid wafts. They knew, they knew.

4

There had been, once, that complaint by the Quint girl that the hermit Emile Gascoigne had followed her home, mumbling. Hands in pockets. Seeming to *soak* at her. The hermit had nearly been tarred and feathered then. Except that too many knew the mind of the Quint girl.

That they did not tar and feather Emile Gascoigne was of little compensation for him, though; for thereafter, wherever the hermit went, there would be the one or some who would spit at him or catcall upon him or drive their stones at his huddled form. It was not only the children who did this. Young or old, they all knew.

Besides, since they had begun to make it known to the hermit Emile Gascoigne that they knew he was the rapist, the attacks had plainly stopped. The people of the town knew they had the rapist of the north-eastern part of the island scared off, even if they could not prove him to be a hermit, the hermit.

The hermit was finally picked up by the police and taken in for questioning that lasted two days. The people of Boobyalla watched the police car drive away with the arrested hermit and came to pleasurably know that at last the authorities had come to listen to what they had been saying all along. Noddings.

Down at the headquarters, the hermit Emile Gascoigne was stripped of his clothing and made to give blood and hair specimens. These were sent to Sydney for analysis. A mere formality. Even the police knew now.

Yet the police who cross-examined the hermit came also to know one very odd thing. It was that, despite his appearance, the hermit was credibly intelligent and credibly not without a credible indignation about being linked with the child rapes. Then the result of the blood and hair tests came in.

On the following morning, some of the citizens of that north-eastern corner of the island were up early enough to see the police car bring Emile Gascoigne back to his shack on the cliff. He was dressed only in an old army blanket.

The hermit probably had expected that the police would have searched his little shack, but soon also came to see that every window had been smashed by the righteous north-eastern islanders of that town who knew they knew the righteous All about him. This was far more than all the threats, all the insults, all the spitting, all the stones. The hermit knew now how he was in grave danger. There was no shuffling away any more.

So he dressed in what few things he had left, then spiked a note to his door that told the vandals that his home was wired with dynamite, though it wasn't. He then made his way down to the bay, where he begged a fisherman to take him out to the tiny Waterhouse Islet, a half a kilometre or so off the coast there.

Waterhouse Islet is only about four hectares in area. It had on it only a few derelict fishing shacks, long ago abandoned. The hermit Emile Gascoigne jumped out of the boat as best he could and forced himself ashore against the sea pulling at his trousers. And the people on that north-eastern corner of the island could realise they had at last removed their children's rapist from their midst.

The hermit Gascoigne's survival for a whole year alone on his tiny islet was seen to be a modern day miracle by the mainland television crew that filmed him as a latter-day Robinson Crusoe. This film of his plight, his persecution and his survival on only what he could gather from the shore was to be shown around the world. In the few rags he had left at that stage and his now hugely-flowing beard, the hermit Gascoigne looked for all the world like a mischievous minor prophet, as one journalist wrote. The resulting worldwide public sympathy anointed that metaphor.

For the people who lived in that coastal town of Boobyalla, this reception to the TV film was the second recent slap in the face by the outside world.

The first time was six months earlier when, while the hermit Emile

Gascoigne huddled his little nestled body behind those slats of his shelter on his tiny islet, a nine-year-old lad was taken from his bedroom in a house near Alberton, piggy-backed to a nearby field and there assaulted. While Emile Gascoigne, windswept and cold-torn, sat huddled in the islet night.

Meanwhile, parcels of food and clothing for the hermit came pouring in to the television station from all over the world. Save our persecuted prophet. The living martyr, the living proof. Only one or two of the parcels reached the hermit, but by this time it did not matter for, a month later, John and Jenny Salem, in a flush of in-honeymoon enthusiasm (he, scooping her away from the glittering world of city nightclubs; she, bowled over by this out-of-towner actually proving true to his words) got to Emile Gascoigne with their offer. In return for fair keep and a fair and secluded cottage, they offered him what they called 'patching work' around the hardier regions of their southwestern mainland property outside of Portland. What they meant was an odd-jobs job. Undisturbed for a hermit's dignity.

So the hermit Emile Gascoigne accepted to wander eremitic in the non-existent pilgrim deserts metaphorically within the Salem property on the mainland. And so, with his paid-for ticket held out in front of him like a food tray, he boarded, finally, the ship that was to fleet him across the rough and awesome-sea'd strait that divided the island from the mainland there for his new life. The television and radio crews were there to see him off, yes, but also to chat against the moralistic persecutors who lived in the north-eastern island town of Boobyalla in what they still described as the sex maniac and rapist's wet-dark moors north-eastern region. A place beyond all decent bounds.

Hidden and watching the hermit Gascoigne embark on the ship was a boy. He verged on being small and brown as he verged on being a teenager. The boy was shaking with premonition as he watched the hermit go up the gangplank. The boy did not know what he was trembling for. He could not know, but perhaps was even then beginning to feel, that in a few months he would be branded as the son of the rapist.

7

The boy, the son, watched, with his mother, the police return to the room with his father. The boy watched his father's face. He could not understand. He was still watching his father's face when his mother suddenly attacked and slashed at his father's face with the knife. That was when they all seemed to start screaming.

The boy, the son, screamed, too. By some shift in the pattern, he found himself between his father and his mother, and found himself down on his knees looking up at his father's bloodying face up there. Way up, right up there. He, the son, the boy, was watching the blood pour out from the slash above his father's eye. He did not take his eyes from it for as long as he could. He, the boy, had stopped screaming.

He was never, either, to forget his father's crutch smell. His face deeply and fearfully buried in there finally. A fiend's miasma. But his father. They told him his father dressed in woman's clothes. But it was his father.

The boy, the son of the child rapist.

Chapter 2

The hermit hesitates only for a brief moment before he steps out of his cottage. He knows the man is watching him from over there. He pulls the cottage's door closed behind him, but does not bother to lock it. Out there, at the far edges of the Salems' property, even when the man has come again to watch him, there is no need to lock the front door of the cottage. There is no point. It is the same about every six months when the man appears to watch him leave the cottage.

The hermit Gascoigne has never known who the man is. He has never challenged the man in all the years, maybe five, that he knows for certain the man has come to watch him. The man appears. The man is no longer there. The man has those eyes watching him or the eyes are no longer there to watch Emile.

It has become as simple as that. Almost. And almost not quite. For Emile Gascoigne has never known who the man is, nor what he looks like from close up. He only knows that there is, again, this moment of hesitation going out into the ionian (he remembers the word actively again) shadows softly mewing against his lonely cottage.

This time when he sensed the man outside, the hermit Gascoigne shivered as he hesitates. A frost a-spike thrilling the morning. And the eyes. Come again there to watch him again. But this time oddly irregularly. Emile knows that. And has shivered. But is still not locking the front door of his little cottage behind him.

He, Emile, leaves in the gum boots that will be needed today. He is still uncomfortable moving along the path he himself has worn up. Agitated as an animal by the give-away of the chocolate slatterny of the mud of it; twenty years of daily plaffing at it since a Tasmanian time televised.

Bare. He is bare. His head is bare. His hair is bare. His old

9

raincoat is bare, threaded and tied. A routine bare. A life alone and bare. A thing wanted called Miss Avery. A falling in love at his age. Oh, bare. He knows his mind should be on other things, like his 'patchworking'. Like nursing that unformed, large and enveloping grudge about something he knows not about, on anyone he knows or knows not, like the eyesman watching him now. Like that surly anger that has kept him half sane and surviving. He should not, either, be thinking yet again about the sighting of Miss Avery half an hour away across a warty granite land. Dripping today. Rainy last night. But he is. His loneliness weak and fervid during the night because he has decided to try to see her again this day. The hermit feeling the tendons of aloneness.

The man is there. The eyes are there. The hermit passes by. He knows what the man will do, because that's what the man does when he has come around again in that watching wait. It's as simple as that, possibly for them both. Emile Gascoigne, arthritic and skin gone to parched clay seemingly to embody a clockwork mechanism as he walks, believes that — that it's as simple as that between him and the eyesman.

For he knows that the man will do as he always does each six months or so. The hermit knows that he will be followed today for most of the day, then left three-parts through the afternoon. He knows that when he will arrive back at his cottage, something dead will be left on his doorstep, on that worn bluestone slab. A carcass, a skeleton, a discarded skin, a socketed skull, but always of something small, like a bird, a lizard, a mouse. Pickup of the ants. Laid to shrine on the bluestone slab of Emile Gascoigne's front door. Laid alongside of, always, a bottle of whisky. It's been as simple as that for each of the other times the man has come to watch him.

Two years earlier, the hermit Gascoigne had arrived home to catch the man redhanded in the act of doing that. From the distance, he knew who it wasn'twas and what the man was doing. So Emile stopped. He stopped and hung his head demurely and hung around at that distance to allow the man to lay what he wanted to on the bluestone step there. Trying very hard not to look closer. The man did not hurry because he too sensed Emile was there. They both let it happen as it happens. It was as simple as that. When the man had finished he walked quickly off, not looking back, and Emile came on, not watching him go. Careful, both, not to break eggs. Besides the whisky was always good for the two or three nights it lasted.

Everything is usually and always relative. The hermit Emile Gascoigne knows that. He has sensed the man following him worked instinctively like that, too. Except this time. As he walks away from the eyes of the man this time, the hermit Gascoigne does not sense the man is there this time for what is as usual. This time he is sensing that somehow this time is different, that somehow the man is there to *know* something more.

He half skates along the wet chocolate mud strip towards the house of Miss Avery. His oldendirty hands swinging stiffly as though he is gliding along two hand rails. The man behind knowing that the black jags that are the old hermit's fingernails are pudging themselves against old man's palms, the lines on which are a seer's dream. Perhaps. Both aware of the sensation of still air around them.

The man Allan Dere stands half concealed and half exposed behind the pine tree there by the hermit Gascoigne's cottage. He always thought it was a gum. In all those years, at those regular intervals he has come, always a gum. He notices now the retinated lumps of the pine bark and knows he has been wrong. He finds that so intense an insult at this time, at this right now, that rage wells up and incarnadines all that he is seeing for this moment. But calming as he leans into and through the trunk of that tree. Half concealed and half exposed. He cannot be more sickened by his perceptions, anyway. And thinks and smiles a half concealed and half exposed smile that he should stay with his new insanity.

Half exposed and half concealedcongealed. As simply usual,

11

except that in his pocket, this time, the man Dere has no skull or skeleton or decorticated skin or tail, nor any somesuch small longdead thing for the hermit's bluestone step. And he has no whisky bottle in his hand for the hermit Gascoigne's front doorstep. And he has no car two kilometres off across that flinty tiger snake country. The man has come with nothing but what he stands up in.

But the man has the perception of the tree being a pine this time. He has the perception *of* Emile this time. And he has the aggression that this time it matters not this way or that if he is half concealed and half exposed, anyway. This time he is here and this time he is not only looking and able to follow. This time he is watching and closely observing. So the man Dere continues to watch and to *see* Emile Gascoigne from the pine. He is not there to be near but to stalk. Feeling and sensing and tasting and licking and hearing and probing at the hermit far more than ever he has. Before. All those times before. All leading up to this. Perhaps. After all, and finally, perhaps leading to this. He could, the man Dere feels, reach out even from this distance and scratch at the dirt caking the old man's filthy, hallowed skin. Unwashed and saintly ascetic in the Nicene desert, perhaps, of this non-deserted mainland land.

Allan Dere, this time not so quite as simply as usual, has come to pay obeisance. To lay his penance on the bluestone front step. This time, finally.

There is no hurry to follow this time. He knows instinctively where the old hermit is going. There will be a time enough to follow after, but first, empty-handed, without the altar offerings, the man Dere moves out from behind the pine he has already forgotten as being pine and trudges towards the cottage of Emile Gascoigne.

Sits there upon the step. The bluestone slab of the front doorstep. His back heavy against the pine-wobbled door. And absorbs the smell of the hermit Emile Gascoigne there. There is, too, a moment when he tries to see from there as Emile Gascoigne might see from there, every day emerging from his cocoon of aloneness and silence. But knowing the perspectives are not the same. The levels of the eyes, for example. A hermit's eye; is it higher or lower? Does it take in or shut out? The moment slips away. The man Dere suddenly realizing that, whatever the why of him coming here these last years, he does not want to get inside Emile Gascoigne's daily sighting anymore.

Allan Dere climbs up in that damp darkish morning to his feet. He walks slowly around the place known as the hermit Gascoigne's cottage. The damp in the walls, the fungal stars on the walls. The fallen plaster like, too, the shed dead skins he has previous times put on the bluestone slab that is the front doorstep. Around the back, the tap from the rain tank drips onto the rust glacier in the bath, stained or never stained, whichever, by the hermit's holy dirt. There, too, the corrugated iron sheets that are the outside wall of the bathroom are twisted apart from each other.

The man Dere turns his eyes away from the gaps between the corrugated iron sheets there on the image that perhaps he is peeping into the inviolable centre of the hermit's cave. The holy and hanging aroma of unearthly uncare. The grubbed piety commended by an unworldly God.

Then shudders. The man Dere shudders, then pulls himself up short. He has not come here this time to peeptom on that image again. He moves to pick up a piece of plumbing pipe, iron-heavy and cast, and swipes into the front window of the hermit Gascoigne's cottage with a wide and solemn arc of a swing.

And as he does so he feels the diagonal searing again across his right eye. It seems to burn and glow even beyond his head. Come to him again. And gotten beloved.

The hermit Emile Gascoigne pulls out the weeds on the side of the

13

road by the fence of Miss Avery. He is working quickly, in-
dustriously, in trying to impress. He cannot know that from inside
the house he only looks strobe-lit. Stiffly shifting by eager little
jerks. He probably knows, but hopes never to be sure, that no one
is watching him from inside the house of Avery. Instead he keeps
worrying at the weeds on the side of the road outside the house of
Avery.

The hermit waits still for a sign from her. There is nothing else to
do when his world, despite the fact that he has left it long ago, is
so fictional. His world is so fictional that he cannot even realise he
is absolutely right about it. So the hermit Emile Gascoigne waits
continuously for a sign from the woman Avery inside.

Beyond him, beyond the peeling palings and across that distance-
apart that is the front yard of the house of Avery, is Miss Avery's
house. Only the old pump to the old water well and the old
remnants of the old front garden path break the odalisque wild
wheat's field there. There are the apple trees to the side called the
left and the drive to the side called the right and the low acacia
shrubs jutting against the front wall of the Avery house. The
house's eyes sunken behind the shrubs and its own front wall as
they fancifully call to Emile Gascoigne from a meekish retreat he
somehow understands so well. And urges to it silently for its sign
for him.

But the house stays obfusc and without ply. It watches Emile
Gascoigne and, yet again today, *blands* at him until he begins to
feel the discomfort of the anonymous stare and begins to get more
jerkily peckish at the weeds. He begins to shake with fear and
hope again that the world of all his life has come to this. The
house of Avery. And does not see the man Dere come out from the
shrub fifty metres down to stand comically, as in comic, glaring a
cartoon glare at the hermit Gascoigne and the house of Avery.
Then to move on across the road and to enter at the far corner of
the Avery property, Miss Avery's property.

The man Dere crawls on his hands and knees beneath the bottom
wire strand of the fence and the silver leaf bush and when he

stands, he stands better for Emile Gascoigne to see him at a closer distance than they have ever viewed each other before. Allan Dere stands straight and large upon the hermit Gascoigne.

The old man is flicked at the edge of his eyesight, whipcords his head around to where the man Dere stands. He cannot see, but can feel, the already-triumph in the eyeman's eyes. He sees for the first time the ordinary height of the man, the ordinary brownness of the man, but not, this time, the ordinary aura of the man. It is after, too, the man Dere has already swung away at a passable trot that the hermit Gascoigne registers what the ordinary brown man has said, finally, aloud to him. He has heard spoken:

'I know this. They'll have to carry me out of here.'

And then has seen the man disappear around the wide side of the property that skirts the Avery house, towards the back of the property. *On* it, unthinkably.

Emile turns quickly towards the house of Miss Avery. The house has not moved. He has expected it to move, but it has not moved. He can only wait and whistle to get some attention which won't come, he thinks, but finds it is himself who has moved. It is himself that is hurrying away from the Avery house. And can feel, but cannot feel why, the feeling of grief beginning to tighten his chest again after these many years. He only knows something has caught up with him with a monstrous overfamiliarity. The olfacts of his own old clothing beginning to rise even to himself, as he jogs away trying to run.

As the old hermit Emile Gascoigne passes the meat work's back door the boy slips on the viscera he is blurting the air out of. The blood and the guts slide down the run off towards Emile Gascoigne's feet. The flies seem to hop at him with it. The boy has let out a 'hey' of surprise. The tacky smell of blood momentarily disturbs Emile's stomach, and the overwhelming pungedom of body gases. He shrivels with the contact but forces himself on, for this, through Salem's Meat Works, is the only quick way from the house of Avery to the Salems' house. Forcing himself into a peopled landscape. This is not any way a hermit should go.

The thud of the .22 bullet and the thump as the bullock's body crashes against the iron railing. Dragged in, still kicking, for the throat to be cut, still moaning, and the blood to be let gush, still bubbling.

The boy hooks his hand in the bloody and now dirt-rendered viscera and heaves them back onto the platform, then stands up and watches the old hermit go past, stamping, absent-mindedly, with the heel of his bloody boot, on the balloon pockets of the guts. Which fart. The boy does not know he is subconsciously making them fart in time with the jogtrotting steps of Emile Gascoigne. As a boy he has never been allowed to seek out the old hermit Gascoigne that he and his mates knew lived somewhere around. The Salems forebade no. He tries to remember if it was lucky or unlucky to have the hermit look directly at him. Should he have crossed himself and then feel a bit of a dope? Instead he moves to the hose and picks up the broom. Another viscera, shoved from inside the shed, slides, half-rotating to wobble upon the first, but the flies, undisturbed, remain at the boy's eyes and mouth. At squint and in pout after the hermit had gone on.

Jenny Salem edges nearer to the edge of the verandah. She was moving from the garden to inside when something at the end of the driveway has caught her eye. She has turned her head and has caught a glimpse and has seen the form of a man slide across the screen of what lies beyond the gate. Now she strains her eyes in peer, but now there is not another movement. Her best feature, as it is said, that neck, inclines as though willing her eyes to see around the corners of the fence up there. That is what it looks like, but it isn't so. Her eyes are now looking for a confirmation of who she thinks she has seen.

There is another movement down by the gate. The movement

itself is a rustle. There is something unspeakably urgent in it, yet unspeakably shy. Still the woman Salem waits from her hide. She is sure now. But does not want to frighten the hermit away. She will wait there within the ease of her growing amusement until Emile Gascoigne comes out into the open. And will wait as long as is necessary. It always, she knows, had to be sometime that he would come out of himself.

When Emile Gascoigne, for the first time in the twenty years since he had been on the Salem property, comes out into the open, the woman Salem almost, then, wishes him back. At that moment she almost would have him go back to his cottage and re-lick at his loneliness until he regains its flavour. His old hermit's mouth is open, as though he was screaming for help. Jenny Salem stiffens, but she would not know it. She wills the old man to turn back. Nothing should turn out as simply unromantic as this.

It is only when he stops that the cynical twist to the woman's mouth returns, as it does now in these days, as it never would have ten years ago. She wants to laugh aloud at Emile Gascoigne's hesitation halfway down the driveway. She feels the urge to go back on to the verandah and jeer at him. Taunt him. Become, deliciously, a child again, and wedgetail at the stupid, silly, dotty, dirtydotty, filthyspitty shuffling old crazy hermit who sticks and stones can break. She will not notice that her knuckles are going white holding onto the window ledge there as she thinks this. For already the hermit has stopped in his tracks. What am I doing? And has taken a step backwards. Then another.

The woman Salem shouts at him. He cannot hear her shout his name from in there. The old man has taken another step backwards. She flings aside the curtain, an automatic gesture of annoyance. And hurries outside, onto the verandah again. But, as soon as he has seen the front door open, the old hermit Gascoigne has turned and has started to jog away again. His heart pounding with incredulity at what he has caught himself doing. As he feels the panic rising, he plunges into the bushes to his right and hears at the same time the woman Salem shout his name.

17

The hermit edges back towards his recluse's shack, again experiencing that particular feeling of shame under the possible glare of all the possible eyes possibly watching him now from all the possible public places he carries around in his mind. So he does not follow his usual path, but keeps among the trees and moves through the scrub. It is never as simple as all usually that.

Emile Gascoigne sits on the single chair he has. Whenever the hermit moves his feet, the broken glass of the window grinds upon the cement floor of his cottage. He has been sitting there now for over an hour, and will sit there. Vaguely his thoughts are on the woman Avery and the man. His hands are shaking as his mind keeps slipping back to an island time so long ago.

With the broken window, he now knows what the feeling is that the man causes in him. Emile Gascoigne sits before the smashed window and sits scared.

The man Allan Dere has moved around the property of Miss Avery. Through the buffalo grass and the gangs of wild wheat, leaving plasticene impressions of his path that won't disappear until the day dries. He has shuffled through the apple orchard, often nearly slipping on the orange surface mud clayed to the soles of his sogsoddened shoes. Almost swinging from branch to branch of each tree to keep his footing. But absent-mindedly and not looking down to watch where he is treading. Rather his eyes scanning the property of Avery for its allness absorbing him.

Right from the outset he has not hurried.

Where the earth was packed and firmer, he has sauntered among the bee hives' two rows, each hive drumming like a city in the distance. Inner workings fascinating him. The occasional bee zipping past his eyes, blurry small and solid cold, he guesses. But doesn't know, can only guess if bees feel the cold, could not have ever guessed, he knows, that one day he would be walking amongst bee hives. Yet now it seems that there could have been no other thing.

The man Dere walks among the image of cromlechs, Druidic mysteries of ancient comings and inner workings. The boxes, the stones; the hummings, the chantings. He lets the images obsess him. Then moves on from the bee hives. The woman that can do with these, what must she be like?

Finally, now, he has come across the line of ruined sheds he has seen from the road. Having closed in on Emile Gascoigne more than he ever had, he has seen for the first time the outback of the house of Avery and spotted the sheds used for nothing anymore much way beyond the house. The sheds pocked by rust and white ant now. Open and twisted. Smelling of damp and mephitic vegetation. Vega Vega vegedom. Dere's senses appalled and fascinated.

But the man automatically chooses a site in the middle shed, against the left hand wall where the centre pine upright stands unbroached. And there he tries to overturn that old straw mattress, but cannot because it spills its contents. Then pulls away a tangle of wood and iron and canvas from against the back wall and heaves it, as though it was bound, all, to one body, to the front of the shed. He watches for a time the cockroaches and the etiolated slugs suddenly scud around in a world of light before jamming this compact of material against a drum to form a barricade to the outside. Then sits back on his mattress. He knows he will sit there in his new site for a while before going back to follow the hermit Gascoigne.

The man Dere knows, too, that he has probably finally gone mad. It does not feel too bad. Even the thought of it doesn't feel too bad.

Emile Gascoigne has moved with a sudden resolution from that chair and the broken glass has crackled beneath his bold movement. Before he has left the cottage he has picked up his treasure of a tool kit and has registered the silliness of suddenly needing to impress her, the woman Avery, by it. Working man, job, tools of mint condition, a battler of the same kind. And is pleased with himself despite the panic he can feel grabbing, now and then, at his windpipe as he has moved again towards the woman Avery's house.

On this all-same day, the hermit Gascoigne has realised that he has noticed the things needed to be done to the front fence of Miss Avery. By a man. Like him, why not? Despite the day, he has registered noticing it and it has been enough to get him up off his chair and to pick up his tool kit and to have come back to the front fence of Miss Avery.

Yet as he has come on towards the house of Avery he has felt the house yawning at him. His steps have become shorter. Behind him, too, has again come the sure feeling of the man unknown to him as yet as Allan Dere again. He has turned suddenly and he and the man have caught sight of each other. Emile Gascoigne has shouted at the person an aggressive 'hey!', meaning all the violation, all the window pain, all the newfound confidence being sapped, all the long hurts against a hermit. At least, this once he has shouted back against the mob at his back.

But the man Dere has from about a hundred metres away seemed to go suddenly berserk and screams abuse at Emile Gascoigne. And has picked up stones and pelted them with ineffectuality and murder at the hermit Gascoigne. Who has moved quickly on, his heart pounding, with the violence again palpable against him. All that murder in all their hearts.

The man follows at a distance. Does shout nothing more at the hermit, a figure of ridicule again. Only follows again as he has done each six months' or so time. Alurk somewhere around. Again. In buzz.

As soon as the front door of the house of Avery opens, Emile Gascoigne dips his head quickly into his pretended work on the lowest strand of the fence, loose and being plierplied at now. With his eyes dancing nervously sideways. Dulia, dulia. It is me, the hermit; there is something I must and do want to say.

But Miss Avery does not look at the hermit enough to notice his eyes. She knows, though, what his eyes would be doing. If she is smiling to herself, she is not smiling to herself. As she steps down the red gummed steps of the kitchen's verandah onto the gravel path there by the hives there.

Emile Gascoigne's eyes brushedly following her hand, almost demurely. It is the thing that can be noticed of her. His eyes and the hand of Miss Avery. It swings so heavily and too large for her body, tiny and broodlike. Filching the attention. Perhaps has done so perhaps for all her years. Say, forty of them, of years. Seemingly her hand, the right or the left, one or the other, never the both in competition, has always been swollen with the bee-sting infection, as now. Seemingly always been larger than the whole of her tiny broodneat pecky little body. One hand at any one time the eye-catcher, and always swollen and rivuletted with pucked and puckery fleshy skin, square and darkgrained at the nails. Her hand. The one or the other. Working hands. The woman Avery.

The hermit's sideways-flung eyes now almost in flutes as he tries to follow, this time, the right swollen hand as it and the neat and broodlike figure of Miss Avery move down the path to the first of the bee hives there.

Her unswollen left hand, convalescently spright, adroitly prods back the hairpin on that side of her auburn-grey hair, whisking itself Victorianesque about the cheeks and the ears of her touch-drawn face, itself so finely sculpted that it seems perpetually in wait for the quiver of a pleasing sensation. Yet shrewish. Not the cleanest of women even to hermit Emile Gascoigne. As she squats her neat drawnforward tiny and broodlike allofaparcel body before the bee hive there. Where she waits. But for what? Where she

21

looks down mesmerically at the opening of the hive as it crawls sugarishly with coldbitten bees flopping in and out on sluggish instinct alone. Seeing, as she finally does, what she has known she would see. The robber wasp. The biggerlarger heavierbully wasp walk bullishly around, magistratingly, the opening among her bees.

Miss Avery reaches down with her swollen and sore right hand automatically, its infection not yet *biting,* and catches the robber wasp among her bees. Without perceptible pressure she crushes the head of the wasp between the nails of her forefinger and thumb. There is no hesitation in the woman Avery's smallcoarse fingers as she does so. And allows her bees to walk over her fingers before she withdraws them. Her fingers registering, still and after all these years, the fur. The woman Avery registering, still and after all these years, the furriness of her bees. Her mind in smile upon itself. Then withdraws the body of the robber wasp, and flicks it away with reflective disgust.

She stands. Now the woman Avery stands upright in one quick and fit movement. It is an alert movement. It is astute. And telltale. She has stood and waits, looking back towards the kitchen door.

The hermit turns his eyes quickly away from the silhouette of her petticoat beneath her whichway thisway printed cotton frock. Not looking might earn ten good points.

The tiny neat and broodlike body of the woman Avery with its back towards him as she waits for the brother Frank to come out of the kitchen door.

It is four o'clock in the afternoon on the day the woman Miss Avery is to remember as long and as short as she will live.

Frank. The man, the boy. He has come awake and felt the silence of the empty Avery house and has screamed out the name of his younger sister. Miss Avery. Younger by one year. But as tiny and broodlike as Frank is huge and gasteropodic. Sleep emphasises his asthmatic features, his eyes sunk between puffy folds. The man, the boy. The heavy clodding of his lumbering body. In wobble and in panic, the one because of the other, crashing down the passageway in a suddenly awaked-upon empty house. Miss Avery! His huge tensed hands pawing away the air in front of him as though his early-teenage mentality has him wading through violently slopping treacle.

Frank. The man, the boy. In wokenup panic for his younger sister not there.

The woman Avery has heard him as she did hear him almost wake up by the sudden change of the movement-hum inside her house. And she waits now for the man, the boy by the bee hive outside. She knows he is to burst out, soon, into the daylight, distressed and dragging at his breathing. Yet she still waits.

Miss Avery!

And comes rolling drunkenly, having glancingly collided with the kitchen door just as he does so, out onto the kitchen porch there. Panic filmed across his eyes seeing only itself. The boy lurching the man's body around. Miss Avery Miss Avery! Spinning him almost off his feet reeling him into the wall of the house of Avery. Heavily, so that he has to stop and gargle a moment for breath. The woman Avery herself trying to force herself to speak, not knowing why, for that moment out of all the perpetual moments that have perpetually been and are to be, she cannot *speak* to her own Frank. Calm now don't be silly here I am. But nothing. A momentarily fatigued thing standing by her bee hives. And fascinated enough by it all in that lacuna of time to observe just how much of an oaf her own littlelarge brother is.

And how grotesque the two of them together must look to out-siders.

Finally it finally comes, flowing forth as electuary; for both, for the sister Miss Avery and the brother Frank, back to a known

23

routine on a known earth. The sound of the voice rather than the sense in what's said and mellifluent:

'Come on here I am where else would I be?'

All right, Frank. Recovering himself and his balance. His eyes flicked to the direction of her voice that springs, yet again, balm and the panic clearing as film from his eyes, so that he is seeing her again. All gone now. There is hardly even a perceptible change in his behaviour. Where he has reeled against the wall in panic, he now comes back off it as brother suspicious brother consuming brother demanding Frank.

'Where yer been? Where yer been, Miss Avery, eh?'

The answer is unimportant. The asking affirms all that is needed. As the birdlike sister Miss Avery is already moving back up to the kitchen verandah from the bee hive, the brother Frank has narwhal'd himself down to sit, by way of collision with the porch post, beside the cat tin. His hands already reaching out for it before his body has even started to lower itself and his fingers already lumbering at it gimme gimme. His head hits itself against the post long after his body has come to a blubbery rest.

Stunned and lost now, I have hit my head. The sister Miss Avery quickly covering the last few paces that gulfs them and holds his head hurriedly against her belly, as well as she could hug a too-large beach ball. She is doing what she knows has to be done quickly: hold the head firmly away from the hurt within it. The man, her brother, the little boy. Finally, surlily, accusingly:

'Where're you been, y'old bag, eh?'

But the asking again already forgetting the answer and the cold contacts of his fingers against the cat tin remembered. Friar. His beaut cat Friar's tin.

Remembering Friar, the manboy shakes off Miss Avery's body from his head, as lightly as puff, and shouts to the hermit

Gascoigne. Who, after the body-jerking surprise of finding himself addressed, and loudly, bobs quickly back down behind the strands of the front fence as though the silver-leaf hedge there could rabbit burrow him out of sight, as Frank, thick and mustardy:

'Hey mug, seen Friar? Seen me beaut cat Friar, eh?'

If he could slink away, the hermit might feel an escape possible. Yet now too late for even that. For he sees with flushing embarrassment that he has dropped his pliers, still shiny, still oiled and still impressive, over the other side of the fence in the confusion. They lie there on the actual property of Miss Avery as plainly extrovertively as he must obviously shout out to the woman Avery if she is to give them back.

And her waiting, with her birdlike body so tense that they both plainly know it too, for him to dare to dare it. Not so shiny, not so oiled, not so impressive now. Instead the hermit Gascoigne speculates scientifically into the air about him:

'I think a man must have dropped something.'

And commencing to *fiddle* at the fence there with his hands as though to show his work needs no fencing pliers. Some things are beneath the contempt of the manual capacities of a working man.

Frank suddenly reaches up and grabs Miss Avery's swollen and sore right hand so that she almost cries out. And might have, if she has not long ago gotten used to the unexpected bruisings his rolling heaviness has given her so many times. So the sister now stifles a cry and quickly grabs at his hand, covering her own easily, to prize it off as gently as the pain will let her, and her voice now lullabying a singsong to him:

'Hair cut Frank you stay here.'

She leaves him there as she plies for comb and scissors inside. Frank, the boy, the man, gets up and walks down the path towards Emile Gascoigne. The cat Friar. His beaut Friar. Where's Friar?

'Hey, mug, you seen Friar, eh? Eh?'

He leans over the top strand of the front fence, so that the whole fence points architecturally to the old man, to cushion his puffin's face only a few centimetres from the old hermit's who-me? averted head. Frank's slack mouth frothing at the side with the intensity of his inquiry with his eyes undeniably tapping a very non-shrinking hermit on the shoulder. For a moment the two men are frozen in cameo. Emile Gascoigne dares not move, can only think frantically that this face-to-face might well last forever, for all of time.

Behind them both, now, Miss Avery re-emerges from her house with scissors and comb. When she sees where Frank is she clucks her tongue loudly against the roof of her mouth and calls Frank in such a way that the hermit, hearing the blame in her tone directed at him, averts his head a few more degrees away from the unblinking and clogging stare of the brother, the man and child. And, as if he could, further cringes from all involvement. Run up a flag and tell the woman Avery I want to tell her something.

And such is the way of her voice that Frank giggles from behind his puffy features there and squirms at a thought as though he would piddle over it, before he grabs at the ends of Emile Gascoigne's coat and tries to pull it up over his own head in a grotesque attempt to hide, like the hermit's body, underneath it too. Going, as he ropes Emile in at the end of a large excited strength:

'Don't dob a joker in, orright? Orright, eh?'

The front fence is now sagging dangerously under the cetaceous weight of the brother Frank trying to squeeze his head sideways into the tailcoat of the hermit Gascoigne's jacket that still contains the squirming body of Emile Gascoigne, citigrade to the spot and truly never having been so close to another human being in all his remembered days.

She comes, does the woman Avery. She is there suddenly looking, from not too much of a height off, down and over the fence at them, before appalling the sensibilities of the hermit Gascoigne by speaking with a stony, accusing voice, ostensibly to the brother but meaning trespasser, oh yes.

'Hair cut Frank I said.'

'Fuck orf.'

Her lips pursed so that her mouth bunches to the front as a tight wad, the woman Avery takes Frank's exposed ear in her good left hand and twists it. She does not need to apply much pressure. The gesture, tried and proved, is enough for the brother's head to come towards her, for her to pull Frank, trotting and half-bent and floppy, alongside her. Back to the house. Not giving one hesitation's acknowledgement to Emile Gascoigne's hurried blurt of innocence too loud:

'Somebody's just been having a look at the fence out here, that's all.'

At the steps to the kitchen verandah, both Miss Avery's momentum and the threatening centrifugality of Frank's dogtrot both combine finally to send him spinning to a neat collision, again, with the porch post. Where he shudders down in a retroaction with the wind that is knocked out of him, even as a thought is in registration in his manchild's mind:

'Seen me beaut animal, Miss Avery, eh? Seen Friar, have yer?' And as she hair-dresses, the cat Friar remains in the mind of the brother. Friar the cat. Who has gone off this time and has not come back for three weeks.

'Friar's coming back, see. Yer oughta see me beaut animal Friar spearing back home. Toldyer, didn't I?'

'Yes Frank.'

The combing, the painfully fumbly fact of the scissors around her swollen hand, the dandruff she has never known how to eradicate

27

from the manchild's scalp. Nor, she knows, ever from her own.

'See, toldyer. Geez, you're droopy drawers.'

When does the man the brother fling her off his head again. Raising petulance and dangerously capable of violence. And as if she didn't know better, the woman the sister literally holds on tight, keeping the contact, keeping his head close to hold against her tiny broodlike body. There, there, it's all right, Frankie.

'All right Frank.' Soothing tones and finally to settle him. 'Fuck orf!'

'Don't listen to the men down at the abattoirs Frank.'

'Fuck orf, see. Fuck orf!'

Miss Avery nurtures a silence of disapproval by holding the brother Frank's head still against her body. She really does not mind his language. She does not really mind. Only that the men down at the Salem's abattoirs would be laughing at her brother. That, and too, the perpetual feeling of guilt that she might not watch over him properly enough.

The hermit pushes his head up suddenly over the front fence and admonishes, so boldly that it almost knocks himself down, Miss Avery's obvious womanly need for a man about the place: 'Yeah, and somebody's seen them egg him on, too, somebody has.'

But Frank tugging, jealous of her attention.

'Whereabouts me hammer, Miss Avery?'

'Under your bed Frank where you left it.'

'Pow! Pow! Like that, Miss Avery! Pow fucking pow, see!'
'Don't swear Frank you could get on with some more hives now if you want.'

'Pow! Pow!' The whole body bouncing in massive mimic. The

28

sister, the woman, small as in flighty in comparison, steps back quickly in case perhaps she is swept up in it and needlessly bruised again.

Now Miss Avery sighs and remembers how she stood suddenly tired, then, at his awakening, amazed at herself that she was, by the hives outside, not able to close in quickly, as she has just done now. With her sister's weight as flighty as a bird:

'Where were yer when I woke up, ydumbcluck.'

But the woman Miss Avery looks up from her brother's bald patch. Her eyes are fixed on one spot far away, perhaps just above the far horizon, if what they were seeing was being registered. It is not. It is just a moment she will remember as long as she will live. It feels as if the reel has broken for an instant. And she will come to think how the reel never did go on the same old way after that moment. Somehow. And, too, later she will come to say:

'The thread of my life seemed to...'

But she will never be able to finish what she seems to want to say about that moment. It has happened. It is happening. Nothing as was is now the same, somehow.

The manchild has begun to squirm once more. Miss Avery notices that she has just about finished cutting the hair, as Frank's leg tries to stretch out sideways towards a line of ants rippling its way from beneath the nearest bush to under the corner of the house. And, as he does so, his giantform man's body, as substantial as a tree beneath her, tries to keep haircuttingly still yet antcatching at one and the same time, with the result that he is now beginning to shake with the strain. And the hermit Gascoigne now is making straddling movements with one leg between the top and the middle strands of the front fence, in and out, out and in, in a very passable mime show of how one could climb in, if one so wished, to the property of Miss Avery and how one could so quickly, if she so wished him to, climb back out again before too many of the delicacies of human intercourse, especially when it comes to relationships that are arguably on the boil, are made distraught. The woman Avery might have had her head cocked as though perhaps she is listening to something far off, but is now whipping her hard stare back onto him. How dare you:

'You keep your distance, Emile Gascoigne.' Punching the air with the scissors between them. Pointing the bone with a finely honed intention. At which the hermit's miserable body drops miserably and automatically onto the second strand and then has to struggle desperately against balance in order to regain rectitude on the public side of the fence.

By the time he can look back at the verandah, the woman has gone. Only Frank is still sitting there, with his torso still held stiff for the hair cut but his whole framework now visibly straining his foot to the ants just slightly more than a Frank's leglength away. So the hermit turns now and walks back across the road on his way back to his own cottage. But gets no further than the other side of the road before he is brought to a halt by remembering again the smashed window and the fear it has dragged up from all those years ago. The presence of the man, unknown to him yet as Allan Dere. About still. Watching still. *Around.*

Emile Gascoigne turns, but does not know he turns, one small, but completed, scanning circle, then sits down on the damp earth on the other side of the road to the house of Miss Avery. Fie does not know what to do. He has just remembered, too, why he has come there today. He wanted to tell her about the man. But has not. There is the broken window and there is the fear.

Frank the body moves and Frank the mind follows. Stretching the leg out towards the ant trail has not reached a satisfying contact with the ant trail. Nor has any amount of concentration of will by Frank the mind made those ants detour their rippling line to pass under the shoe of Frank the body. Aw cmon cmon. But still the mute inaccessibility of animal life.

A sudden boiling over of killing rage makes the manchild's body spring up in an obscene display of power. The manchild screams and froths, obscenely too, fucks and fuckingbastardcunts at the ant line. He stampstomps and wilddances along the ant trail there. In carnage and grunting and screaming at a pitch so high that it can almost not be heard. He flings himself against the house and still stamps upon. He throws himself at the bush under which the ants' line disappears and still stamps upon. He still stamps upon until he has exhausted the needs of a boyish tantrum. Now, as instantaneously as he has started, he sits giggling again on the kitchen verandah, oblivious to the fact that Miss Avery is not there and firmly holding on, where he fights silently for breath. His eyes slowly calming down and beginning to see again.

Frank sits in exhaustion and could, now, be thought to be asleep sitting up. The line of ants has now no flow, at least for a while. Here, too, the quietus. It does not ripple along again just yet. Instead, it wriggles and jerks as the ants convulse among a whole universe of dead squashed bodies.

Slowly, as Frank the body regains its breathing, the line from the house end and from the bush end, begins to pulse, slowly and confusedly at first, then to ripple and then to flow again. Soon it is as though the manchild has not ever moved from where he is sitting quietly, head between his forearms and his arms leaning on his knees, against the porch post now.

Inside, Miss Avery has heard, has been to the kitchen window, has seen that Frank is all right and has withdrawn. For the second time this afternoon she cannot understand why she hasn't hurried to Frank when he is having another of his fits. She turns away from the window, perplexed and annoyed at herself. The reel, having stopped and restarted itself, is not quite in *thwack* with the must-to-be.

31

Jenny Salem has completed her nursing rounds. As usual, when she has completed her nursing rounds, she is hating herself for continuing to agree to be the same old nurse on the same old rounds. She feels she has become so deliberately countrified that she has locked herself within her own cliché of what a city gal should do for the *people* having married the 'lard'. (He likes the word 'lard'; she and her husband have mixed up 'laird' with 'lard' so many years ago that they now cannot remember that 'lard' is in fact wrong. Instead they use it and, both, mentally spring into the pantry and laugh at the lordly word lard; lard is for spreading — up profits, ha ha.)

The woman Salem has found it acceptable, and not a little amusing, to broach the house of Avery with the bonnet of her car so that she virtually gets out with one foot on the roadside verge and the other foot on the property. It is a gesture of compromise that has become a matter of exquisite form between the two women over all those, all these, years.

Even so, today it is odd for her to be feeling so hateful at herself. Not that she minds that. She has long known that her major virtue in life is a healthy cynicism. She would never confide in anyone either, certainly not the lard, that, sure as shooting, she is an inthere stickitrightup'em survivor. Always will be. The feeling of feeling hateful at herself in fact only helps to sharpen her tongue which helps her to survive a little more. She could, as the truth is known, lick herself she feels so deliciously miserable.

Emile Gascoigne sitting on the opposite road verge. She nods to herself before she bails him up. She was right to connect his aborted visit to her place as something to do with the woman Avery. Poor little poor Miss Avery and the poor old funny little bugger. Funny little worlds of flat earths. And then, flip: 'Emile Gascoigne, you horny old thing, you.' Finger snappingly.

The hermit recoils not only at the saying and the thought behind the saying, but at the unspoken truth in them. He groans loudly and tries to back away from her. But already the woman Salem is already bending. She picks up. Now she impishly tosses the fencing pliers beyond the front Avery fence and straightens to throw back to the recluse Emile a winning smile. And knows, too, that she has the figure, still, for turning her back and walking off in a way that can leave things nicely up in the air with her serve to come.

Frank alone still on the kitchen porch. It is the first time in all her years of trying to teach the manchild breathing lessons against the asthma that she has found him left unattended. An undoubted target for the next thunderbolt that is due in the area within the next one million years. The woman Salem smiles at the thought as she walks towards the house. She knows how well the smile is one of familiar insolence.

'How's my Frankie?'

'Whozzat?'

'My God, you're hands are cold.'

'Hello, yold bastard.'

'Where's Miss Avery, Frankie?'

'Got any goodies, mud guts?'

'You won't find any up my dress, naughty boy.'

'Youghta see me bowl over a bloody great rat yesterday. Pow! Pow! Like that, see, with me beaut hammer. Pow.'

The woman Salem pats the manchild on the top of the head, amusing herself. He has not moved or looked up, but stays there letting the life seep back in. She moves up to the kitchen door, yoohooing in her heppedtoned, highly-amused housewife's voice put on for just this occasion. She knows Miss Avery is undoubtedly inside cringing away from the mocking in the tone. Singsong an invasion. You have to laugh; keep a straight face.

Finally, Miss Avery bursts out to almost breast upon Jenny Salem.

33

And as usual it looks as though she has made her headlong dash from the back of the house and arrived just in time to stop the woman Salem from putting any invading portion of her body inside the kitchen door. It is always like this. It is always Miss Avery who is caught off balance because it is always like this. And, too, the dialogue:

'A week gone already?'

'Can't you see a week's worth of extra lines under my eyes, Miss Avery?'

'Didn't mean that.'

'Of course you didn't, lovie.' They turn together, as if on cue, to look at Frank.

'Has he been doing his exercises?'

'You don't have to keep coming around here, if it's too much trouble.'

'Oh no, it's no trouble. I've only put in about two thousand million hours on him already, haven't I?'

'Your men down the abattoirs still keep egging him on.'

'I'll speak to my lard and master about it. Won't we, Frankie?' Ruffling the hair on his head. She is on top of the tease again.

'Getorf.' Making a backhand, back sweeping lunge with his left arm for the calf of Jenny Salem's leg cmon here and: 'Get em down on the workbench, slackguts.'

The woman Salem skips with a practised step out of the way of his groping arm. Miss Avery, with equal practice, half-turns her head at this moment to look as though she is staring at the far horizon. Demurely:

'How's the bees, then?'

And the dancing amusements around the corners of her eyes.

'You can come in for... something if you want to.'

'Miss Avery, lovie, what if I said yes after all these years?' Knowing that this always-the-same line will the little sister's hackles rise for what's not been said yet again. Yet this time the woman Salem has only backed, deliberately as usual scuffing the gravel of the path, towards the front gate a few paces when the man not yet known by them as Allan Dere appears from around the obverse side of the house. He comes from around the back and has glided there even before either of the two women has seen him. He stands apart from them, but his feet are planted determinedly on his ground. His eyes fletching at Miss Avery. Intolerable.

The man Dere looks at the little sister Avery within a fascination of seeing closely for the first time what he has, at every six months' interval give or take, only peered at, latritant, from behind wherever the hermit has stationed himself. He looks at the woman and his breath comes deeply. He says:

'Miss Avery?'

Miss Avery does not answer. She stares fascinatedly back at the man unknown as yet as the man Allan Dere. Her neck pulse throbs familiarly at yet another invasion. The robber wasps. Jenny Salem answers for her.

'Who wants to know?'

The man Dere slowly swings his eyes around on her. His eyes move up and down against her. The woman Salem poses superciliously for him.

'No, you're not Miss Avery.'

The woman Salem shrugging the clown:

'Take it or leave it.'

But Dere is back on Miss Avery. She feels him pressing closer. The manboy Frank tensing with her, exploding panic against the skirt of her frock; the manboy in folds:

'Miss Avery... '

'It's all right Frank ssh.'

Again the man Dere:

'Don't want to trouble you.'

Now Miss Avery, with Frank again held against her legs safely and tightly, is back on the firm ground that is the land of her known routine. Stern again against all presumptions. She holds her brother Frank and remembers again how to erect the verbal barricades.

'Help you?'

'Don't want to trouble you. All I...'

And stops there.

The man seems to have suddenly run out of puff. Is nodding at Miss Avery. Is looking and nodding at her again, so that her hand flits to the old cotton shirt she has on under her cotton frock. Up to the neck and down. And is dreadfully shocked to find the top three buttons undone. Her chest showing tit spoutings. She suddenly feels obscene and slatternish. Her fingers dive for each button, while the man Dere is saying, impudently:

'Don't cover up on account of me, Miss Avery.'

'If you're looking for someone, he's not here.'

Angry and flustered now, she goes to move aggressively forwards towards the man Dere, but Frank feels the movement away from him. He holds her tighter, whimpers Miss Avery Miss Avery so that now she has lost her momentum towards the invader. And her eyes, in a moment of weakness she will come to hate in herself, dart to the woman Salem for help, who is amusing herself by staying there and watching the funny people in the zoo.

'That's right, Miss Avery lovie. You go him.'

But the man suddenly has turned and run. He turns and he runs across the property of Miss Avery, lances through the front fence. On his way he startles the old hermit across the road with a pretended rush at him. Instead dummies around him by twirling him around and shouts into his ear:

'Boo! Boo!'

And is gone.

The woman Avery gathers Frank up. She does so by an action that makes her look as though she is hauling in a huge rope. Nevertheless the manchild stands weak-kneed. He has to fight for breath for a while, but both the women know it will be all right this time. Nor does the little sister give time for the woman Salem to say what is obviously on her mind; she has already bundled her manboy brother back inside and has closed the door behind them both. The door, the portcullis. Even by the time Jenny Salem turns back again, the hermit Gascoigne too has slipped away.

A gal gets very little thanks.

The eyes are watching Miss Avery through the window as she moves through the house cleaning up. She could not reason why she might be cleaning up at this hour, nine o'clock, at night. At the corners of her mouth, she is even slightly amused with herself for doing so. Has never learnt it a vouchsafe against probabilities of a woman living alone to automatically lower the blinds when she has the light burning in a room at night.

And the eyes watch her from outside as she flutters, broodlike, from one room to another. Alive and throbbing outside there, the

37

house of Miss Avery. The eyes. Finding rooms for themselves.

The woman Avery is cleaning up the place, but it would be impossible in a half hour or so to say she has cleaned up one room let alone the place. What she is doing is really clearing pathways to make them more visible through each of the rooms. Each room is piled with on-top-ofs, from generations of the Averys *piling*. It has always been so. By now the whole upstairs is one large junk room of old furniture and crates and cases, pressured and squeezed to be up there almost as if by the pressure of the incomings on the ground floor. The stairs themselves are a windy task, and as sticky underfoot as the room they lead up from. It is in this room that the woman Avery has kept her honeyed combs. The honeycombs, the boxes. The new honeycombs, the old honeycombs there in that room. The hives waiting to be cleaned and the hives washed up, washed out, waiting for the manchild brother's hammer for this or that. The room littered with honeycomb and box. Its lino slippery and sticky, by turn, under her feet. The luscious ooze from the sensual hives. Her bees. Her hum. This room is the central cell of the Avery hive. And, from outside, the eyes are watching how her chest is showing the tit spoutings and her thin arms have not yet got flubbery. Broodlike, hiveish and humming. Frank got to bed and already snoring. It is only nine o'clock. And the eyes have already come.

She moves, clearing such paths, through the kitchen, too, so encrusted with junk that it resembles a garage rather than a kitchen. It is as though every little minute of every little kitchen ware time-used has frozen it in that spot. The weldings of time. The sink rusty and concreted. The fridge rusty and concreted. The central table rusted and concreted. The weldings. The woman Avery not knowing that the eyes have followed her into the kitchen. As she clears paths. As she bends and her frock rides up to her crutch.

Each stocking is a bunting loose at the top where only one suspender clamp now holds for each. It gives her a Dick Whittington-in-boots look. But the eyes do not think so. Drinking in the alabaster of the top of her inner thighs. No, she has never learnt, the eyes learn, to pull the blinds.

Miss Avery moves out of the kitchen. Bustling with contentment. In happy charge again. She moves down the passageway off the kitchen into the parlour. Her father used to say the parlour. Just a lounge really. Drawing, outside, the eyes around the flower beds against the walls of the house after her.

Where she bends again. Bends to tidy the arrangement of the newspapers lying all over the floor there. Morning papers from years back neatly tiling the floor. The eyes cannot know the untidiness of the newspapers on the floor there is the result of the tidiness of the mind of the woman Avery. The precious carpet underneath where she sat at the feet of her father. A girl. In wonder about her largehuge brother Frank. But a girl. And then there was father to look after Frank. And the carpet hugely warm and comforting. Precious and never to be worn out. So she, Miss Avery, bends and straightens the long-ago morning papers she has strewn around the floor to protect the only thing of the house that she thinks must not be worn upon. Her knees do not bend as she bends over. Her nates, suddenly firm and solid stretch the material of her cotton frock. And, again, the bunting hang of the stocking tops.

The eyes, the eyes. From outside the eyes watch the woman Avery finally move out into the passageway. She halts at the door, reverently, of Frank's bedroom and listens to his snores. His great frame sucking hugely. The eyes cannot see her now. They wait outside her bedroom window.

The woman Avery moves, inside, into her bedroom. The eyes have her outline against the lit frame of the passageway. The light outside the bedroom for Frank. The woman Avery now for a moment framed in the doorway of her bedroom for the eyes. They open wider in expectation. Where there is her radio, her one entertainment. Where she will sit in bed and listen to the radio, listening for Frank, and has ever done. She is not a book reader. She will sit in bed and just listen, broodlike. The sweet smell of honey through the house long accustomed to. In the bedroom she will at last pull down the blind. But so casually that it is up a few centimetres above the bottom window pane and casting look-in light into the night outside. The eyes, the eyes.

As she undresses her young girl's body never been touched.

Miss Avery hears the cry of alarm first. She thinks. She thinks she hears what sounds like a cry of alarm from outside and then she hears; she thinks what some bumpings outside the house are. She sits up in bed and quickly lowers the volume of her valve radio and listens. She thinks, too, she hears the swish of branches of somesuch. The night is frostily still outside, but dark, no moon.

By the time she has reached the kitchen door, the man holds the other man forcibly still out by the side hedge. His arm is around the other's throat; his other is armlocking a silence. He coarsely whispers a threat into the ear of the held man. They stay there. Stilled. The one watching Miss Avery come worringly out onto the kitchen porch, looking and listening. Her sharp senses radaring beyond the perimeter of the electric light's influence. The other not able to see her through the tears in his eyes. The arm about to snap. Oh, the eyes, the eyes.

But nothing. The woman Avery listens for a while more. But nothing. She moves back inside. She cannot ever know how vulnerable she looks and has looked. She wears a pink woollen nightdress that is surely very old. She goes. Switching off the kitchen light and leaving, now, the outside to the outside. The one man to the other man.

He lets go the other man's arm slowly and deliberately. In the very deliberateness of the movement there is a threat. The other man remains rigid and afraid, while the man moves around in front of him. Holding him closely so that the hermit Gascoigne cannot escape.

The two men stand there in the night on the property of Miss

Avery. Not a word has passed between them. Emile Gascoigne is trembling with fear. The other man is looking into his eyes fiercely. If the hermit Gascoigne was not so full of fear, he might have been able to see the compunction in the other man's eyes. Boring into the hermit Gascoigne's. Speaking a remorse. The violence does not come unto Emile Gascoigne as he is expecting.

Suddenly the man has bent down and is kissing the hermit on the lips. The man as yet unknown as the man Allan Dere has bent down and kissed Emile Gascoigne on the lips, then has spat revoltedly out onto the ground. He has gone again even before the hermit can react, and in all that time he has only spoke once. He has said, or so Emile Gascoigne has thought he heard:

'Have pity.'

At first the hermit Gascoigne, from across the road from the Avery house, has not seen the man Dere sitting with his back to the old water pump there. Not until the sun has come up well into the arc of the sky and thrown Dere's shadow. It is then Emile notices that Allan Dere has beaten him back to the Avery place the next morning. The sun shining a better day.

The scar across the man Dere's eye seems to blow his head up balloonwise. It is throbbing like that as he sits and watches the front door of the house of Avery. He has come out of his shed at first light, but can hardly remember getting there to sit with his back against the old water pump. He is still finding that what he is feeling doesn't feel too bad, after all. He has thought sometimes in his life, long ago, that all crazy men convulse at some time or mainly. But he doesn't feel too bad at all. And what's more, he hasn't felt the cold and the damp much at all.

Inside, the woman Miss Avery takes Frank's breakfast plates away from him and darts a look out of the kitchen window to see if the man unknown to her as yet as Allan Dere is still there leaning against her old water pump. Lying on her house with those eyes.

Frank playing race tracks in the butter he has dropped onto the table from his breakfast rmmmmm rmmmmmm brrrrmmmmppp. The man Dere is still there by the old water pump.

Miss Avery rinses out a flannel at the kitchen sink. She returns with the flannel to wash Frank's face 'off', as she would say. The manchild, as always, is caught from behind and wriggles while his little and businesslike sister wipes his face, then, turning the flannel over, wipes his eyes and ears. Pissorf, pissorf. Rrrmmm rrrmmmmm. Where she stands, having finished with his face, with her hands on his shoulders, looking thoughtfully out of the kitchen window to the old water pump and the man Dere. Soon, she knows, she must go out and start the raillery. But tired now. Again. Like yesterday. Tired for a while and letting the man sitting by the old water pump be for a while. After all, Frank is safe beneath her hands.

'Friar's coming back ternight, Miss Avery, isn't he, eh?'

'He might Frank he might.'

'Betcha he'll be thirsty, Miss Avery. Cats get thirsty, don't they, Miss Avery?'

'Yes Frank.'

'Fucking old Friar'll be drier than a camel bum, won't he, Miss Avery?' The chuckle cut off abruptly by another thought jabbing. 'Betcha Friar's been a long way this time, Miss Avery. Betcha he's been to... Darwin.' The thought, the chuckle, both, on line:

'Darwin. All that fanny up there, eh? A bloke can't go wrong up there, kiddingyer. Geez, waltzing back from Darwin... that's why the silly bastard's tin's out on the porch, ain't it, Miss Avery? Eh?'

'That's why his tin is there Frank.'

'Toldyer, toldyer, see yold ratbag.'

The woman Avery pulling herself up with a visible jolt. She takes

42

the radio and sits at the table with it. The man Dere outside can wait.

'Watcha doin', eh?'

'You shouldn't go around smashing things with your hammer Frankie look at this plug.'

'What about... what about when there's fuckin' murderers in me flamin' room, eh? What's goin', see? What's goin'?'

Miss Avery sighing, but a long wedge off exasperation: 'There's no murderers, Frank.'

'Cut off a bloke's dick, give 'em half a go, Miss Avery.'

Now into whine, having truly frightened himself.

'Don't listen to the man down at the abattoirs Frank.'

Frank leans his face into the gap between the plug and her bosom, with his neck twisted and his eyes large and browncow up at her. Now, by habit, she knows it is pointless to try to fight the brother off when he is after possession. She puts down the plug. Dropping it all, always the best way.

'My fuckin' screwdriver, see.' And snatching it from her hands.

She can only answer wearily, 'Don't be like this Frank please.' The little sister Avery gets up from the table, lightly pecking the manchild on the cheek as she does so. Now she moves off down the passageway. The dim early morning light is in there and the woman Avery is vanishing within it. By the time she has reached the bedroom, the manchild's head has rotated twice in the stern concentration of following a fly's groggy winter's flight, and his body has raised itself. Arms flapping way too late for the swat and his swaying body rocking the table as he gets up. Frank Avery on his feet. Facing the door. The kitchen door. The door must be it. Outside. Got up to go outside. Now the manchild's body follows the mind and in its eyes is a gazey look that seems to be almost

43

saying whoops and watcha and watchawhoops.. But cannot.

Allan Dere sees the kitchen door of the house of Miss Avery open. He stiffens for a moment, then lets himself relax again. There is nothing to stiffen about. He has made up his mind; this and that doesn't matter. He sees, yes, the manboy Frank, the mammoth brother, roll out of the kitchen door and onto the porch. Stumbling slightly from the one step down and steadying himself against the porch post. When, suddenly, he sees the man Dere sitting there against the old water pump. And is caught bolt upright in his tracks, petrified. Then, when his mind has caught up, the whimpered cry-for:

[1]Miss Avery...!'

This is what it is all about. The man Dere watches from closer in than the hermit Gascoigne is watching from as Frank ululates to his birdsister. Miss Avery! The man Dere watches and sees the figure of Miss Avery plunging out of the house to her brother's side. Now her hand grabs upwards for Frank's shoulder and squeezes it's all right. All right now Fm here. The fleeting gesture that is all that is needed. Then the turn with arms akimbo to confront the stranger sitting there with his back against the old water pump. The invasions. She has, now and again, the iciness in her voice for it:

'I asked you yesterday, can I help you?'

But only the man Dere rolling his sad eyes, brown and ordinary, at her. Communicating to her what she does not yet understand, yet disturbing her enough that it is all she can do to just look back. Finding in herself a quiet amazement that there isn't all that much of a hurry really. But Frank's voice. Suddenly Frank's voice, because the bogeys haven't come this time. He has been able to tell from his sister's voice that the bogeys from the white places have not come this time:

'Pissorf! Pissorf!'

He jumps like an ape down from the porch and picks up a gravel stone, so small in the pincers of his huge fingers. He throws. The stone digs in at the man Dere with surprising force and accuracy. The man Dere might not have been able to dodge it anyway. The stone thumps into his chest with a dull, hollow thud. With the pain, the man Dere's head slumps onto his chest and his shoulders hunch protectively. Miss Avery is appalled:

'Oh Frank.'

'It doesn't matter.' Dere comes to quickly reply to her.

He knows instinctively it is important to. Mesmerising, probably trying to, a silence, and Miss Avery is silent. She moves down to place herself between the man Dere and her manchild Frank. I, the shield. I, the absorber. She moves down closer to Dere and sees him for really the first time and answers his question of yesterday, as though it had hung importantly in the air for all that time:

'I'm Miss Avery.'

'Your hand...'

The swollen hand, the great club of a hand now. The woman Avery whips her hand out of sight before she can stop herself from whipping her hand from out of sight. The cotton top of yesterday and the brown freckles on her chest; today the hand. What is this?

'*Miss Avery...?*'

Protect Frank, Frank's voice goes; protect Frank. And the man Dere is nodding at her, but she cannot comprehend what for. She is even hearing him speak as softly to her as she does herself to Frank. Soothing tones:

'Ever since I was a boy, I always wanted to come to the wine valleys of the South country. This isn't one, is it? It doesn't matter. It's somewhere near enough.' And then: 'I only want the quiet, Miss Avery.'

45

'No!' This is intolerable. You let the world in and its appalling questions. Questions, questionings. 'This isn't a wine valley.'

'My name is Dere. Allan Dere.'

'This is where *we* live!' Before she wheels Frank around and with her. Fighting with him a momentum towards the kitchen door. Forcing him up the porch steps, *get orf get orf,* and into the kitchen.

The house blank against the man Allan Dere again. After a while comes the sound of Frank's hammering from inside. He suspects, but cannot know, that the woman Miss Avery is keeping an eye on him from behind the muteness of the kitchen window there. He stays seated against the old water pump, his mind made up. And stays there a long time.

It is on the fourth day that the woman Avery has decided to collect the honey, despite the presence of the man Dere or no man. When she announces that they are to collect some of the early honey flow, the brother Frank claps his hands and beats down on two of the hive boxes with whooping delight. Pow pow pow. Me beaut bees. Eh? Eh? Until it is now time for the little sister to put on his mask and gloves. She tucks his trousers into his socks and ties the gloves well up over his frayed cuffs. Get orf, get orf.

The brother Frank stays beyond the circle of the hives while his sister collects the combs and applauds with his hands as he instinctively tries to compete with the buzzing of her bees at her. Delighted when his sister opens up a hive and disappears beneath the crowd of bees. Almost. Is mainly, though, for a spine-chilling moment, mounted by panic that she might never again reappear.

It rains. Now it rains. Half way through collecting the combs of the early honey flow, it is raining suddenly. A shower coming as a burst. But enough to send Frank rolling into a fattumble of a run for the shelter of the house, his legs splaying uncoordinatedly as though he was in slew. And behind him the little sister too engrossed in finding herself alone and having to take the stack of combs inside so quickly. She tries to gather them, but her thin arms are too thin and her slender arms too slender to pick up them all. She calls out to Frank, but he is gone.

The man Dere has not heard her 'Oh!' as though she has cut herself. He has not thought about the possibility of bee stings, either. He has been watching and now he is there beside her, grabbing up the rest of the pile and running through the once-back garden and along the side of the house to the lee of the kitchen porch. Already the rain is stopping and already the thin furls of sunlight.

The man Dere and the woman Avery stand, gasping not too slightly, upon the kitchen porch together. Both of them feeling foolish now that the rain has short cut so abruptly. The chuckling of Frank far away, deep inside the house. With an abrupt turn, he, the man Dere, turns to face her. He speaks to her from that so appallingly-close far away.

'It's strange, isn't it, Miss Avery, when you look into someone's eyes? Yours being grey now.'

The woman thrown off-balance. Her mind whirring to make things stand *up*. At the same time she hears her voice almost in outcry:

'I didn't ask for grey eyes! You get off the place, please!'

The man Dere acknowledges the shift. He raises his arms in surrender and laughs and steps backwards off the porch. Is raising his arms again and she hears him say:

'You can stick me up, but you're stuck with me, Miss Avery. So get a posse. Gee up.'

And whips his imaginary horse to trot back down to the sheds at the bottom of the property of Avery.

The woman Avery places her honeycombs on the pile left by the

47

man Dere and strides down the path towards the hermit. When he sees that she is making a beeline for him, he is horrified. For a moment, head down, he digs at the earth at his feet as though he would dig a hole for himself to hide in. It makes matters worse for him that she stands and waits until he shyly peeks up, a pantomime Quasimodo. But she no beauty herself. Except when he looks up and sees she is more beautiful than what he has imagined. His mind singing not bad by half. 'You got any idea who that man is?'

'No. Promise!'

The woman Miss Avery, having broken such new ground so near to him, is already turning away and retreating to her house. Give a man a chance. The hermit mentally beats himself, whips himself, but all he can come out with is a hoi. 'Hoi!' What a thing to say to a lady. But unbelievably the woman Avery is stopping and has turned to look back and wait. Her features swept back by a flush and those lips pertpacked tight.

'Dyer want someone to get him out of there, lovie dovie?'

And knows already he will never forgive himself for calling her that. Where, oh where could he have possibly got 'lovie dovie' from?

'You keep off my property, Mr Gascoigne.'

Bitten and bruised, the hermit cries back to her:

'It's no good you encouraging someone. A person's not saying who, either.'

But the woman Avery does not stop, only walks upright through the arch of the porch of the house of Avery. Whereupon, the hermit Gascoigne moves away from the verge outside the front fence of the property of Avery. He moves away from being out of his emotional depth and from needing, now, help. The man who has brought back the old fear to him has taken the place where the hermit would have had himself hide from that fear.

The hermit is coming to realise they will never leave him alone. All that that is now past is returning. He is going for the only hide he knows.

The eyes, the eyes. They waver around the nightly outside of the house of Miss Avery and manchild Frank inside. But Miss Avery does now instinctively block out the sighting with the use of blinds. So the eyes move around the outside of the house of Miss Avery and guess where she might be. The eyes move with the switching on and off of the lights inside. Pretending sight. Hoping for. Only the manchild Frank to be seen through a peer rift between the blind and the window frame, laying in bed, a little boy lazing into sleep. And tracing the patterns of his mind with his fingertip on the wall by his bed. But no Miss Avery. No joy through her bedroom window. All bunged tight.

The eyes. The eyes. Outside. That night, yes, and the night after. And the night after that.

The lardlump husband of the woman Jenny Salem drives into the realm of the hermit Gascoigne's cottage. John Salem is feeling proprietary, but only by aggression, by having to remind himself that this cottage is his cottage, not the hermit's. It has been so long. Underneath his jutting exterior, he is actually feeling uncomfortable. In all these years he has not put a foot on this piece of his land. A part of the unsung bargain of giving the recluse a mainland refuge from all that island persecution. Felt sorry for him; still does. All those years ago. Twenty? Yes, somewhere around twenty. The husband of the woman Salem has to guess, been so long ago.

John Salem is there because he has ridden about the property for the last two days looking for the hermit Gascoigne and not found him. It would have been the easiest thing to have come straight to the cottage, but the original promise in the agreement all those years ago was privacy and privacy the old man Gascoigne would get.

So John Salem has driven around the property, off and on, during the last two days to corner the hermit so that he could ask him the what-for about what seems to be going on with him. Why has he hung around the front gate of the Salem's residence, first four days ago and then two days ago? Moving a few determined paces up the driveway and then stopping to hurry back. Edging and inching and *asking* from the bottom of the driveway. This smell is from a woman's wifely nose and nothing to be laughed at. The egg cracked.

So John Salem has insisted he will see Emile Gascoigne before his wife points her feelings to confront Miss Avery directly. He wonders, as he approaches the front door of the hermit's cottage, what happened to the window. Brown cardboard has been placed over the broken glass. The wind is hushing at the row of pines around there. He sets the box of rations on the front doorstep and knocks. There is no reply, nor a feeling that there might be one. John Salem walks around the cottage, musing, as he always does, how the devil the old place could be still standing on such a damp little plot. But no sign of Emile Gascoigne.

The man Salem knocks at the front door again. There is no reply. John Salem leaves the rations on the front doorstep and returns home for lunch. He has no inkling that Emile Gascoigne still remains crouching in a corner of the front room just a wall's width away. He will shuffle around at night, but it will be many days before he is seen in daylight again.

From the back of the rear shed where you can see the road burst into clearview for some fifty metres, the man Dere has looked up and has seen Frank chugging down the road, with only his left leg striding forward. His right merely steps up to the left leg, so that the manchild is literally waltzing forward on the run on one leg. This is not common, nor is it playacting. It is just that this time this is how his body has coordinated itself. And even from where he stands Allan Dere can see that Frank is chuckling. Naughty as naughty is, he has obviously got out without Miss Avery's knowing. Heading down the road to the meat works.

The man Dere is now following Frank, but does not know as yet that the manchild is heading down the road to the meat works. He keeps to the shrub off the side of the road without giving himself a good reason for doing so. It doesn't matter. It is enough for a madman to have the impulse to follow. Nothing is comparatively reasonable, anyway.

In the doorway of the meat works' shed, the men sit having lunch. The flies hop at them, nuzzling into the pungent odour of hot blood in their airs and upon them.

Apart from Kellet and Fraser and the boy, they do not like very much baiting the manchild Frank. It is just that, when he is there and when he is taking the bait, you can't help laughing. Yer have to laugh. The man Kellet and the man Fraser, both in their early thirties and both with the caught-on philosophy that it pays not to care a shit, know that the other men there have to laugh. They know also that how the loony Avery is baited can make the most of the rest of the day. The boss Salem takes no notice anyway. So the man Kellet and the man Fraser and the boy smile slow smiles at each other when the manchild comes goose-stepping half-way across the yard, past the shed where blubber-backed skins hang in racks for the drying, and pants his way ecstatically up to the eating group, going:

'Beauty beauty beauty...'

They do not see the man not yet known to them as Allan Dere stop at the shrub's edge and casually lean against a sapling gum to watch. With the men Kellet and Fraser already beginning their priming with watcha Frank old buddyboy old pal old oppo:.

'Here's bloody old Frankie! How the ferg, Frank?'

'G'day, g'day yold bastards. Any of you mugs seen me beaut cat Friar, eh? Eh?'

'Yeah, we skinned and gutted the bugger, ha ha!' This is Kellet, sitting up in the shade of the shed against the offal barrel and warming to his task. 'It's hanging up there on a meat hook.'

Frank rocking slowly on his heels. His mind is working at trying to figure what the ginger-haired man means. Friar? Hanging up in there? His heavy mind urging forward wording, his heavy brow knitting in consternation so that he does not, as would normally be the case, laugh with the men down at the meat works. Bait the bear. Yer have to laugh. As Frank blunders his way up the ramp to look inside for his beaut cat Friar. Urged on by the man Fraser:

'Run, you silly old bugger. *Run.'* ('Run, run!', echoes the boy; jejune, but not old enough yet to feel so.)

By the time the manchild Frank has reached the top of the ramp, he is running as best he can. He is lurching and clumsy, exploding the name of his cat Friar Friar Friar unintelligibly with each breath. The man Kellet has winked at the rest and quickly skidded the palm of his hand against his other. The other men from the meat works surely know how slippery the floor is and yer have to laugh and this is all so instantaneous in any case. The floor in there still running with water and still with the long pole-axed, seemingly, riverlets of blood. All this and only this just before Frank hits the slippery floor inside the shed and skids.

For a moment the manchild tries to correct his balance. He hangs in the air delicately before his legs shoot forwards and his body crashes backwards. Then, with arms flaying and legs convulsive, the giantform of the manchild comes down on its back, bum first. The head whipping backwards and cracking against the concrete floor. Eggshell against concrete. Each man's heart there jumps fearfully. They freeze, all, before some get up to help. But the man Kellet has recovered the quickest and is now laughing. So the men from the abattoirs, even those who have started to get up to help, remain sitting there. They laugh weakly, too, but they don't like it too much. Their eyes nervous, but unadmittedly, for Frank lying dead still there. Yet the man Kellet still leading as he leans towards Frank on one elbow and jibes with a twilling timing:

'Whatcha doing down there, you silly old moll?'

'Beauty. Beauty.' Softly, hurt, stunned at first. The manchild's mind staring upwards towards the roof of the shed. 'Beauty. Beauty.'

The manchild finally gets grinningly to his feet by rolling over onto his side and hauling himself up on, possibly, an imaginary Miss Avery. Erect and rigid, supporting and invisibly by his side. On his knees, now, he crawls back out of the shed to the sunshine part of the ramp. Friar forgotten. The colour comes back to his cheeks as the men applaud. It is a genuine applause of relief, but they too are caught once again in the bear baiting. Even now Kellet with a sausage in front of Frank's face:

'Here, Frankie old son, tuck into this.'

'Fuckin' oath yeah.'

The huge-soft, soft-huge hands of the brother reaching out for the grab and is toyed with. The sausage put here and there each time Frank goes to grasp at it, until the giantform is making painfully uncoordinated lunges for the sausage that have become childish flappy-hand swipes. And with such a look of puzzlement on his face that most of the men are about to turn away, when the man Kellet decides to stop. He holds the sausage still, but still out of Frank's reach. Who rolls questing spaniel's eyes at the man. Kellet shrugging simple and:

'Wash your hands first, Frankie.'

53

The spaniel's eyes of Frank for that instant flicking at possibilities of taps and hand basins and towels from Miss Avery standing by. Kellet taps the barrel he is leaning against. There, flung into the bloody water, are the beasts' livers and hearts and brains.

'Wash 'em in here'll do, Frankie.'

Frank has climbed to his feet totteringly at last, is giggling as though he could feel, and not stand, the expectancy in the air. Then plunges his arms in the blooded water gone gluey viscous, where he washes them so studiously that even the most unwilling of the men burst out laughing with the man Kellet. The more they laugh, the more the manchild washes exaggeratedly, smiling and nodding yeah yeah over his shoulder.

Now Frank removes his arms. The hairs on his thick arms are curling bloodily from the liquid. He wipes his hands on his shirt, on his trousers. Then stands for the sausage. The man Kellet still laughing. He taunts Frank with the sausage, then tosses it to Fraser over Frank's shoulder, and Fraser tosses it to the boy and the boy back to Kellet. All this before the manchild's brain can get the body on the move. Frank swings a belated full circle, comes rocking to a dithering halt. He laughs but this time there are tears in his eyes and this time a grunt from him of confusion and frustration. Kellet holds the sausage towards him. Frank swipes again and knocks, as he should have done anyway, the sausage across the yard, where the red mongrel sheepdog swoops on it and has bolted it down before Frank can pissorf pissorf get to it. He stands looking down at the spot where the sausage was, trying hard to register how come the sausage is not there. He resolves it into the low moan of 'Aw'. And cannot move from wishing it staringly to come back.

'Never mind, Frank. Have a man's meal.'

This is the man Fraser who is holding out his palm. On it is a squashed blowfly. The manchild spins around with an urgent wanting.

'Beauty. Beauty.'

'Go on, we don't want it. Get it into your guts, mate'

There is the urging of them all now. Frank, go on, mate. Get it in yer. Frankie old cob. More flies being caught and placed, half of them still in twitch, in Fraser's palm. Come be, Frank, one of the boys.

When he eats the first one and all cheer, the manchild looks around and grins widely. They clap and stomp their feet when he eats a second. He laughs vacuously at their appreciation. Skips, wanting to piddle his pants, a little pre-empting dance of joy. His friends, one of the boys. And is about to eat the third, when the man Dere reaches him.

The man Dere has put on a slow smile that won't disturb the workers too much, takes Frank by the arm and walks him away. He is almost halfway across the clearing before Frank registers that he is being led away. Then he tries to get his arm released to go back to his friends back there, one of the boys, and out of his mouth:

'Pissorf, pissorf.'

Yet he is not trying to free his arm too much and his words do not have much energy in them. He does not, this time, as he would have with Miss Avery, dig his heels in and sit down refusing to budge then and there on the spot. His eyes puffily darting little looks at the man Dere forcing him along and trying to register where he has seen him before. Probably a mate of Friar's. His beaut cat Friar.

Allan Dere, as though it were his own, closes the gate carefully after himself. He has guided the manchild through it before him. Even so, such is the indusium of behaviour of Miss Avery upon him that Frank has a moment of doubt about the man coming so owning-like onto the place, but the moment is swept away when he registers the playmate possibilities. Still it is enough of a disruption for Frank to start all over again:

'G'day, Mr Dere. How the fuckareyer, eh? Eh?'

'Your sister's calling you, Frank.'

She is, her voice a bark from behind the back of the house, searching the orchard for her brother's bulkform probably hiding behind the trunk of an apple tree. She has realised that he is not on the property, must have escaped down to the meat works again, and, is girding herself mentally to have to go down there and fetch him. It is a thing she hates. Has always known about the sniggers from the men behind her back. Their half-baked sexual innuendoes about the sexlessness of her and how those explosions of laughter plop up behind her. Knowing that is what hurts the most. So the little birdlike woman calls again just in case and wishes the telltale wriggle of her brother's flabby bulkform to show itself I am here, I am here.

Now she, the woman Avery, the sister, gives up looking for

Frank and is returning to the house by way of the far side, when she hears the voices. She stops. She is at the corner of the house such that she can peer around the corner of the house without giving herself away. Again the feeling the invader makes her sneak. She peeks and sees and hears and listens.

The man Dere is back to sitting with his back against the old water pump. He is sketching in the earth between his legs. Alongside of him Frank squats, rocking back and forwards on his heels, agile in the children's squat. He is asking, she can see, 'Whatcha doing, whatcha doing?' And she can hear the words 'Mr Dere Mr Dere'. And:

'Miss Avery's after a bloke, Mr Dere. Stupid old moll. Don't give a bloke away, Mr Dere. Orright? Gotta keep a posse out for me beaut animal Friar. Orright, Mr Dere?' Delivered only a few

56

centimetres away from the man Dere's left ear, as though he was trying to hypnotise him. Miss Avery smiles at seeing Frank so objectively like this. The good and funny and lovable old boy. Can even catch herself at it; it has been, she thinks, a long time since I've smiled. Passing strange; she has never thought herself a smiling person.

'Who's that, eh?' Prodding the earth and knocking Allan Dere's finger away from the drawing.

'That's Miss Avery, Frank.' Miss Avery starts to hear her name. Said like that. Caressed. She never thought she would hear it like that.

'Where's her scrawny arms, eh, Mr Dere? Eh?'

'Can't you feel them around you? Let's say she's lost them, okay?'

The manchild chuckling orright, orright.

'Silly old bag. Cripes, y'oughta see the skinny old bugger having a wash all over. No bull.'

'Tell me, Frank.'

Miss Avery watches the man sit up and pull the thought of her washing all over towards himself, and feels the colour rise in her cheeks. Frank chuckling; he knows the response. It is, after all, a standard meat works' reply:

'Slack as a yak and twice as salty, see. Fuck, y'oughta see her legs. Get em around a bloke and he'd need a blowtorch to cut his way out, eh? Eh, Mr Dere?'

'No, I mean what's she like when she's washing all over.'

The man Dere's voice is now raspish as though his mouth has gone suddenly dry, so that Miss Avery cringes back against the wall of the house. Feeling herself really naked before him. Her

57

own woman's body. That thin and unmentionable thing of hers. Brown freckles on her chest. The taut skeleton that she washes all over. All that running of blood for all those years, and now the hand. The swollen and brutish hand. Intolerable. She struggles to disengage herself from the wall, is already mentally forcing herself to take one step towards showing herself. When, now, the woman Salem, too, arrives. The car swung into the drive to exactly, as usual, broach the property.

Miss Avery drops quickly back against the side wall again. The colour in her cheeks rises again in case the woman Salem has seen her spying on the man Dere and Frank. For a panicky moment she wants to run. She wants to come out and fight. She wants to run. But she stays rigidly where she is, not even daring to peer around the corner. This is intolerable, yes. Stupid. *Stupid.*

Frank, the man, the sister. The three of them caught in separate frieze by the woman Salem.

Jenny Salem climbs out of her car. At first she does not see Dere, only Frank. He looks so funny sitting by the old water pump and staring at it that she does laugh by way of a bubble bursting. Now she sees that Frank is staring into the face of the man Dere sitting with his back against the old water pump. And moves towards them. They do not look up, only the man Dere nodding at the ground at her feet and:

'You'd be the slut showgirl.'

'I beg yours?' This is all not going just as it should.

'The showgirl and the farmer offer the hermit... what did they call it?... "patchwork" around their country property and a cottage. Showgirl makes country society. Hiya, *toots.'*

'Where do you come from?'

She has remembered that she can mix it.

58

'I read old newspapers, *toots.*'

Jenny Salem swings wide of Frank and strides from them now to the kitchen door. There is no smile at the corners of her cosmetic mouth now. There is now only the kitchen door and Miss Avery undoubtedly somewhere inside. She calls Miss Avery and bangs loudly on the door. And, around the side of the house only five metres away, Miss Avery waits fearfully. Intolerable to think of being caught out now, like this, split and spilled out into the open. Feeling as naughty as Frank.

The woman Salem is so engrossed in flushing out Miss Avery that she has not noticed Frank crawling after her on all fours up to the kitchen door. Where he is now imitating his beaut cat Friar by licking at the filthy cat's tin there, then is turning to crawl up to Jenny Salem and to shove his purring head up her dress. Meeouw, meeouw. The tom's on the lick. The way the woman Salem swings around, in shock, causes them both to reel and pitch against the kitchen wall. Frank's body stopping while his mind registers whether he is hurt or not. She pulls her dress back from over his head and, in a pique of absolute fury, grabs a handful of his hair and twists. Frank screams for his sister in great lumps of childishness. And Miss Avery, embarrassment instantly forgotten, comes running. Regained all the push she has ever needed in the world again.

'Help you?'

But her cold and hard eyes say to the woman Salem don't ever do that again, even as Frank rolls back onto his buttocks and reaches for her to reel her in with one single movement and to pout from there at Jenny Salem. Who has not come here to badinage words, so that the tone of her voice, dipping in sharply, carries an accusation:

'Emile's been hanging around our place and now he's gone bush or something.'

Miss Avery's eyes narrow. She pats Frank alright alright and her eyes narrow in concentration. She answers in a voice that will only answer once:

'That man sitting there just brought Frank back from the meat works.' It is no answer for Jenny Salem, but it is for the man Dere. He looks up sharply from the old water pump. And watches languidly as Frank thrusts his hand up the woman Salem's dress again. She cannot react as forcibly as she did last time, can only grab his stiff and unbending arm with both hands and try to either hoist herself off it or pull it from under her. With, now, Miss Avery irritably assisting her. Their four hands small against the manchild's arm. And he trying to shake them off as a large dog might shake, bodily, rabbits:

'Pissorf, pissorf.'

But the little birdlike sister, having finally achieved the pushing herself off the wall, will not now be shaken off and refuses to give in. She grabs Frank's ear and twists you naughty boy. He cries out but it is still in her name. Miss Avery, Miss Avery. Then is led by her, by the ear, by her will, by all the years of what must have been and must be, back inside the sanctuary of the house he and she should never have left given such invasions. Only stopping momentarily in the doorway of the kitchen to hiss at the woman Salem:

'You tell him this is no wine valley. We don't let rooms!'

The woman Salem stands, staring furiously at the door. She is willing the woman Avery to return and apologise, then finally turns and walks back towards her car. Stops for the second time alongside of the man Dere. This time he is smiling and smally nodding, even though he still does not look up at her, and will not. She whips it at him with a cultivated chill:

'Why don't you just bugger off, whoever you are!'

Now the man Dere answers so softly that the woman has to bend slightly so that she can hear him. His mouth barely moving:

'Yes, *toots*, I know you all right. You've leered at me for how long? For as long as I can remember you've swept your face across my eyes, sneering and knowing when the light catches the lewd side of your lewd profile. The lipstick gash and the bad cigarette breath. All those corridors of private hotels with your purple fingernails on the come on. And in your eyes always... quiet perversions. Who's been following who?'

'You must be crazy or something. I'm not going to listen to you.'

'Today, you put them on especially, didn't you? Today...' Now looking up now and catching the woman Salem with a demeaning smirch, '... you're wearing your bum-bouncing G-string briefs just for me, aren't you, bitch.'

Jenny Salem swings her hand. The man Dere has already ducked. Her slap merely catches him across the back of the head. Now she is already storming away from him and is already backing her car away from the property of Miss Avery. In the car she is thinking, I am not dead yet. Yet still swiftly glances at herself in the rear vision mirror. She is not weeping for the insult. She is not in rage because of what she is seeing in her eyes there. She is weeping in outrage because she is tired and tired and so very tired of seeing the sameness of herself in the eyes in the rear vision mirror there. Coming, lard.

Frank climbing out of what the man Dere presumes to be the sitting room's window. There is not so much of a dummy there, after all. The way the manchild has silently opened the window, has even slithered through and fallen, yes, but without too much sound, and then has quietly reclosed the window is an observation for the man Dere that there might not be as much of a dummy in the giantform of Frank as first might be expected. The man Dere will remember it. Frank giggles as he half-trots almost sideways

61

back up to the man Dere. Holding, as he comes, presumably his penis and certainly a handful of his crutch, as though he would hold back on the peeing in his trousers. He has the excitements.

'Beauty beauty beauty, Mr Dere. Me cat Friar come back, eh?'

And resumes his squat at the side of Dere. Gazing, once more, with absolute intention at both the profile and the sketch and wafting at Dere a nameless food taste of the last thing he has eaten. Fishy. The man Dere shifting his position so that he can pull out two coins from his pocket. He holds up the coins in front of Frank's face, so that the manchild has a desperately irresolvable decision at that moment of whether he should go for the dirt sketch or for the two coins.

'Toss you for your sister, Frankie. Odds or evens.'

The man Dere calling as the coins rill through the air. They land as he calls them. Frank clapping his hands, not understanding, full of delight; a game, a game. They land after the second flip not as Dere calls them. And not as he calls them the third time. Two to one. Dere hesitates, then lies. Two to one for him, not Frank.

'Best of three, Frankie. You've lost.' Hard. This is no game. The manchild's hand shoots out in a quaking wantness, gimme gimme my turn, but the man turns hard and no-nonsense eyes onto Frank's puffy puffing face.

Miss Avery has seen it all, again from the kitchen window. She will soon work out how Frank gets outside, but not quite yet. For now she stands and looks at the man Dere with her biglittle brother and wonders about the tossing of the coins. She waits, too, for the second move. It comes, finally, in a way that makes her hurry out onto the porch. The man Dere suddenly reaches one arm sideways and hooks Frank around the neck. He pulls him in to nestle Frank's head against his neck, rocking slowly so that the manchild feels the lullaby and hears the whisper in his ear:

'I've just won your sister off you, Frank.'

He continues to hold Frank's head there, even though the manchild is now starting to fidget to be let go of. Images of coins floating in the air. And Miss Avery, now, from the porch:

'Frank!'

But it is Allan Dere who gets up as soon as she calls. Frank sits there, rocking on his haunches and still staring intently at the space that has recently been filled by the man Dere an eye blink ago. Carn, carn, Mr Dere. Who has walked so boldly up to Miss Avery that she feels the twinges of panic begin to pull at her stomach. There is a stranger between her and her Frank. How has this come to be?

'Frank's not to talk to strangers!' And suddenly feels exposed, as though in the rush of these words she has made an intimacy. This man speaks to her softly:

'Miss Avery, where I come from, the city, the rain cannons off brick. Someone's mind breaks and you all avert your eyes where I come from. When you listen at night, in the early morning, you can hear faint cries for help. Their faces, you know, as grey as dead ashes.' The woman squirming in the sudden realisation of an unsaid submission. 'Miss Avery, listen. Your hand.'

And then suddenly has it in both of his; she doesn't know how come. A man is holding her swollen and clubby hand, his thumbs caressing the swelling. She has never seen, in all her life, a hand so ugly and revolting, and is appalled at what is happening beyond her control. The man's thumbs working towards the small scab in the centre of the back of her hand. The point of the sting, at the sting, where the sting. He must see a nail head, for he speaks down at the hand she would gladly have shrivelled:

'Stigmata.'

'It's only a bee's sting.' Her voice too loud, but unheard?

'You have the stigmata,' his grip firming when she tries to pull her hand away and his face turning up to hers. 'So have I. The scar across my eye, you see.'

But Miss Avery cannot see. Even when the man Dere

blessedly lets her hand go and traces a diagonal line across his left eyebrow, she cannot see any scar. She does not even know what a stigmata is, so she looks and nods and steps away so that her hand, herself, her all-thing is out of reach of the invader. Yet will dwell on, soon, the fact that a man has never felt her like that, in all her long and feeling life, never. And that so sad. But for now she hears herself in an unknown tone:

'What can I do for you, Mr Dere?'

The man Dere shakes his head, nothing, nothing. He steps back, hesitates only for a moment while Miss Avery takes the opportunity of the room to breathe, then goes to walk away around the side of the house. She knows where he is going.

'Wait.'

He does not turn, nor inquires, but does stop and does wait. The woman Avery hurries back into the house, such that her body hops along with urgent little bounds. The birdlike. She is not thinking about what she is doing. It is the way it is.

Her sudden thrust of movement disturbs Frank. It is as though he senses, rather than sees, his sister move away from him for a cause not for him. Slowly he forces his eyes from the spot where the man Dere was sitting and returns to the present from dreams of coins floating in the air and games and a playmate Friar to come back. With a tilt of alarm, his mind pushes him near the man Dere once more and the sighting of the cat's tin crazily caught between two of the porch boards. He chuckles. Friar. His beaut cat Friar coming home. The manchild clucks approval as he picks up the tin. Then bangs it triumphantly and repeatedly against the verandah post as he calls loudly and rhythmically for cat cat Friar cat. But stops in trail-off when Miss Avery returns. She carries two blankets and a pillow and an intention that takes her straight past her brother. Frank's eyes narrow with a squirt of jealousy.

There is, though, no grace in the manner she thrusts them into the man Dere's arms:

'It's the best I can do. Another night, that's all.'

Allan Dere shakes his head, and walks away around the side of the house. He should have surely, she wonders, have nodded.

'They're my blankets, see.'

'Yes of course they're yours Frank.'

'Ain't his blankets, see.'

'I only gave him a lend of them Frank.'

'Mine, see. Mine.'

'Yes Frank.'

'And this is my house, ain't it, Miss Avery? And... and me beaut cat Friar, he's mine, ain't he, Miss Avery? The sheds're mine. Miss Avery? The sheds're mine, eh?'

'All yours Frank.'

'They're not Mr Dere's, are they, Miss Avery?'

'They're not Mr Dere's, Frank, no.'

'And... and you're mine.'

'Yes.'

'And you're mine, see, yold drip. You're mine, see. Geez, I like

Mr Dere, don't I, Miss Avery? Real beaut, ain't he, Miss Avery?'

'Don't go near strangers Frank.'

Allan Dere lays thinking. The early morning's weak dampness is upon him. He has used the pillow Miss Avery gave him, and has done for the last three nights. He hasn't used the blankets. The blankets are folded between the pillows. He shivers deeply and re-feels the biting cold of the six, seven or eight days, whichever it has been, he has been sleeping out here.

For the moment he lies there. Again, today, like the other mornings, he cannot bring himself to care for anything, let alone his own bodily wants. He remembers how, yesterday, he found a flea on his chest. He smiles to himself now, remembering the flea he found yesterday on his chest. That gentleman's companion. There will be other gentleman's companions on his body, he knows. He has found the one lodged uncomfortably on his chest and has thrown it away, but he did not look for others on other parts of his body. Knowing they are there. His mind sees them crawling up his legs, but he no longer reacts itchedly to the image. It is what, he supposes, he is there for. The holy dirt of the martyrs. The holy lice, the lice on the body of Thomas a Becket, the filthy rags of St Francis, stigmata, stigmata. Atone by letting in the worm.

So the man now known as Allan Dere lies there. He has not quite got used to the stench that is starting to rise from his own body, and would find it quite pleasant if he couldn't smell the other. The foul musk that rises from his unwashed crutch. It has been like this as long as he can remember, but now threatens to overpower him. Rank and nauseating. Perhaps, he thinks, it might finally absorb me. And smiles, not against it.

The man wears a grey, well-tailored suit, with waistcoat and black leather shoes. He is not so tall, but is heavy and squat. Dark and simian. But his jaw does not jut too much and his eyes are brown and trustworthy. He looks odd, rather than displaced, as he walks along the track to the cottage of the hermit Gascoigne. Facially and from a distance, he looks too solid and dependable to look out of place anywhere.

He is both those things, too, as an investigator; that's why he is such a good operator. At college, they called him 'Mane' Sloane because his body hair not only darkly covered his chest but also his shoulders and down his back to his shoulder blades. Nobody, even in the city from where he has come, calls him Mane now. Now it's just Sloane. He has long ago only had acquaintances, has disliked the sentiment that goes with friends. Male or female. He has far preferred the cut and thrust of people disliked and half-liked than, again the word, the invasion of people taken in-board as friends. And it has been this distance between his motives and his actions that has made him, first, an exceptional crime reporter and, in his later years, what he has called a 'contact man'. For Sloane is a resenter. Resentment has been the one final pouring of his life of forty years. He knows of no single reason why he should resent, nor does he care to waste the time to try to discover a reason why he should resent. All he has come to realise is that he *hubs* best when he is being resentful.

The operator Sloane tries to lay no ghost, nor build up any images of ghosts. He only works on the margin of existence that is given by resenting, calculating and fighting. As an operator the first gives him a worthy skepticism; the second gives him a unique incentive; and the third, a means that usually gets an end.

Sloane also knows where the police, having to rattle the bones of a large form-filling organisation (papphagous, he has called it; oh yes, Sloane has the substance which, too, has given him researching ability), begin and where the police end. Even as a city detective he had done one or two victims' families favours by hinting at solutions that they would not get if they stayed on the police organisation's roundabout. Those favours led to repute and repute led to demand. So that, today, the operator Sloane operates on the one or two highly-paid assignments he gets a year from well-heeled people. Some of these people are respectable, some notorious but all have no faith whatsoever in the processes of the normal forces of law and order. Sloane is a distinct man for distinct jobs.

The operator Sloane isn't going out of his way not to be seen making his way towards the hermit's cottage, but he knows he will not be seen, for that somehow is a constancy of his life. Only when he opens his mouth has he found that he is remembered. It is not only that he speaks spectaculously out of the side of his mouth or that his voice is so deep that it is vibrant. It is because he calls everyone, male or female, 'citizen'. An affectation, but a stock-in-trade. It has never stopped amusing him. Its anachronism goes with what he knows as an anachronistic job. Good. That furthers the resentment and that in turn makes him better at the job. Free and easy. Unillusioned and very, very patient. Has found himself empirically to be.

At the same time as the operator Sloane threads his way towards the rear of the hermit's cottage, the man Kellet from the meat works finally manages to catch the manchild's attention. He has been waiting for the best part of an hour for Frank to come out into the front garden. He has waited, has squatted and is cursing his luck for having to be there. But his blood pumping and eager for the fight.

The manchild has seemed to have lost his bearings. It is always like this when he comes outside or moves inside, as though the change of light lets go the grasp his mind has on the idea. And as usual he steps off the kitchen porch to walk a few paces up the gravel path, then turns, walks back and clomps back onto the porch. There to wait for the reason for being out there to come back or for some other kinesis to take its place. Having quite forgotten that the thing he is usually muttering in cadence with his paces is the thing he is trying to remember. This time it has been 'Water, water, water' said so many times, it has lost its meaning.

Now the manchild calls out, 'Miss Avery?'

It is a cry into the air, not a direct asking. He has known for years that if you cry that name out to the sky, the answer will come back, immediately responding and all-knowing. The mothersister, the brotherson.

'Frank water the bushes.'

From Miss Avery inside. Deep within the house. And factually and ready with the answering. The little sister has known the question will probably come, and has in fact waited for the question from the manchild to come. So now she calls to her brother about watering the bushes and settles back at the sewing of Frank's shirt.

When he sees Frank, the man Kellet backs away a few careful paces from the boxthorn bush he is hiding behind, then turns and ambles freshly back about fifty paces. Then stops. And then calls Frank's name as he would a dog. Here, boy, Frank, here boy. Here, mutt.

The three men from the meat works even further down the road draw back into the shrub so that they cannot be seen from the road and snigger amongst themselves as Kellet approaches. The dog call amuses them. Trust Rusty Kellet to play the fool baying at the moon at a time like this. Even so, even with their odds, they are, each, a bit shaky.

Frank hears his name called; it is a wonderful thing floating in the air. Pan pipes, the piper. The body follows; the mouth murmuring yeah? yeah? yeah? His eyes wide open with the wonder as they could puffily be. The manchild follows. Down the path and out of the gate and sees, to his delight, one of the abattoirs' men beckoning him with wide sweeps of the arm. Promising magic and mateship, man to man. The manchild trots after, scuffing along in his slippers, flopping at the heel, mandarinate.

Now Frank's name is being hailed by all four men in the same way, lilting in the air, as clear as a sounding bell, increasing the urgency of Frank to go faster. But actually slowing him down, the slippers flopping crazily and impeding any faster.

The men from the meat works do not care if Miss Avery hears it. They do care if the man whose name they have learnt is Dere hears it.

He does. From his shed the man Dere has clearly heard the calling of Frank and has clearly seen the manchild hobbledy shuffle along the road crazily eager. And so the man Dere moves out. To cut across the orchard. To keep Frank in sight. His elective earning of the shed's keep, he supposes, as if it matters why he is doing so. Following Frank.

Now they have the manchild there at the turning of the bend in the road, the men from the meat works prod at him in the ribs and make him squirm and laugh and wriggle. They are doing so so that he won't suddenly get bored and turn around to go back home again. Then, when he begins to frown because they are beginning to hurt him and is becoming confused and muttering for Miss Avery, the man Kellet begins to tell him about his beaut cat. His beaut cat Friar. That his beaut cat Friar has run into that boxthorn bush over there and won't come out. From Darwin? Yeah, all the way from shit-kickin' Darwin.

Only the man Kellet is in immediate sight when the man Dere arrives at the place where Frank is down on all fours at the box-thorn. The man Dere pulls up short, nods to the man he has recognised from the meat works, but the worker only stares at him cat-transparently. Dere notices the vein in the man's temple throb. The sighting disturbs him; it is so physical. And when he goes into the scrub for those few metres to heave Frank to his feet, the four of them come for him.

It is an untidy beating. The four men try to fight individually and get in each other's way. But the man Dere has no chance perhaps, not even the presence of mind to fight back even a little. He can, and does, though, get to his feet for two of the three times they knock him down. It is the man Kellet who finally has the nous to go for the throat to keep the man Dere down the third time. It is, too, the man Kellet who says the reason:

'The Boss doesn't like how you talk to his Missus.'

At the start of the beating, the manchild has clapped and laughed at the funny show, but has then slowed and soon got frightened. His hugeform incongruous as it tries to cringe back into the boxthorn. Wide-eyed and frightened. The sight, here, of human blood mightily enveloping. He is turning right and left as the man Dere is hit and is mixing little laughs with his whimpering. Vestiges of flight, vestiges of to-stay. Miss Avery? The whimpering.

All quiet now. The four men from the Salem meat works have snorted at each other, each with a vague dissatisfaction that he might not have pulled his weight, and have now gone. Frank stands. He does not look at the form of the man Dere directly, but only out of the corner of his eye. What comes out now is a high and sharp giggle. Displacement. Nor does he walk directly up to the form of Allan Dere but steps sideways, as though he is hoping that he won't be seen. The man Dere hunched around himself protectively, sucking in air past his bloody lips. Is nudged gently, once, twice, by Frank's foot, but does not respond.

'Whatcha. Whatcha, Mr Dere, eh?'

Frank scuffs at the dirt by Dere's side. The answer he is waiting for, by word or by sign, does not come from the man Dere. He backs, then, a few paces away from the man Dere, then, when loosed, when not commanded back, turns and trots back home as ungainly as he came down the road. His slippers still flapping, but this time has thumb clenched firmly between his teeth.

Behind him the man Dere can only roll painfully over in his first attempt to get to his feet. He succeeds in his second attempt.

71

The little sister knows that something has happened. It is not only that Frank has come inside frantically fighting for breath so that the very alarmed way he is trying to catch his breath is in itself likely to bring on an attack of asthma. It is the way he has blunted his way into the house and has moved himself against her. Her voice now not of a rhythm to him, but shouting up to his ear commanding him to stand up straight. To breathe. In, out, in out. She hangs on, her arms full of his chest, forcing as much air out as she can. Using the pressure of her thin, strong arms to mount a regulation upon his wheezing.

It is only when he has sat, quieted, the rhythmic breathing inducing itself, the overflush of blood returning to his head, that the woman Miss Avery leaves him to go outside and look for the slipper she has noticed he has lost. She becomes alert when she finds the slipper just outside the fence by the side of the road. Looks now suspiciously up and down, but nothing and nobody. A bogey man, she will probably say to her largeformed brother that night. Not before. A bogey got Frankie today, eh? And he will probably laugh and his bulkframe will bunch expectantly for his sister to call him a silly old thing and to tickle.

It is not the same this time, for when the woman Avery turns back into the front garden, the manchild is coming out of the house. She calls but he takes no notice. Has to actually hurry after him around the side of the house to find him standing there, a look of bemusement on his face of a fact trying to stay fixed in his memory, and his eyes fixed on the sheds. He will not, either, be led away by her.

She lifts Frank's leg up, as much as if she was shoeing his hoof, and puts the slipper back on. Then pats him on the shoulder with the gesture that he knows means wait here. This time obeying it without a murmur.

At the entrance to the second shed, the woman Avery looks down on the man Dere, lying filthy on the old filthy mattress and holding himself in a foetus position. There is the smell of man in there. She shifts uncomfortably, wills herself to stay. The empty cans of food he has eaten have been tossed into a pile in the corner and are now alive with ants. She knows in the night there would be the rats. The sun strikes the damp brown earth in there through a few nailholes in the old corrugated iron roof. Hard flints of beams, cold and mean.

The man Dere looking up at her. There is no movement in his eyes. No asking, no wanting. And when she looks back down to his bloody face, he answers her with a short shake of the head. A gruesome and tight smile. Miss Avery, the invasion goes on. But her heart hurts deeply at the sight of him, so that, not daring to touch, she has to turn away.

The woman Avery returns to the shed. The man Dere has not moved. The manchild, the brother stands behind her. He is murmuring something she does not understand. The man Dere murmurs something, too, that she does not understand. She does not ask the one or the other what he is saying. She merely places on the ground, within easy reach, the dish of warm water with antiseptic and cloth, and the plate of cold meat and salad she has covered with a cloth.

She will feed the man Dere, both as unceremoniously and as carefully, as this for the next three days. On the third day, the man Dere is not there, so she will nod with satisfaction and just leave the food.

She will not yet have realised she has accepted him by then.

But she will catch herself up looking now and then for the little signs of him moving around the place. And begins to feel coy when she still remembers to pull down the blinds at night. Cubby holed.

The operator Sloane, intensely disliking the muddy damage being done to the shine on his black leather shoes but would never show it, comes up to the cottage of Emile Gascoigne and knocks heavily on the back door, as a matter of principle. He has always tried around the back first. It is not just because he has the sleuth's cliché in his mind that they'll always try to escape out of the back door while you're notching your presence into the front door. The operator Sloane has no flipperies of images like that, but is attracted to the offbeat by nature because the offbeat is not really the really different way of looking at things. That is why he is a good operator. He has been known to loathe the word hunch when it has been connected with him. That was in public. In private, which is only to himself and never more than a passing feeling of quiet amusement, he likes the sound of the word 'nose'. 'Nose' is hunch, hunch is 'nose'. The nose for. So the operator Sloane bangs no-nonsense on the back door of the hermit's cottage. It is a knock that says let's not shit around, citizen.

He gets, of course, no reply. Expected none.

Now the operator moves around the cottage. He stops and listens for sounds of movement inside. Looking at the ground around for signs of living. Cigarette packet, paper, tins, something carelessly or innocently dropped. For his first circuit, he keeps a few paces away from the walls of the cottage. He does not want to press. Don't tread on the eggs when you first move into an environment. Slowly, slowly catcha da monkey. For the first circuit around.

Back at the rear of the cottage, the operator Sloane prises back a sheet of the old iron covering the back verandah and just manages to see the edge of the bath and the side of the bucket toilet. He smiles as he lets the sheet spring back into place. The old portable toilet will tell him if the hermit is still around or when last the hermit Gascoigne was last around.

Now he is moving around the building touching its walls. This is a man who goes by a sense of power in the divination of feeling. Thigmomancy. Yes, he knows his words, believes in the lysis given a little human nudge along, rather than the crisis. Is moving past, without touching, the window behind which the cardboard is pasted. It would be easy to shift the cardboard and get the entry, but he does not want to do that. The 'nose' not to is enough to prevent him.

At the front door, the operator Sloane now stands listening for just a brief moment and seems caught instanter by the senses. He quickly kneels on the doorstep. A quick efficient brush of his dark hand has swept it first for the kneeling. With difficulty, because of his thickset torso, he bends right over and sniffs in the air from under the door. Then straightens and smiles. This is no deserted cottage weeping draughts of unfettered dampness. The operator has caught, he would bet, the pungency of something still living in there.

So that the man Sloane walks away from Emile Gascoigne's cottage's front door. He does so noisily. Where, a few metres away on the blind side of the cottage, he picks up a short-long, long-short broken branch of pine and breaks off the too supple end. Then quickly slips back to the wall by the front window again. There, he prods the thin end of the branch between the cardboard and the window pane and levers the one away from the other noiselessly and abruptly. And sees the outstretched legs of startled Emile Gascoigne, sitting crouched in the near corner, retract urgently.

The old hermit has been laughed at many times in his life, but not so cruelly nor contemptuously as now. He has had enough experience of the ring of authority to open the door almost immediately to the operator when the operator stopped laughing and commanded the hermit Gascoigne the citizen to open the door pronto.

Twenty years earlier the hermit Gascoigne had walked the streets of the island town and was pursued by murmuring voices. Mostly he was spat on and sometimes he was stoned. When the police took him in that day in regard to the attacks on the boys and girls, he had for two days never swerved from his jumbled, inarticulate, stumbling protestations of innocence. He had been released two days later to start a path that would lead to the lifelines of the Salems.

But during those two days, he had spent unendurable hours being soaked by one thing he could not endure — the *pry* of other humans. During those two days he had been stripped of his clothing and had blood and hair specimens taken. And when they dropped him back at his broken-down shack after those two days, all he had on was one old Army blanket. The morning was cold and he knew how dirty he looked to them. Them all. He was as naked as he had never wanted to be and they had accused him, abashed and encrusted and naked, of the unmentionable. And he felt guilty of every crime that any and every man has ever committed in all the human lives-time during the all human story. They had taken away even his underpants.

These things, ausculated monstrously from the past, does the hermit Gascoigne remember so shamefully as he answers, nakedly and exposed again, all the questions that the operator Sloane asks him about the man Dere.

Chapter 3

Her name was Selma Youngstein and she was nine years old. She was the first out of the class that day by five minutes because her essay on last weekend was the best and the neatest, so she was let out of school those five minutes earlier than the rest of her class. She had run across the schoolyard, had opened the schoolyard gate and had dutifully clipped it to stay open for the others when they were let out. Happiness blushing at her cheeks. And was running across the side street that bordered the primary school when the car hit her.

She didn't see it before it hit her. She was in dancing spree towards her mother's waiting Jaguar and had been just about to cry out joyfully, 'Mummy!'

Mrs Sally Youngstein was flipping through a copy of *Time*. She would have normally been out of the car and waiting for Selma at the gate. She normally would have been talking to the other mothers, but it had not yet got to the time when they started out of their cars and gathered for a few pleasantries that would end abruptly when the child came, and when the passing remark, laughed and waved on at, could be made. They were all Jewish mothers waiting for little Jewish children to take them back to, generally, excelling Jewish homes. And because they were all Jewish, they waited until the time school got out to be almost arrived before they got out of the cars. They knew it all over too well to informalise a formality. Get in, pick up, get out. Economise the action.

So Mrs Sally Youngstein waited in the Jaguar and didn't hear the dullingly thick thump of little Selma being hit by the car. But she did have the horror of having to come to terms with coming to realise that the heavy thwack on the side of her own car, on the back mudguard, was the almost-then body of her daughter landing. When she had finally overcome the shock to open her door to see what had happened, she could not get the door open more than a few centimetres, but not enough. Something was blocking it.

It took Mrs Sally Youngstein at least two heaves to realise that the something jamming her car door was the something solid and the something soft of what could be a human being — and then another moment of whirring absorption to recognise the parts of the cardigan and frock she could see beneath the partly-opened door. There was no one there to hear the first moan come out of Mrs Sally Youngstein. She had closed the door back again by an instinctive reaction. A part of the red cardigan and the pinkly printed cotton of the frock had caught, like lewd tongues, in the door at her feet. Stuck out fast and up at her.

She began screaming then, hermetically sealed in her car, all doors locked except the one her daughter was caught in. The mothers, the children, the teachers, the people had to stand outside this vacuum flask and watch helplessly. Horror pulled at all their hearts. The children ushered quickly away. But Mrs Sally Youngstein sounded so far away that they could have almost been watching her on television. Sound and grief muted.

Mrs Sally Youngstein was still screaming when the police arrived a quarter of an hour later. The officers took one look at the situation and rang for another ambulance. They could not open the door for fear of moving the child wedged under the door, nor could they free the child's clothing from the door because that needed scissors. They had tried hacking for a while with a penknife, but they didn't have scissors. So they turned their backs on what they didn't want to see and ushered everyone away from the car. And the further the bystanders moved away from the car, the more, too, they turned their backs on the daughter, the car and the mother screaming in there.

The car that had hit Selma Youngstein had not stopped.

Mordecai Youngstein was the son of a son of a son of a son. The wine-making business had been in this, the local branch of the original German-Jewish family, for that long. Longer than anyone else in the whole *shittim* country, he would joke. And now, and since for a long time, the largest in the shittim country by far.

Mordecai Youngstein had the bearing that went with that position, too. It was a bearing that, he the son, had aped from his father, who had aped, as the son, that same bearing from *his* father. That bearing, as Mordecai Youngstein had realised a long time ago in a basically Anglo-Saxon country, was a bearing of the neck. The European bearing, not the parsimonious English bearing of the mummified face they called the 'stiff upper lip'. A minor point of realisation. But it gave to Mordecai in particular and the Youngsteins before him in general a paradigmatic bearing that smacked a neat difference in this fundamentally British country. A European carriage of body, yes; that Mediterranean, oleaciously-shaded carriage, yes; but a bearing of true aristocracy for all of that.

Other than that, other than the darkly European bearing, Mordecai Youngstein was an ordinary man, physically and intellectually. He was, too, ordinarily Jewish, which meant, even if ever he had wanted to, he could never have passed for anything but Jewish. Alternatively, he was thought of, even at a passing glance, as archetypically Jewish-looking. But he had his bearing, tried and ancestrally proven, and that alone made Mordecai Youngstein a very unordinary man. It simply, like a hypnotic key, made him aware of himself and his line all the time and, by that, aware of his essential dignity that must be maintained all the time, no matter what. If was of no consequence if that dignity to Mordecai Youngstein really only meant a way of holding oneself. The point was that it had *worked.*

And it had worked in the simple way that it glossed upon the hard, hating, disdainful and, beyond his family, xenophobic character of the man. Being born rich and having to work hard to get richer had not 'made' Mordecai Youngstein; it had only cemented in the acquired characteristics of aping the father of a father of a father. He loved or he hated; he admired or hated; he allied a cause or hated; he helped or hated. He would say he was callous, not hating. But, whatever, the drive-right-through that the ever-spectre of his own dignity gave him had made Mordecai Youngstein a civic leader of the greater Jewish community in the country. A leader in the Zionist Association and the Jewish National Fund equally and unequivocally.

That, and being a leading industrialist in a public-eye industry (the slosh industry, he would call it), made him a potential terrorist target as much as any such influential persons in any part of the world would be. And Mordecai Youngstein was well aware of the fact as much as any of his counterparts anywhere else would know themselves to be.

And now, he was to soon come to believe, they had got to his one huge love. Selma. How could that ever be?

Mordecai Youngstein thought the pain of grief in his chest would surely explode. He felt huge and fixed beyond air, beyond breathing. He had not seen them take his little girl into the operating room. He had only heard from the general surgeon first, who had drawn him aside from what seemed the swollen family to tell him the child had been busted, like a china doll, all down her left side. Her leg broken; her pelvis broken; her left arm broken; her left shoulder broken. He had whispered that to the tall, strong, stiffly-bearing man of a Jew and had said there was more but please wait for his colleague. Youngstein waited there apart from the family and waited for the colleague. The colleague was a neurosurgeon and he, too, whispered to Mordecai Youngstein, as though Mordecai Youngstein could take it but the rest of the family obviously couldn't. He wasn't to know. He told Mordecai Youngstein that yes, like a china doll, yes, the left side. *All* of the left side. Including the head. Yes, including the head. And he told the man he didn't know at the time to be the father to expect the worst.

The wine merchant saw his daughter wheeled out of the operating room and he ran for ten paces beside the bed. The little form was all bandages. All he could see of her was half a closed right eyelid, half the right cheek and half her chin. Then slowed to a standstill as they hurried his Selma away. With the recovery room's doors swinging closed on him and the family moving up soggily behind him, Mordecai Youngstein registered recognition of the shape of the little cheek. For the first and last time in his life he exploded with the grief. There, landed in an open hospital corridor he rocked for his daughter and he rocked for his wife. It left him with a monstrous hatred.

And when, the next day, sitting alone, his jaw clenched so pendragonly tight, they rang to say his daughter had died, he said, 'Thank you'. Then put down the phone, never to answer one again directly as long as he lived. And vowed a curse like a beast of prey.

The lead on Selma Youngstein's death being an act of terrorism rather than an accident came at first by mistake. The oldest B-grade journalist for the evening *Standard*, Bob Blewett kept his general reporting position by adhering to the good old snooping ways of newsgathering. Time inefficient and sloppy, yes; but

Blewett, no intellectual and not one to turn metaphors, did come up with the occasional unexpected coup, even if most of the time that coup would prove to be wild speculation. His answer to that charge would be, 'Prove it was'. The reporter Blewett was therefore not a great advocate for old-style journalism, but he was at least a *reminder* of it — part of the time in journalistic culture when one was supposed to have 'an inkling' for a story. In Blewett's case that normally meant he had blundered or had blundered into.

Blewett took his coverage of the little girl Selma Youngstein being run down one stage further than he normally would have straight off because of the mother having to be admitted to hospital as well. With the late model Jaguar it had to be one of the topgrade Youngsteins. One of the mothers on the scene confirmed that the Jewishly-blonde, the Jewishly-coiffured, Jewish woman Sally Youngstein was the wife of *the* Mordecai Youngstein. Blewett chose, then, to go to the hospital and wait for the father and husband, rather than go back to the police station first for details, as the other newer journalists did. That was the 'inkling for news' part of the reporter Blewett's coup.

He missed Mordecai Youngstein hurrying in to the hospital, because he was on the phone at the time filing a Stop Press paragraph. That didn't matter. He was too late for a story for that evening's late edition anyway, so he waited reverently to one side of the Youngstein relatives and friends until they knew the extent of the injuries and the probable fate of the little girl. He waited two hours before he got to talk to the father. Then it was only a three sentence exchange and a brush-off. But Robert Blewett had got used to brush-off in his reporting life and, anyway, he knew he had a punch line that he could let others follow up tomorrow. For tonight's story for tomorrow's edition he had the leg opener. He could not have known he would get it by hitting directly on the nerve of Mordecai Youngstein's central fear in life:

'Blewett of the *Standard,* Mr Youngstein; do they know who did it?'

'The bloody swine.'

'What do you mean "they", Mr Youngstein?' By way of fixing it as having been said.

'They'll live to regret it.' Lodging the 'they' into the father's and husband's mind.

Thus the reporter Blewett was left, brushed aside by the father the husband, with a statement that a 'they' had been responsible and that the Jewish celebrity Youngstein knew more than he was saying. A 'they' meant an agency; and an agency meant deliberation, a calculated act.

The next day the *Standard* carried a front page story in all its editions that an act of terrorism, probably with international machinations, had been committed against the nine-year-old daughter of one of the most prominent, active and influential members of the Jewish community, the wine magnate Mordecai Youngstein. The story by Robert Blewett quoted unconfirmed sources. It cited, too, the macabre circumstances of the little girl's body wedged under the mother's car as being too horrific probably to be believable as pure chance. It all smacked of perfect timing, the most precise execution of a master plan.

Blewett's 'inkling' had done it again. The news editor might have chuckled that that old bugger Blewett had zinged it again, but one person to believe him implicitly was Mordecai Youngstein himself. He would comment no further. But he believed. And he would have revenge.

By midday of the next day, Mordecai Youngstein had visibly shrunk into grief. He sat like a gargoyle on the edge of his chair, alone, shrivelled, ugly, fearful of an appalling physical world. He was just entering the phase in which he was to be able to smell, touch, taste the desolation that was to be his for the rest of his life. He had not read the early edition of the *Standard* as yet. His sister, discreetly doing what has to be done downstairs, brought the paper up to him. The implications in the report demanded nothing less; that is why it had been relayed so quickly to the Youngstein's house.

If terrorism it was, it had the reverse effect on Mordecai Youngstein. It helped shake him out of his fearful cowering before a sense of monstrous deific callousness and returned to him a purview. It was a warped, hating purview, but it was a measure of objectivity at least. In one very real sense, his mother should have had it so good.

Mordecai Youngstein put the paper down. Having read the piece by the reporter Blewett he might not be able to more fully *absorb* the reality of having lost his little girl, but he had totally and objectively realised that 'they' had done that to his wife and daughter. He did not care why 'they' had done it. He was not going to wait around until 'they' told him why 'they' had done it. Mordecai Youngstein had the cold calculation of the professional soldier in him and so had his father and his father's father and his father's father's father. It had kept them rich; but mostly it had kept their bearing and therefore their Jewishness. So that when the terrorists took on Mordecai Youngstein, they took on the whole line of his descendants, not in a dead letter sense but palpably truly.

It was no longer than ten minutes of being alone with the newspaper that Mordecai Youngstein had gone through all that catalogue of prescribed emotions and had got up, his own man again, and dialed Chief Inspector Tony Luellen.

It was not the least of the ironical facts of his own existence that Chief Inspector Tony Luellen had become, with his last promotion, one nodule of the net of protection the influential monied people of the city had, perhaps understandably, thrown around themselves. It was, in fact, the measure of the man, rather than an indicator of his corruptibility.

Being Welsh, being a postwar migrant, being near both to the Catholic Irish and near to the bland-faith English, being from the Gaelic half-light of Europe, being poor himself and of poor Calvinistic stock fervoured-up, being one of the few coppers of the post-war world who *knew* about the phrase 'a cultural minority' without either chewing on it to spit it out or ever allowing it any substance, together with, because of all these things, always being posted to 'ethnic areas' (as they had latterly been called) or the shitheaps (as they used to be called when a name actually *mattered)*, Tony Luellen found himself rising steadily through the rank and file because he was a champion of minority groups. Just so. And if that meant he liked them, that he liked dealing with them, that he liked colourful human webs in the spin, then he was most definitely a champion of minority groups. A stubborn, hotly-Calvinistic one at that.

Tony Luellen wasn't so dumb, though, that he didn't find it ironical that he was eminently promotable for doing what he really loved. Police forces, of good men against bad guys, really oughtn't to be about all that. He thought so and he had said so. And though they felt uneasy about him at first, the influential people convinced themselves they admired his integrity. Besides the men of influence were mostly of minority groups anyway.

So that Mordecai Youngstein knew that, to get a straight answer to something that involved his Jewishness, he should ring the proscribed man, and friend, for this sort of thing. He gave neither the switchboard nor the two secretaries a polite word, save his name. And, when the Chief Inspector eventually came onto the connection, merely his name again and the question 'Why?' Luellen could hear the white anger in the voice and could hear all the reverberations behind the question. A copy of the *Standard* was on his desk.

'Mord, I want to say how sorry I am. I know I can't say how deeply sorry I am. I don't know how you must be grieving, but I can guess. I don't know what to say, but I know why you're ringing. I've got the *Standard* in front of me.'

'Why?'

Just the question again. Coiling.

'I don't know why, Mord. Listen, I don't know if there is a why. What's the source of this fellow Blewett? He won't tell us, so perhaps there's no source, have you thought of that?'

'No, there's a source.'

Flatly, the tone flat and pre-emptive over the phone. The Chief Inspector recognised, however, that it was purely instinct as yet.

'Listen, Mord. I want to speak... removed. Will you let me speak removed? What we've got here is a hit-and-run. We've got no witnesses about the car. Maybe a white or cream, maybe a big heavy car like an English car or a large Japanese car of its type. We've got a hit-and-run, Mord. We've got to treat it like a hit-and-run, not a set-up. I don't want to say an ordinary hit-and-run, but you don't need any poker face to know what I mean, right?'

'There's a source.'

The man Youngstein on the other end of the line was obviously hardly even listening.

'Mord, if it's a set-up we've already got the right people looking into it. What I'm trying to tell you is to look first at the accident. Do you know how hard it would be to set up a hit-and-run? A kidnapping, a shooting, sure. But how can you set up a hit-and-run? Sure, I know it can be done. I just don't want to add to your troubles, that's all. We're doing all we can, in the absence of knowing the car. We're even leaning as heavily as we can on the Blewett bloke, and we'll lean harder for his source if we have to. I know he won't give it to us, but we're trying. What you've got to remember, Mord, is that most of our hit-and-runs are solved from *within*. The family notices the dents in the car and whoever it is acting oddly. Or whoever it is breaks down and confesses, and they advise him to go around to the police. All we can do is damn well make sure we publicise it, ask publicly for information and all that. We've already done that, too. Listen, Mord, I'm talking too much. I'm just trying to tell you most of our hit-and-runs solve themselves; most hit-and-runners are just ordinary joes.'

There was a silence on the other end of the phone. For a moment the Chief Inspector had thought he had been talking to a point at infinity, when:

'How many of *your* hit-and-runs are *all* hit-and-runs?'

The policeman Luellen tightened and had answered out of practice before he had even realised he had: 'We've got a good record and we do all we humanly can'.

'There's a source.' Mordecai Youngstein's cold tone had not

changed, but his hatred had. It was shifting around to knowable proportions by shifting on to an objective. He had just realised why he himself had to act.

The second time that Chief Inspector Tony Luellen spoke to Mordecai Youngstein on the phone, he could tell that the industrialist was going to go his own way. The Chief Inspector could not bring himself to warn the father the husband Youngstein not to go his own way in this. He knew about threads of sanity and the strengthening to those threads that self-motivated action can bring. He was just worried about the tangible power that a man like Youngstein had. He had thought about this for a while and then thought about phrases like *inalienable rights* and *individual's unaccountability within the law* and decided that whatever Mordecai Youngstein did was beyond his, Luellen's, duty, to interfere anyway. In that sense his last promotion had made him farewell the palpable meaning of phrases. The compromise had started.

The Chief Inspector was frankly amazed at the information he had to tell the father the husband, but he also knew it had to come from him, now that the man Youngstein had established contact, rather than it being read in the morning paper. The information had come from the news editor of the *Standard*, who had himself been in a quandary. When the anonymous caller had rung through it was too late to change the late edition story and, although he had a promised exclusivity, it was clearly ridiculous to sit on the information until the next day. It was equally ridiculous in his eyes to give a scoop to the morning competitor. A call to the editor, another call to the publisher confirmed that, in the absence of newspaper mileage, civic duty should be addressed.

The news editor rang his contact at CID and that contact had passed the information through to the Chief Inspector Luellen. It was only four hours after Mordecai Youngstein had phoned Tony Luellen that Tony Luellen picked up the phone through to Mordecai Youngstein. And had to bark to get through to Mordecai

Youngstein as much as Mordecai Youngstein had to bark to get through to him.

When he did get through, he told the father the husband that the *Standard* had received a call from a group that called itself the Palestinian Red Brigade. The group had claimed responsibility for the 'assassination' of Selma Youngstein as a curtain-raiser only to a future move directly against the 'Zionist thug' Youngstein, and his like.

Tony Luellen heard the man Youngstein moan from the depths of his being. It was a moan so deep, so perpetual, so much like an animal in pain that the Chief Inspector felt his own heart freeze. He waited during the fearful silence that followed before he went on to say it was an even chance that the phone call had been a hoax, that his people had never heard of nor had on file a group of that name operating in this country or anywhere else, that, even so, the Special Services Branch and ASIO had increased their commitments to the case, just in case. The play or, words was accidental and made the Chief Inspector stop himself short before repeating to the father the husband Youngstein that the main thrust of their investigations was still going to be from the straightforward hit-and-run angle. That was where, in his opinion, the breakthrough would come.

This time he could hear the man Youngstein's breathing on the other end of the phone and waited for the reaction out of politeness. When it came, it was still the flat and the cold tones of a man whose mind had not been changed either from what he knew as a fact or from what he had decided to do:

'There's your source.'

It was a long time before the men Mordecai Youngstein and Chief Inspector Tony Luellen were to speak again. The father the husband had no need for the policeman after that. The *Standard* still miraculously got its scoop and manifested it with apt professionalism. It referred to the Palestinian Red Brigade, for example, not as an unknown, but as the 'little known' group and was therefore suitably suppositional about its existence, without leaving any doubt about its existence or its role in the killing of little Selma Youngstein.

The operator Sloane was glad to leave the house of Youngstein. He hadn't liked the prospect of meeting face to face the man who had lost his only child in that way and whose wife was going to have a very long way to go before she recovered her sanity. He had never liked being around people who had freakish things happen to them, good or bad; it just made them freaks. Freaks set your teeth on edge.

But the operator Sloane hadn't been prepared for the obsessional glint in the man's eyes. Because Sloane still knew his words the term *idée fixe* popped into his mind. Nor did that make it any easier to meet the father the husband's eyes, especially when they belonged to someone who was obviously going insane about his grief, as though the actual cause of the grief was becoming already not real, was illusory.

Sloane decided, as he stood outside the house of Youngstein, that the husband the father Mordecai Youngstein was the most tangibly dangerous person he had ever met. There had been no pleasantries, only business and a lot of money. Money down and money promised, and a hint of money if and when any crunch came and if and when a few people had to lose their lives. And bodyguards. That part, there being around bodyguards, Sloane had been amused by; were they for real or only playing a game? He came out with a few guesses. One bodyguard was openly watching him walk down the long driveway at that moment. As the operator passed him, he slowed just enough to deliver clearly:

'It's too late watching me come out, citizen.'

Sloane did not hear the expletive the man had answered him with. It didn't matter. Very little that citizens said ever did. It was just good to feel ballasted again. Back inside the house, the man

Youngstein's presence had dislodged his sense of reality.

The operator Sloane had learnt about the death of little Selma Youngstein before he had arrived. He hadn't been surprised to be offered an assignment to track down the Palestinian Red Brigade or those who had been contracted by it. Hit-and-runs were the unmotivated or motivated, whichever, explosions of violence that made the authorities the most impotent. Most times there were no witnesses and most times there were witnesses they were so impressionistic as to be useless. Sloane had only been surprised by the amount of money and the fantastic possibilities of blood retributions the wine maker had offered.

Normally the operator who called himself just Sloane would have sat tight-lipped, maybe have grunted a few questions, accepted or not accepted the assignment and left without saying much. A client wanted to assign beyond the cops, then a client had already made up his mind. Yet, this time, the operator Sloane had stayed and talked possibilities to the man Youngstein. He had done so because, with such a fixed idea about the result wanted and being paid for, he didn't want that dangerous quality in Youngstein to turn on him, if reality and obsession resolved themselves into being totally separate things. It was the professional thing to do and Sloane did it, and did it by way of warning as professionally as the Chief Inspector had:

'Mr Youngstein, I don't know about your little girl and in-ternational politics. If it's there, I hope I find it and I hope you'll let me help you crack its head. I won't need any extra incentive to help you do that, either. I'm just telling you that, with a hit-and-run, I can only do my best. It's not like other situations. A hit-and-run is here and then gone. If it's some citizen, some drunken sap, say, then he's usually either caught or not caught by someone near him ratting on him or he does the guilt thing and owns up. Occasionally the police might have a witness and be lucky. If it's a group so well trained that it can spot and then execute this kind of thing with that touch of sadism in the right timing, then the citizens who keep tab on political crackpots in this country have got the best chance of busting them, not me. I'm just telling you.'

90

'You find the source, Sloane.'

'There's... avenues. I just want to make sure you know the situation.'

'You find the source.'

'If I find the source you want me to find, Mr Youngstein, I'll help cut off its head, free, like I said.'

The client's eyes had not shifted from the operator Sloane's forehead. For the first time the operator had really felt as dehumanised as the thing he boasted as being best — an agency. Already, inside the house, he was beginning to file away a warning about Mordecai Youngstein in his mind.

The operator Sloane let the shower water pour off his head and roll caressingly all over his body and did so for almost a half an hour. When he had come out of this pre-assignment ritual, he had cleared his mind of any preconceptions he might have had about the case as a whole or bits of evidence in particular. That was the way it had to be.

He dressed, too, carefully and meticulously, almost formally, in white shirt, tie and blue suit. He had laid out the items before he had gone into the shower. He knew it was a ritual of ceremoniously layering on an alter ego as a warrior would have done his battle dress and arms. It even amused him that he did it, but he felt like doing it and that was important. It was the instinct he was calling up; it was as much a part of the assignment as the sleuthing itself. It was, too, a ritual of escutcheon merit, in that repeating it would keep the need to keep things *tidy* during the coming days. But, most of all, it served to purge of the preconceptions. It was why Sloane was good.

By the time he was ready for what he called the *tipple* of the world-made aberrations of his assignment, the operator Sloane was not seeing things from the standpoint that the father the husband would have wished him to be doing. He was going out to investigate with no thought that he was after an internationally-connected, if not activated, anarchist organisation. He had, in fact, no thought about what or who he was after at all.

He started as he would have usually started. The foundation was to know what there was to know phenologically about the event as it happened. In some cases, this might not be getting to know what the police knew, but getting to the 'insiders' in the professional criminals' world. In the case of little Selma Youngstein he needed to know whether the police knew more than the *Standard*, for instance, knew.

As usual, for this, he rang Lieutenant Erny Roberts, knowing he would be invited, as willingly as anyone could be, around to CID headquarters and given all the fundamentals he would need to know. It wasn't only that Lieutenant Roberts was his friend.

It wasn't for Erny Roberts, either, that the operator Sloane was *his* friend. Friendship had gone out of their relationship like the term romantic love had gone out of Roberts's marriage, yet he would still say his wife was still near and dear to him. She was also Sloane's sister, but that fact had become over the years as remote of emotion as the friendship between the Lieutenant and the operator had become. The fact was that Sloane operated 'good'.

So it was that both Lieutenant Erny Roberts and Chief Inspector Luellen had decided that it was okay for Roberts to be the operator Sloane's professional friend. It was okay, too, if Roberts did overtime with Sloane and got paid for it at the end, providing Roberts only advised on what information Sloane was working on and did not add gratuitously any confidential Department information. To an outsider there was a vagueness about the arrangement, but to the man Roberts and to the man Sloane it always had a clearly definable edge that was never overstepped.

Lieutenant Roberts had his own contacts. He had learnt, just about the time Sloane was putting on his white shirt in the dressing ritual, that the father Youngstein had assigned the operator Sloane. So that when Sloane rang his best friend, he was told immediately that there wasn't any need to come along to the office, what they had was what the *Standard,* Mordecai Youngstein, the general public, with the exception of the reporter Blewett of the *Standard,* knew. There were no clear witnesses. It *might* have been a white or cream car. It might have been a Japanese station wagon or a large and heavy English or American car. He told the man Sloane to come around to dinner sometime but expect nothing from him with this case. Routine enquiries, even conjoined with the pressures of a rich man and the speculations of a newspaper, hadn't come up with anything. The police were *broadcasting,* that was all. As for the international connection he had nothing, had been told nothing.

Sloane didn't want him to make further interdepartmental inquiries regarding the international possibilities. Sloane wanted to start first. There must be no clogging. He got none. Waiting itself is a presupposition.

While he was in the police force, the then detective Sloane had never once been asked: 'If you had committed this crime, how would you feel; and how might that affect your behaviour after the crime?' Yet he had always held it to be a truism that every criminal, apart perhaps from the true professional, was affected in some way by the crime he or she had committed. It might be morose guilt; it might be overdue care; it might be excessive excitement; it might be a desire to suicide or a desire to absorb life a little more vigorously for a while; it might make the person more normal as to be abnormal or more exaggeratedly preened as to come to be obvious and ludicrous. It might only be one unusual slip of the tongue. Whatever it was, Sloane had always believed that it would be, for that person, a difference to his everyday normal reaction, and therefore telltale. So the first thing you looked for was for something odd that might have happened somewhere near the scene of the crime. It could be before the crime was committed or afterwards. It might not even look to have anything to do with the crime itself in any direct sense.

About two hundred metres from where Selma Youngstein was hit, the side road to the school met Franklin Road, one of the hardier feeder arteries into the heart of the city. The city was downhill. Uphill Franklin Road allowed the city traffic to spend itself out into the south suburbs and finally into the southern countryside. The operator Sloane knew that the police inquiries would have been, and would continue to be, both around the scene of the hit-and-run and in shops around the T-junction of the side road and Franklin Road. All well and good. But he also basically knew the police would assume the driver, having decided not to stop, would have swung with, as it were, the natural course of things, by turning left with the flow of traffic and, despite having to go uphill, have made for the suburbs and anonymous distance.

Sloane stood at the T-junction of the side street and Franklin Road and didn't figure it that way. For him the most *natural* path of get-away would have been letting the car slide downhill at the junction, even if it meant turning against the traffic. That was the path of least conscionable resistance. Turning into or away from the city centre would not have come into it.

Finally, he crossed the junction and walked downhill along Franklin Road towards the city. As he walked along, he scanned the road looking for a natural test situation where the driver would have had to react to a situation as a driver of a car again.

He knew well before he got to them that the first likely spot was the traffic lights up ahead. He was now something like half a kilometre from the junction. It was a long way from the junction, sure, and there were so many other possibilities. The driver could have done a U-turn in the meantime or swung off into one of the side streets or just halted somewhere between here and there and left the vehicle. Yet the operator still felt hunch-good as he approached the traffic lights. He let himself 'nose' towards the lights.

At only the second shop at the traffic lights intersection, he was lucky. At the first, the delicatessen owner either had personal experience with the police or he was quick to thrust telefiction into streetfact; Sloane could read the script line telling the man: you've got to hate operators and give them the bum's steer. The owner resolved the two alternatives into mutely shaking his head no, I saw nuthin of nobody, so buzz.

Across the intersection diagonally, trying the least obvious automatically, the operator Sloane teased at the oranges until Joe, as it turned out, the owner, presumably, of the greengrocery with Joe's name signwritten upon it, came out and listened to the operator Sloane respectfully. Joe thought, nodded un-sensationally and remembered a cream Datsun station wagon, not sure what model exactly, doing something odd at around four o'clock on the day the man Sloane was talking about, sure. It turned so many heads, Joe almost humbly explained in an Italianate voice too impatient for the English cultivated economy of syllables, that there was 'milla-iones' of people who could back him up.

The cream Datsun wagon had come to the lights just at the changing of the green to amber. Fifty metres away it had accelerated to catch the amber, then from twenty metres away it had been screeched to a sliding halt when the driver had obviously decided he couldn't make it. Yes, it was a he. And why it had been noticeable was that it was done so thiswaythat. Sloane knew what the shopkeeper Joe meant; he meant panicky. It wasn't only that but the 'bast-tard' had suddenly went to start off before the light came back on green and then had to jam the brakes back on when he realised one of Joe's regular customers was still crossing in front of him. The woman had shouted without articulation before she had time to think up an abuse and Joe, seeing it all, had run out onto the footpath to add his own 'hey!' at the driver. But the car had been driven off — kangaroo hopping at first as though the driver couldn't regain his co-ordination.

There was no registration number and no description of the driver. The model was all that the operator Sloane got from there. He spent a few more hours interviewing the other shopkeepers and checking with Joe's regular customer, because there was no other testing situation on past the traffic lights there, nor other traffic lights for another kilometre or so. He gained no more information, yet it was enough for the operator Sloane to feel a small and tight contentment. He had a leg-in, he joked to himself, for his nose.

There was only one thing left for the operator Sloane to assume. That was that the hit-and-run car was stolen. Again, it didn't matter if the hit-and-run was an organisational set-up or a mug's accident. *His* only chance of breaking it down further was that the vehicle had been stolen, because, if it hadn't been, then the driver would either be caught out by his own kind or his own overwhelming guilt. Or he wouldn't be caught out at all. Either way, the operator Sloane knew he had no resources to tackle that sort of situation.

That was for the cops.

The next morning, giving a decency about morning coffee and the filtering back of energies for a coming and boringly CID day, the operator Sloane rang back his brother-in-law, the Lieutenant Roberts, and, from out of that one assumption further on, requested a list of all the cars reported stolen on the 'Selma Youngstein' day and the two days previous to that. He knew the list would now have been made for the total city area, if not for the State itself. To have called in all the car theft reports on that day from every station would have been the first thing that his ex-colleagues still in the force would have done. The ways of desk jockeys you could read.

It was there waiting for him by the time he got to the Lieutenant's office. Roberts had opened the door and then bowed, with mock subservience, his brother-in-law into his office. But they smiled, fleetingly, at each other, before the Lieutenant Roberts left the operator Sloane and before the operator Sloane tucked himself into an hour's immersion with the stolen car lists left on the desk for him.

He sat back at the desk. The operator named Sloane had come to the conclusion that there was only one possibility. He got up from the desk and moved to where he could lean his forehead against the coolness of the glass partitions of the office. In his hand, talismanically, he held a piece of paper on which that possibility had been written. He tried to force the willfulness of his 'nose' upon the likelihood, then had to smile to himself on the image of the kind of grotesque silhouette he must be making for the citizen sitting at the desk in the next office.

His 'nose' told him nothing one way or the other.

In all practicality, there was a likely nothing to lead a likely anywhere. Mrs Joan Rankin's car, in fact, hadn't been stolen. It had only showed in the Balmain lists because she had rung there to report her cream Mazda, not Datsun, 'missing'. She had then rang back an hour later to say that she had 'found' it again; that she had just mistaken where she had parked it. That was quite probable. The lists from the stations showed numerous such dummy calls from panicky citizens about their cars. Yet, Mazda or Datsun, the vehicle of Mrs Rankin, probable or improbable, was the only one reported that approximated with the car the operator Sloane was probing for.

The woman Rankin was home and agreed to see the operator Sloane. He would have liked her to have been a little bit more impatient with his request to meet her regarding her 'missing' car. That she was not reluctant in any way lowered the probability even further for him. Someone with something to hide, he figured, would have been even slightly irritated and probably would have bleated something along the lines of having an embarrassing mistake dragged up again. Joan Rankin did not. She was just a voice that edged a certain sharpness at him for an uninvited inconvenience, but that was all. This afternoon, yes; but this morning she would be out.

The operator Sloane made sure he arrived at her apartment block in the morning. He wanted to see her driving the car, if possible. He had a feeling that this would be enough for his nose. Knew it was irrational, but cared not. He waited.

As she pulled in to the block's car park, the woman Rankin stared back momentarily at the man she did not yet know as Sloane who was in turn watching her so openly. She parked, got out without turning around to look at him again and made for the lift. Sloane waited even after the lift doors had closed on her. He smiled when, after a time, the lift doors opened again and the woman who had to be Mrs Rankin stepped back out into the car park. She started towards the car as though she expected to see something and then quickly swung her attention to Sloane again. He had not moved but continued to stand languidly where he could be seen quite openly. And knew, too, it was irritating her.

From the boot, she got out a few packages and then returned to the lift and only looked hard at him again as the lift doors were closing again.

The operator Sloane smiled to himself. He had not moved because he had guessed the woman would try that manoeuvre. By the way she had stared at him, she either was on the run from something or thought he was up to no good there at the entrance. He discounted the first to some degree, although it was interesting to feel that she had become used to being watched in her time. What he *had* seen, however, was a bit discouraging. His 'nose' told him that she had emanated comfort in driving the vehicle that Sloane really felt would somehow be impossible if the woman had smashed against little Selma Youngstein. For the moment he put that thought out of his mind.

The operator Sloane moved away from the apartment block towards his own car down the road. He got in, lowered the back of his seat down to a lounging position and shut his eyes. He had an hour to wait, had decided to daydream it away thinking of nothing or, alternatively, thinking of the woman Mrs Rankin that he had just seen, whichever. Mostly he dozed, yet still kept the sense of the liveliness he had seen in the woman. He guessed she would have been in her late fifties. A small, squat woman with a nondescript, if not a plainly ordinary, body with legs that were going bandy with the years; but a body that did not somehow go with the long, erect neck and a head that moved quickly and alertedly. Her features, too, were darkly fine and drawn on bone contours. It did not have the fleshiness of the body. It was as though, fancifully, the brain had stayed finely-honed because there were good reasons why it should still remain so, while the flesh of the body was beginning to sag because there were no good reasons left why it shouldn't.

The woman Rankin was, Sloane decided, someone who was still figuratively on the run when she no longer had cause to be. Not primarily anyway. And decided, dozing there, that, yes, he was actually interested in seeing this face close up that afternoon. Futile, perhaps, but in prospect not too much of a bind.

When the woman Rankin answered the bell and saw that the man standing there before her was the same man who had stared at her as she had driven in to park, she reacted so immediately that initially the operator Sloane could only absorb her anger, not her features. How dare you, she had thrown at him after only a brief hesitation. There was no need to elaborate; they both knew what she meant. Sloane allowed himself the excess of an uncommitting shrug, and inwardly braced himself for the verbal langrel that must follow. But no. She held her full lips tight together, as if they generally remained like that in an attitude of schoolmarmish impatience. And in her silence, he instantly recognised that in the game of hunt and be hunted, this woman had had a long enough experience to know that one doesn't over commit a showing emotion.

He appreciated this instructive show of inherent professionalism in her. She must have had quite a lengthy experience with the hunt at one time or another. She was good. And with this recognition, the operator Sloane's own sense of 'nose' lifted with a pleasing tingle.

99

There was something there. He knew it just as he knew he was going to see her again.

He had inspected the car more closely before coming up in the lift, but hadn't expected to find evidence of anything conclusive. He had had enough by way of sighting cars that had hit people to know how little damage there can be outside of Hollywood. Sometimes there could be almost nothing at all. A glancing blow that gave no perceptible damage to the car was just as lethal to the victim. It all depended on the angle and the reactions of the victim at the time.

The woman Rankin recovered to demand who he was. Sloane felt very tiresome as he reached for his identification card and wearily waved it in front of her face, up and down since the door was so narrowly ajar. Her cold, blue eyes were not drawn in to the ruse:

'Hold that still so I can see it or go away.'

Sloane momentarily felt a silly desire to nod well-done at her for the professional sureness in the voice. In any case it pleased him greatly that she knew enough for a mere glance to tell a proper police identification from a one that approximates, however closely, to the real thing. That was good. It meant she has been in the hunt at some time, certainly. It meant, too, his 'nose' was still good. The woman Rankin was talking:

'If that was you on the phone you were impersonating an officer. I've got a good mind to complain. About that, and intimidating me in the car park.'

'First thing first, citizen.'

'I beg your pardon, who?'

'You're the Rankin citizen I'm here to see?'

The need to throw her and get back on terms. The hunt's different with one of your own; there is a need for greater gamesmanship. He wanted to smile:

100

'You report your car missing and then a couple of hours later ring to say mistake. You got damage to that car. Question. How? Don't bother with the courtesies of asking me in.'

'I'm not asking you in.'

'The damage, citizen.'

'So you say, probably to get me come out there. No fear. If there's damage, it's the ratbags around here, always thieving. I don't know about any damage.'

'What happened to the car during the two hours?'

'I'd forgotten my son had arranged to use it. His wife just had a baby.'

The operator Sloane could see very obviously that the woman caught herself up on saying that.

'Had she?'

'This is ridiculous. I'm going to ring the police.' And slammed the door in his face. That didn't insult the operator Sloane. Had come to rather like having doors slammed in his face; had come to call it over the years 'getting a reaction out of the jujubes'.

The operator Sloane did not glance at the woman Rankin's car again, felt no need to, as he left the apartment block. He had enough direction.

He felt in high tune all the way to the *Morning Globe's* basement library. Where he could nicely burrow and hide from the world for a pleasing time in the bustling and baggy company of Barney Lagadu, who, in his twenty-seven years running the newspaper library down in the same basement, really only ever enjoyed the off-centred, bookish company of the man he first knew as the copper Sloane but now equally enjoyed helping as the operator

Sloane. For the operator Sloane, the librarian in turn seemed to breathe life into all those records, lovingly filed and alphabeticised for all those twenty-seven years while not once, otherwise, ever having a sense that he was doing something that was *alive*.

That is why the operator always brought a small bunch of flowers each time he came to the library for help. For all the little dead things. They had their little joke between them.

The other dailies had taken up the *Standard's* raw assertion that international terrorism had arrived so bloodily and so madly in the country and had exploded, against the name of all reason, the life force of the little nine-year-old Jewish girl Selma Youngstein.

The day that the operator Sloane visited the woman Rankin for the first time and had afterwards retired to the library of the *Morning Globe*, the first of the national weeklies carried an analysis of how the bloody path of international blood-lust had come to these shores, how ill-prepared the country was as a unity, and the probable credentials of the Palestinian Red Brigade. It was obvious, came the assertion, that the curtain-call for this country being dragged into the midst of the world's terrorist stage had been planned well in advance — and executed in a cruel demonstration of intimidation. The (now called Jewish) industrialist and Zionist Youngstein had been marked as an arch-enemy. Lop him and his and the tree would fall. Actually, the metaphors in the article were rich and so florid as to be blindly apt.

Later weeklies speculated whether this was the start of a new phase of international terrorism, which was being termed Third World Reprisals. Other editorials hinted that this newly-notorious, previously unknown group, alloyed with the acronym PRB, was a prototype cell for distending the new dimension of terrorism to spectator countries in order to keep the international threat of violence sharp-edged. The greater impact was made by those who ran handsome speculations.

The proudly a reporter, 'don't give me journalist', the man called Blewett had therefore finally had his moment's influence on the press of the nation. He had always known, assured alone, that he would one day. Also, the man the father the husband Youngstein had read every single word of every single article. Also, the operator Sloane had read one. The first. He had not read any of the others.

The first of these articles was waiting on the newspaper library's desk for him. Barney Lagadu had put it there. It wasn't purely to show the operator Sloane that he, Barney, hadn't lost his instant-recall touch, although he, Barney, loved to be able to demonstrate just that for the operator Sloane; partly it was because he, Barney, always liked to have an attention other-getter so that the joke of the flowers would not overstretch itself by being too long at any one time a centre of distraction between the man the librarian liked and the man the operator liked.

So the operator Sloane and he the librarian performed their curt little friendship rituals, but not so passingly that the meaning of the ritual diluted. Enough. Barney nodding to the cut-out item about the international aspect of a hit-and-run on a little Jewish girl; and nodding meaningfully.

And, as usual, as expected, the operator Sloane nodded gratitude to the librarian and sat down, in something resembling a respect, in front of the librarian's offering. He glanced quickly at the feature lines, took in the meaning of their presence there and nodded a quick recognition of the astuteness of his friend. And had it, equally as shortly with a nod, accepted. The operator Sloane picked up the article and read for the required moment, put it down and looked meaningfully at Barney Lagadu. As if by rote, they both settled down to an equally economical run-down by the man Sloane to the librarian. He left out nothing he had found out or thought or where his 'nose' would lead him or who he was working for or what was in it in all the various ways. Barney Lagadu appreciated the frankness in all confidentiality and the frankness in all confidentiality was meant. When the operator Sloane had finished, the librarian nodded yes and smiled a crafty smile at the operator that promised a leave-it-to-me as much as Barney Lagadu would ever promise anyone anything along those lines. He punched from a distance at the operator Sloane's shoulder and turned away to shuttle himself from cranny to cranny of the folly of a clipping empire he had built himself.

In his hand was the name Rankin and the address of the woman Rankin.

The operator Sloane ran his eye over the article again and got its drift. He put it down, shook his head and silently vowed not to read anything for the next few weeks. It was bad enough having to tell the father the husband Youngstein that he had nothing for him. Yet.

'Nothing as yet, Mr Youngstein.'

'Mr Sloane. I want you to try the traps. Try the vine. Try the small yobs, the big ones. Root around, Mr Sloane. You especially try the police. I want sniffs. I want the source. Read papers, Mr Sloane. Just get me the source.'

'Mr Youngstein, I'm trying to get at a crime.'

'Mr Sloane, get to the source, then we'll have the crime.' 'Take it easy, Mr Youngstein.'

'You're just one man of many thousands, Mr Sloane. Don't get important. Just get the source.'

At home (a dry word for the apartmented side of him), the operator Sloane dialled each and every hospital listed in the yellow pages of the telephone book, and each time he forced himself to make a fresh-sounding inquiry to the maternity section. He made ten calls but had no joy, even as a distraught new-mother's father just got back from a bush trip.

After these, he settled back in the chair by the phone and squeezed the glands at the inner corners of his eyes against his nose, but, more especially, against the likelihood that the son of the woman Joan Rankin might live out of town. Might live in a country town somewhere. Might live, leaving, in another State. The graft, the hard work, the hunter in the operator Sloane's flux, when he becomes, and feels and knows it, an ordinary operator. And therefore contemptible to himself. This part of the hunt he so hated.

And was trying to gather up all his energies for another blitz on the telephone when it rang.

'Mr Sloane, nothing on the woman by way of Rankin.' It was the way the librarian Barney Lagadu had phrased it. Sloane smiled. The game between them. Something alive, something dead.

'But?'

'But I got to thinking about your assessment of this lady. Who knows where she's come from? Know that, might hold something in "Regionals" or something. A lot of interstate stuff not cross-referenced. One day I'll do it, by way of time allowing it.'

'One day you'll do it, Barney, sure.'

'Rang a certain party used to be in the same game. Discreet. And a bit bent.' And laughed his dry librarian laugh, a sort of surprise to himself and dispatched with, before: 'He's in the Titles Office. You need to know his name?' A bit fearfully asked in a magnificent concession to friendship.

'No. But he looked up the title of her apartment, right?'

'Thought it might come in handy to know where she came from. Strata title. She owns it. Her previous address given as Kirribilli, which might be of some interest. Doubt it. The thing to hear is the title was conveyed twelve years ago for a transfer of deed. From a Mrs P. M. Dere to a Mrs P. M. Rankin. More than initials the same. The Kirribilli address, which is a single house, is the same.'

'Guess, Barney.'

'Guess is that twelve years ago the Rankin woman had her name changed from Dere. Suggest a further search, but up to you.'

'Barney', the operator Sloane knowing the approach so well that he needed to vary it a little each time, 'unearth what that newspaper of yours probably should have unearthed a long time ago if they'd asked you. Personally I can't believe you could possibly take it further.' He could almost hear the chuckle on the other end of the line. And made a mental note that he really ought to buy a *Morning Globe* one time or another. Help with the salary lump out of which is paid the librarian Barney Lagadu.

Pretending to be doing up a shoelace, the operator Sloane quickly cased the house of the son of Mrs Rankin across the street from the side lane there. His 'nose' could sense a hiatus there. Would have wagered that the house of the son Allan Dere was empty. No car and the windows shaded. And moved towards it.

The librarian had rung back with the address of the woman

Rankin's son ten minutes after Sloane had asked the librarian to get it for him. After receiving the name Dere, the operator had rung around the maternity hospitals again, this time inquiring about mother and child by name of Dere. He had, finally, at the Ashford Community Hospital, been told that a Joan Dere was still under sedation but was better than could be expected. The matron, to whom the operator's call had been redirected, had questioned him closely about his brotherhood of the woman Joan Dere before she had squeezed out for him even that piece of information. Obviously a mother of mothers.

Sloane had then rang the librarian Lagadu back and had hinted that an officious sounding newspaper inquiry, for the sake of their records, might convince the Administration of Ashford Community Hospital that the address of the Dere family was one of the most vital things the general newspaper-reading public wanted in all the world to know. When the librarian rang back some ten minutes later, the operator Sloane distinctly heard the chuckle on the other end of the line. But did not upset the delicate balance of their interplay by commenting that he knew from the chuckle that the hospital had indeed been very pleased to give the Dere's address to the great and greater newspaper reading public.

And now the operator Sloane knocked at the back door of the house of Allan Dere. He knew in advance that he would get no answer because he had already worried from the outside by walking around the garden of the house first before knocking, and had got the clear signs he was looking for. A neighbour, a woman, had come outside in the yard next door. Noisily, but not too noisily. Not watching, but watching, the stranger Sloane.

The operator guessed by the way the neighbour straightened up for him so quickly with such a certain breathlessness that she was in a suburban state of loneliness. Large and blonde and healthy and thirty, she oozed the look of a mother whose predeceasing line of duty to evolution would have commenced with the locking of a Visigoth horseman and a tenderly-bruising German dairymaid. Her children, soundingly in a many multiple, throbbed the inside of her house by way of background hum to her presence — as they probably would have done so for the last twelve centuries. The varicose veins on the thick shapely legs beginning to show already. The disloyalty, too, to what had previously been her permanent neighbours after all, just beginning to show enough. The feeling, as she would later no doubt say, that there was always something wrong.

So the operator Sloane concentrated his attention on her bold blue eyes, knowing that hers was the generic type that loved lusty looks.

He learnt that, as far as she could neighbourly tell, the wife Joan Dere had gone into the Ashford that last Monday and had given birth on the next day, the Tuesday. But was allowed no visitors; funny that. That the husband Allan Dere had been at home on Monday night but, since then, had not been seen; funny that, too. She, the neighbour, had been taking the milk and the papers in for the last four days. Neighbourly. And yes and no; sometimes the man Dere did have a car and sometimes he did not have a car; that was odd. Right now she believed he did not have a car, but anything could have happened since she last had been told anything.

He, the man Dere? Briefly will do. Untall, unfattish, with the balding coming flaw and the ordinary brownness of the man promising an unusual sandiness in a few years. Unstraight, unstooped. Silent generally and generally a proper 'niceties' sayer at the right time. Unshort of the compliment, but you could hear occasionally the violent bursts of temper from inside the neighbourly house there. A mover in alertness as though he expected the pounce, but that's just an impression a neighbourhood girl had got. His eyes generally not looking directly at you, suddenly *flashing*. Sharp and fighting directly at you. An architectural draughtsman. Yes, a neighbour might report as being respectable; but funnily, a bit odd. Always some qualification when you speak about him. You know? No. A bit odd...

The operator Sloane sensed there would always be an 'if about the man Dere, whoever described him. And knew now he had what he felt to be a truism about citizen Dere. So he looked, with almost as much admiration as he had contempt, at the neighbour woman, that blonde mum-perpetual who was such a feeler for what was being said by eyes that she could divine much through feeling. An oracle of the horizontal position.

Her? The wife Dere. Briefly, too, would do. Pretending to be a detective of the police, the operator Sloane listened to a description of the wife who he next planned to see. Was said to have been crying a lot lately and heard, too, to have been raising her voice, uncharacteristically, a lot lately.

The matron, whose shoes with magnificent regard for clichés

actually squelched as she rolled her clichéd, buxomy body along the corridor with the operator Sloane, had required nothing more than a policeman's grunt or two from the man alongside of her who had claimed to be a CID detective. The operator would have been surprised if she had required, and scrutinised, identification; he was so good at the official mouthings required that citizens rarely dared to be impertinent to what obviously was a senior detective and to express doubt that he wasn't. Mrs Joan Rankin, a notable exception.

He had been careful to tell her three-quarters of the truth — that he was investigating a hit-and-run of a little girl last Tuesday— so that, should it get back to Chief Inspector Luellen or Lieutenant Tony Roberts, their displeasure would be mitigated by an unspoken admiration for the operator's sheer gall. He kidded himself that he tried to operate in a way that his existence would brighten their dull lives if how he operated should come to their attention.

By the time they got to the ward, the visit had already preceded them. The other three patients were lying back, halfgroomed, picture patients, but eyes flisking for the listen-in. The curtains had been drawn around the bed of the patient Joan Dere. Sloane stood back respectfully and waited for the matronly cliché nod okay from the matron. He was beginning to come to love her sham. And then, invited, entered, solemnly as befitted the crime, upon the bedside of the woman Dere there.

He found Joan Dere sedated beyond emotive lift or deflation. Indifference was a far too negative description of something that was holding her back so fastly. Her dark eyes, widely bracing against her dark hair, absorbed him instantly and accepted him as something infinitely occurring within her environment. The sheet fixed her figure to a bed as being trim enough and small, but as perhaps spreading too much at the hips and loins, as swollen unsensually at the breasts. Yet the operator Sloane mostly felt an urge to leave her as quickly as he could. She lay there deathly grey. So grey and so static that he knew he did not need to waste time on preliminaries.

'Why hasn't your husband been around, Mrs Dere?'

She turned, finally, large lizard eyes upon him, and, finally, spoke seemingly from a long way away. Yet it was with a mounting excitability, as though even to remember some earlier process was thrilling:

'He wouldn't believe about the child. I had to come to shout at him to believe about the child. He wouldn't believe about the child and I had to make him believe about the child so he could make me believe about it, you see. I didn't do it deliberately. When it hangs leeching in there and won't go away and when you come to envelop a dead thing, you have to start raising your voice, don't you? You'll understand. He wouldn't come near me and it's a funny thing to wake up in the night and find him staring at you, there, in the night. Listen, *in the dead of the night.* He is making me scared and I can't tell him that it isn't my fault. And I can't tell him, can I?, that it doesn't mean anything when he can't take his eyes off me and he can't help vomiting sometimes in the dead of the night in front of me and. Oh, that scar across his eyes weeping raw. It's not there in the morning, is it? The nights and the middays when he cries out how his head across the eye is burning white hot and weeping steam from between his fingers. It's true, you know. I know you think it's all my fault but I couldn't help the child and I couldn't help the scar that came like a river's tide across your eye. You shouldn't be staring at my belly in the dead of night like that, Allan.'

Where she stopped what had been the babbling, casting help-me glances at the operator Sloane. So that she, the wife of the man Allan Dere, when she had suddenly turned matter-of-factly towards him, looked quite like she was commenting on the part she had just been in such an Ophelia floating for:

'I don't know who you are. Are we talking about my husband? He had always seemed so mad the way he washed washed washed himself, his hands hands hands. When he learnt of the child I stopped him scrubbing his hands raw. I swear to the scar that came over his eye. Do I have to? He had said just recently all the things

110

about his childhood. I know now how he could be mad. I would never have guessed, you know. Don't make me think about it, will you? Will you?'

'No.'

'He had said that the hermit was in the measure of his filth the holiest of men. Can't you scrub it away from him?, I asked him. No, he said. You know...?'

'What?'

'I came to know the times he had gone off to his holy man.'

'To wash his feet?'

'Yes. I had come to know when he had gone off those times to see his holy man. Like now.'

'Yes?'

'Yes. He has told me how he truly knows the child is his, you know.'

'You haven't told me.'

'Because it died in my womb at five months and stayed there.'

There was the quietus there then. The woman wife's eyes dead on the man Sloane, flat as their own metaphors. The matron's hand reached out to touch the operator's arm to come back to the realm nosocomial and treatable. The matron felt a fear for the first time in her life. But the man Sloane kept at the eyes of the mother, there, of the dead.

'Mrs Dere?'

'Yes?'

'Where's your husband?'

But she had gone from them:

'You are swollen, aren't you, by what I envelop in my womb. There is no need to scar or run and dirt die. I did not know about the source, you know.'

Then the operator Sloane turned back his asking look to the matron. The matron not of cliché now, but in cliché, dreadfully fascinated, so much so that she recidivated with a cliché pinch on the woman Dere's cheek, when she should have, by normal helplessness, sent for the needle tray. Yet it was enough to bring the dark little woman Dere's eyes back into tune with the eyes of Sloane. He was to remember this as an inversion of eyes, depriving him, her and him, both of them, of anything *real*. Now trying to reach her urgently before she goes off again:

'What is this source, Mrs Dere?'

To see her reflexes shiver as, perhaps, he thought, he had never seen the muscles quite so shiver. Nor the wife become such, suddenly, the wanting wife.

'The source. The him. Are we talking of my man? I don't know the source for you. The island. Listen...'

'Yes?'

'Who would have guessed?'

'You?'

'No. No. No. No.'

'Mrs Dere...?'

'Yes?'

'What's the hermit, who?'

'Emile.'

'Is that a name?'

'Emile Gascoigne. Oh.'

'The island and an Emile Gascoigne a holy man?'

'Oh.'

'Tell me this source, Mrs Dere.'

'Oh.'

Such a sigh that the matron was dragged from being mesmerised to the need for a matronly performance again. She peremptorily laid a hand on the operator Sloane's arm and that was it. It, with her peremptory nod, was enough; one of the few timings in her life perfectly, and without cliché, judged. Sloane nodded, touched the woman the wife briefly on her pale and limp hand heavy seemingly upon a classic sheet in a classic pose of a classic stillness from a deathing inner pain, and got up with the matron to leave there.

They walked silently back down to her office. They both knew what was to follow, so there was no need to ask to be invited into her little cubbyhole. The operator Sloane sat down. He did not have to ask, but waited for the woman he would only remember as the matron to explain. They both knew she would. Her voice was tight, could have been speaking about the unspeakable.

'It's the only case I've personally come across. I've heard of them, but you can never understand when you hear about them why they're not prevented. The answer is, I've found out, everybody keeps hoping the body will do all the nastiness itself. I'm talking about miscarriage. Normally it does. Mis-carry. Normally you'd have the body do it for you. Mrs Dere's baby died at five months. We don't know why it died after five months. Perhaps we won't. Perhaps we will. But it didn't abort. It just... stopped. The doctors knew it had *stopped*. She had a week of kicking. Then it had died. But the body kept going on. Her womb, her reproductive things

113

kept going as though it was a living baby in the womb. It wouldn't seem to recognise that the foetus had died. Even her belly kept swelling. They kept waiting for the miscarriage, but it didn't happen. At the end of nine months she even got birth pains. She did. Her stomach was as huge as any normal mother's would have been, too. She even gave birth biologically perfectly. But it wasn't a baby; it was a four-month-old dead carcass we had to test then burn. That's what she gave birth to. She carried a dead thing for four months and knew it. She knew it. Her husband came to know it. It makes me sick to think of it.'

The operator accepted the implied wrong of being a male. He got up and left the matron looking bitterly at him. She was no cliché hospital figure now, merely a small and plump woman who needed more foundation garments and less mouth tide.

The coquettish voice from the switchboard told him that the librarian Barney Lagadu wasn't in, I'm sorry. The operator Sloane knew that the librarian would merely be submerged somewhere in his warm and enfolding library and refusing to emerge to answer the phone.

'Ask Mr Lagadu to try the name Dere. Ask him to also try the name Emile Gascoigne and being a hermit. And an island. And dirt.'

'Did you say "dirt"?'

'I said dirt.'

In his phone call to Mordecai Youngstein, Sloane again informed the father the husband that he had nothing to report. The man Youngstein put the phone down without talking. His jaw was set with annoyance. There was no breakthrough being achieved. It didn't matter who was ringing in. It could have been one of Chief Inspector Luellen's lackeys merely indulging an influential member of the public with a regular progress bulletin on the

114

routine inquiries that were routinely going on, or perhaps the operator Sloane who annoyed because he didn't seem to be part of the overall co-ordination, or it could have been either one of the two vigilante groups formed of his angry and young associates. None of the intelligence the Jewish wine maker was getting was anything that would lead to the breakthrough. He, Mordecai Youngstein, knew that.

The beatings had started. Men and women known to be prominent in the likely anti-Jewish, anti-order leanings around the country began to be found bound, beaten and dumped. 'With such leanings, we too lean', the father the husband had said almost for the laugh. His hating predisposition was beginning to be spiced by what had begun to look very much like a paramilitary operation directed by him. It had only been a few days since Selma had been knocked down yet his contacts had already moved quickly. The result should have been more *interesting,* but it definitely was not. So that, Mordecai Youngstein, irritated beyond congress, had listened and had slammed the phone down on the operator Sloane.

The operator Sloane had not cared. He had only rung because he was sitting near the phone and had thought to ring while he had the mournful instrument close at hand. He had been sitting, and now continued to sit, there half supine, with his legs straight out and his eyes closed. He was waiting for the librarian to ring. Even though it was early evening, he knew the librarian would not have left the library until he had rung. So Sloane used the waiting time to breathe deeply and rhythmically. If this was a disease, he mused, this point would be called the crisis.

When the phone call came, the librarian did not even measure his words for the usual preliminaries between them. The operator Sloane hung up and left immediately.

Barney Lagadu had said, 'Mr Sloane, I think you'd better come over here.'

On the library table, stacked neatly in a leather tabloid folder, not in chronological order but in a sequence for dramatic unfolding, as the operator Sloane later realised, were clippings. They had gone only slightly hepatic in colour in the twenty or so years since they had been current. From across the room, Sloane could approximate their age by the layout and design of the top piece — a page one from the *Standard,* with a large and heavy Fifties-style headline.

Beside him, he could palpably feel the mute elation of Barney Lagadu. He was not pointing to the folder, but had, rather, his arm outstretched towards it, hand open and palm upwards, as though he was solemnly and proudly inviting the operator Sloane to step forward and sign documents of public testimony to the justification of a lifetime devoted to the principles of a newspaper library. The librarian had been waiting for him in the reception area of the newspaper building and had shepherded him downstairs in a manner that suggested the operator Sloane had a habit of losing his way.

Sloane nodded to the librarian, went over to the setting, sat down without comment and began to read. It took him an hour to absorb the basics of the pile of clippings. Neither did, for one moment, the librarian stop hovering around him all that time, but had nodded with almost a demoniacal cackle each time the operator had glanced up at him in utter amazement. There could be no better enlivening than this, and the librarian knew it.

When he had finished, the operator stood up and for a while looked up at the skylight that reflected back the lights of the library itself. Then he held out to the librarian a clipping that contained a photograph of Emile Gascoigne in a woollen Norwegian cap and duffle coat. Behind him was the rocky, barren coast of an island.

'Mr Lagadu, can you find out where he is now?'

The librarian laughed for the first time that Sloane had ever heard him. It was a check-mate laugh. Next time, Sloane knew, there'd have to be new rules between them; the game had changed from one of proof to one of adventures.

Barney Lagadu opened his fist in front of Sloane. In his palm was a crumpled piece of paper, as though, too, he had won at a short burst of Guess Which Hand. And he said, as the operator Sloane read the address of the Salems' property:

'South-western telephone book, name Salem. As simple as that, Mr Sloane.'

Sloane conceded a look of appreciation that was enough of a concession for both of them. He tapped the folder containing the clippings:

'Keep this for me, will you, Barney?'

And left.

He had not closed the folder. The top clipping was still the page one of the *Standard* datelined September 15, 1959. The headline was: CHILD SEX MANIAC CONVICTED. Beneath it was a close-up photograph of the rapist who had terrorised the island's north-east corner for so many years. The photograph's caption read, and in italics, as though the very emphasis needed emphasis: Louis Edward Dere.

He had a feeling he was going to enjoy this because he had a feeling that he was going to be able to get nasty.

The operator Sloane could hear her footsteps as she approached the door. He stepped away to one side out of the field of survey of the seeing eye built into the door. When he could sense that she had her eye to it, he reached for the doorbell and rang it again and smirked to himself when he heard her jump with fright.

The woman Joan Rankin pulled the door open angrily, thinking it was the children baiting her again, becoming more and more for her an obsession the older she got. It took, theft, a perceptible readjustment to the fact that it was the man Sloane who had swung around to stand before her in the doorway. Sloane felt a twinge of disappointment in her confusion; the way she had swung the door open so aggressively had pricked at the feeling of admiration for a fellow pro he suddenly felt for her again. Confusion showed an embarrassing uncertainty for that instant. But thankfully not for long. Her eyes narrowed into a meanness that he appreciated more.

'You.'

'Fleshily, citizen.'

'What do you want, before I call the police.'

'I'd like chatties, citizen.'

She looked at him with an admirable sneer of contempt, and her regard of him seemed to hover midway between his face and his groin for a time that she deliberately let lapse. Then she stepped back so that she could slam the door, with a promising viciousness, in his face, but the operator had checked her before she even had it moving. The forward parry took him close to her, just close enough to slap her with the name of the man:

'Louis Edward Dere, Mrs Dere.'

The operator Sloane moved back in order that he could watch the effect a little better. The woman Rankin had been literally set back on her heels, so that she stood sedentary and *thumped.*

'I'm sure you'd prefer me inside than standing out here in public, citizen.'

Her reaction to that was so unexpected that the operator Sloane did not have time enough to block the punch she made at him, but could only start. The man, the woman collided untidily, then struggled momentarily against one another as though contact was revolting. Sloane grabbed her arm and pushed her into the passageway of her apartment and closed the door behind him. He

118

didn't follow her immediately, but stood with his back to the door hating her for making him act so sloppily. By doing it, she had somehow got back at him, and he suspected she knew very well she had. And she an old woman. But that acquired sense of the professional.

When he entered the lounge, she was standing with her back to him looking out of the window. The operator Sloane watched her for a time from the doorway. Black jumper, black woollen skirt, her dark hair combed but not elaborately. There was no reference point, no sharp contrast of colour, no untidy or excessively tidy thing about her. She was anonymous, flat, even though she had not been expecting anyone. It was the same with the room. It was furnished with pieces that reflected the number of years she had lived there, but his eye could catch upon nothing that could have been said to be odd, whimsically hers. There were no knick-knacks, no little or large arrangements. The room was as anonymously unnoticeable as the woman herself. The man Sloane's voice, when he did come to speak, would at first come out louder than he intended it. Hers was mean and hating and was to stay that way.

The woman Rankin held nothing back, either; and the absolute hatred in her voice spoke plainly that she did not have to be pressed on any point. It afterwards puzzled the operator Sloane; he left her with the sense that he had been hearing a vicious and voracious confession that she had urged upon him when it really wasn't wanted. He came, much later, to the theory that she could only now survive by others' destruction. But for now she spoke without turning:

'You're after something smutty. All you private detectives deal in smut.'

'That's right, citizen. I've got a client who wants to make a proposal of marriage to a child rapist's widow.'

'I've even had those, too. I've even had people like you who deal in smut accuse me of driving them to it, too.' Had turned and had

119

confronted the operator Sloane by then, ready to pour the acid.

'Them?'

'Yes, *them*. If you want to know anything about that filthy and disgusting thing... twenty years ago... what do you want that I can remember? It had nothing to do with me. You want to know, you ask my son. He's always *itched* at it.'

'Like the name.'

'Yes, the name. I changed his to Rankin, but come twenty-one, he changed it back to Dere. Dere made the shame enjoyable, I suppose, just as his father had enjoyed...'

She stopped. He could have sworn the leer she turned on him was lewd. But he was not there for the mother Rankin.

'Like the mania for things clean. Scrubbing his hands. A phobia. I know one of his terms is "holy dirt".'

'You've been talking to that little cheap-mouth wife of his. She would have been thinking the wind in her belly was a baby from kindergarten onwards. *Pathetic*. Both of them. Yes, the scrubbing. You want to use the term Lady Macbeth and damn spots, use the term Lady Macbeth and damn spots. It's been used before and they've been right. My son is pathetic. Get out. Go and talk to him.'

'Like his father?'

'My son and his father.'

Snorted. And half a do-you-know on her lips.

'Like the father's scapegoat? The hermit.'

'Your type says "who took the can for him". Right?'

'Right.'

'I've been around your type for twenty years, Sloane. I know you flinch at having your name identified, Sloane, you all do. Smuts. You've all prodded me and pulled me and even wanted me in bed. You're all as disgusting as that son of mine's disgusting father. *You — are — disgusting*. Every one of you. Degrees of weakness. Yes, my son is the weakest and the most pathetic. Yes, I despise him with his itch, with his scab-picking. Never leaving my life alone. If you want to say the name Emile Gascoigne, you say the name Emile Gascoigne and say it like a man.'

'Emile Gascoigne, the man who took the can for your Louis Edward Dere, citizen.'

'He was not mine.''

'Emile Gascoigne, citizen.'

'Ask my son.'

'Why he was so fascinated by the innocent getting hurt that he tracked the poor sad dopeheaded hermit down? And has gone on regular pilgrimages? I'm guessing. You tell me, citizen.'

'That's right. That's not smart.'

'That persecution equals exile equals the dirtiness of a saint.'

'Oh, who cares? I do not have a son. He is so weak that he won't even let me tell him that he is not a son I want to recognise. But he comes here and he *itches* at me, too. Get out and ask him.'

'About his scar over his eye?'

'What scar? What are you on about?'

'The scar that comes and goes?'

'You mad?'

'About the dead thing born to him, citizen?'

121

'If you like. Dead. Ha. They could have had it cut out. Dead and death. He actually thinks death follows him. He came here and he took the car and you know what he actually said?'

'No.'

'He had the sickening nerve to say to me after what I've been through, what I've had to live down from people like you, that he thought it was going to be born dead, aged twenty. *Twenty.*'

'And he took the car and he came back in a panic.'

'Wrong. He came back with that damn tail of his between his legs. He sat there and he cried. He wasn't in a panic. He was just more pathetic. He made me want to be sick. Sitting there, talking rubbish about Death surrounding us all and innocents and dying and the devil. All that maudlin rubbish he has scratched at for all these years. It was filth and it made *me* sick.'

'So his mother threw him out.'

'So she did not. His wife had just done that to him. I once felt like his mother. When he sat there and wept so that his pathetic heart seemed to burst and when he sat there and asked me to forgive him, I forgave him. I don't even know what I was supposed to forgive him for...'

'Don't you, citizen?'

'No, Sloane, I don't. When he did that, despite all *I've* been through... me, not him... when he begged for my forgiveness right here, I gave it to him. When I did, that weak and pathetic thing stood up and... the disgusting creature tried to spit in my face.'

The woman Rankin pierced at the operator Sloane with her eyes for a disgusted reaction. She got none, was not to know that the operator was as surprised as she had intended him to be. She swung from him and stood, again, facing out of the window. She was not to turn back while the man Sloane remained.

122

'I am investigating a hit-and-run of a little girl last Tuesday. Your son did it in your car.'

'He did nothing in *my* car. Get out.'

The operator stayed silent there. It was the time for her to talk on, he thought. He was right, except that she started and then, professionally, cut off her flow. She said:

'My son... *my* son... he was caught, you know, one time...'

'What?'

'Watching in a woman's bedroom keyhole. He was seventeen. I knew then he was no better than his disgusting father. Weak and disgusting and... shaming.' Then: 'You'll have to ask him about your hit-and-run. *If* you can find him.'

'I know where to find him, citizen.'

'Then bugger off, *Mr* Sloane.'

'I think I'm on to something, will be out of town. A few days. Give me a few days.'

'Wo!'

The father the husband Youngstein barked the command down into the phone and, as he did so, he stood up by autonomous reflex. Here was something *interesting* at last, and the fool was telling him to give him a few days before he gave out the information. The father the husband could not believe it. Yet there he was, listening to the same kind of schmaltz from this so-called pro operator called Sloane. You co-ordinate against the cartels, the anarchist thugs; you don't play cops and robbers all after Maltese Falcons. So Mordecai Youngstein had lost his temper and stood by reflex action and shouted a command down into the phone.

You find the source. You collect the data. You intelligence away at the opposition's strength. You parry first and then reconnoitre. You do not go off waving the banner for private-eye fiction. You were playing murderous modern power politics, in which the total bloodshed would come as sweetly as it was carefully organised and planned. You informed, for Christ's sake; you do not Lone Ranger away and compound reason. But the operator Sloane had gone from the phone. Disbelievably.

The operator Sloane had put the phone down as carefully as he cared to. He had hoped it was careful enough to make the father the husband Youngstein remember the next installment due for services, but he had also hoped it was not so careful that his employer Youngstein would forget having the phone put down on him.

By the time the 'agents' of Mordecai Youngstein had ripped at the door of the operator Sloane, the operator Sloane was already packed and on his way to find, outside the country town and on the property of the Salems, the hermit Emile Gascoigne.

Chapter 4

It is just two hours after the operator Sloane has introduced himself into the Salem household and told, by way of swapping information, something about the man Allan Dere that Jenny Salem pulls up to again carefully broach with the front part of her car, as merits habit, the property of Miss Avery. It is eighteen days after the little girl Selma Youngstein was run down.

The woman Salem is breathless. This time she is not so amused that she can barely keep her amusement from showing, as she normally is. This coming time there, she is as agitated as her fidgeting with the obstinate mute inanimation of the *things* needed to stop and park the car would perhaps show her to be. So much so that her consciousness is dwindled to so low and close a threshold that she does not notice the woman Miss Avery up on the roof until she has jumped out of the car, forgotten something, plunged back into the car for the something that, when there, she finds she can't remember anyway, then has re-emerged and has looked up by way of a self-annoyed gesture.

And when she looks, she is brought back to the present time with a kick of an involuntary cackle that bursts to sound. Miss Avery turns her head to give a frozen stare back and down at the woman Salem down and over there at the damn half invasion of her car on the property again. She cannot know how spiderish she looks from down where Jenny Salem is. For she is spread-eagled over the corner ridge of the gable, prone upon the corrugated iron sheeting, as though she was locked in a stunning moment of vertigo in which she can neither carry on up the mountain side or come back down. Stilled, actually, by the Salem woman's encroachment in the act of trying to nail down a sheet over to her left and higher up, and a little too far over to her left and a little too far higher up for her to do anything. Racked there with the sheer determination that she will do it. Her legs are widely apart and the painted print frock is riding.

Her coarse cotton, orangebrown stockings hanging toothlessly from one-only suspender lifeline to each leg, flashing reddish back-o-thighs against the grey of the roof and exposing her high, rounded buttocks so pertly erected by her crutch straddling the corner flashing. Her knees are too broad for shapely legs. And she continuing to look insanely to the woman Salem as though she was a semi-lewd, semi-cartoon drawing on the side of an American bomber.

The woman Salem waves and retaliates with a singingly inarticulate greeting. She suddenly feels she could break into a stomping and a cheer. This is the first time Jenny Salem realises she is elated by the news about that man Dere she has heard from the person called Sloane. The extension possibilities it gives to the telltale of their own hermit Emile suddenly wings in her a little thrilling delight. She realises, too, how much she has missed the cut and thrusty emotions of the living-in-the-city game, where skins are shed seasonally and used for spicings.

Miss Avery seems to come to the reluctant conclusion that she cannot stare the woman Salem away, after all. So she turns her head back to the nail hole and the nail and the hammer and the annoying roof sheet. She is aware only of the need to concentrate on the nail in order to suppress a suddenly mounting feeling of panic against the invasions once you turn your back or lay helplessly spread-eagled on a roof. It does not occur to her that there might be a perspective of her up there that might cause a cheer. Instead she carries on to try to reach the place where the roof is obviously leaking quite oblivious that this stretching makes her frock ride up further to peepshow the promise in her buttocks.

As she does so, the woman Salem comes on and skirts the two beehives automatically, but does not complete the half-circle detour around them that she normally would do to get to the kitchen porch. Instead she stops at the point of the detour at which she can see down past the side of the house to the sheds at the other end of the property. And though she speaks up to the woman Avery, her eyes, cut out of mascara but not too roughly, press for the man Dere down there:

'Thought I'd call in while passing. It's time.'

And waiting, with half an ear cocked, but not too metaphorically, into the air for the Avery funny answer, invariably to be some variation of the non-variable 'Time for what?' or somesuch dressing. Yet the straddled figure of the lit-tie reddish ladysister does not answer. She is too intent now on inching the hammer slowly towards the offending nail; even so, the negation of the expected causes the woman Jenny Salem to reluctantly draw her eyes away from the sheds and push them upwards towards the stranded-bird, surely-exhausted figure of Miss Avery up there. The pure routine of response makes her answer anyway:

'Frank's breathing lessons.'

Once up and upon there, Jenny Salem's eyes remain fixed to the sight of Miss Avery, just as the form of Miss Avery up there seems to remain fixed to the roof up there. It is a moment that, for all of her fluttery excitement, Jenny Salem cannot make to pass or to alter. It would seem impossible to move her eyes from looking upwards. Her mind wanders from the image as those fruity drawings of women on the side of old Yankee bombers to the image of birds stepping off the migration trail to rest exhausted on the corrugated roof. The silence between them becoming fixative, and in it begin to come through from inside the house the heavy and sluggish thuddings of a hammer on wood. They come regularly at first until there is one blow that evidently thwunks upon something that half dampens it. Immediately there is a cry of pain and a half scream of rage. Both women prick up their ears, but still seem unable to move. It is as though they can only listen to the sound of wood being tan-trumly smashed by the manboy Frank inside in a destroying rage at being struck on the thumb by his own hammer. The agony of inaction more obvious in the broodlike sister up on the roof. She seems to have got herself caught up there within the mothlight of the eyes of the woman Salem. Pinned to an unmoving. And quivering to move.

When Frank suddenly reels out from the inner folds of the house, sucking his thumb and whining loudly for his sister. 'Miss Avery,

127

Miss Avery.' He lurches out onto the kitchen porch after having cannoned off one, then the other, side of the kitchen doorframe. Blundering towards the mothersister image whereareyer whereareyer, blinding groping for.

He stops stock-still when the presence of the woman Salem comes to his perception. At first his eyes strive fiercely at her as they try to radar a danger, but soon there is the recognition. Soon the geez, fucking you, eh? Soon the geez geez of plaything delight in his mind as it tries to motivate his whaling body towards the visitor, gathering, finally, momentum enough to fit his hugeform to his eager mind and pumping the greeting howyer going howyer going into the air in front of him, as though it was a steam whisper of traction. And she, half-feeling and half-seeing the Frank bulk steering wobbily towards her in a gathered momentum, is half-flooded with a sense of panic about being flattened; yet, despite that, is totally ineffectual at being able to lower her eyes from the Miss Avery's gimcrackish form up there on the roof. Not even for survival.

It is a frozen moment of no apparent rhyme nor reason, which the woman Salem will remember, without fully understanding, all the few days of her life, she, too, nearly has left to her.

The manchild Frank manages to pull himself up just in time for a neat front-to-front confrontation with the body of the woman Salem. His belly, leadish as one half a dew drop in fall, forms a physical bridge beneath her breasts between he himself and she herself, so that he blocks out her viewing of Miss Avery by the sheer proximity of being no more than three centimetres away from a tangible nose-to-nose with her. And not even his little puffs of whispered howareyer howareyer exploding in her face, threatening to gas her with bad breath, can make her desperate enough to turn her face away and get *moving* again.

It is only the sheer desperation of her inner urging that spurs the woman Salem to break the spell that is threatening to land her into a re-enacted fairy tale of come-to-life reality. She prods with her finger, mentally, at the manboy's ribs so self-urgingly that, with an indescribable relief to her whole being, her actual finger actually follows to prod the chassis of Frank in the ribs. His instant recoil and giggle makes the world begin to spark back into motion again so instantaneously that it could just as well have been re-activated by a flicking of a switch.

The woman Salem keeps prodding, ruefully, the ticklish fleshiness of the manboy Frank; the manboy Frank keeps recoiling inanely with each prod, gone helpless in physical noncoordination and hopeless with a giggling fit, as though the woman's finger carries an electric charge. And as he teeters backwards towards the kitchen porch, his broodlike sister has begun scrambling the instant that the Salem woman's finger is laid upon the person of her brother, back into life too, like an old motor with the start-splutters, and is pawing at keep-holds to climb down at once to the rescue. Her roost to protect.

Frank is already staggering against the porch step and falls back on to the porch, squealing at the woman's prodding so shrilly as to confound Miss Avery about whether he is in hilarics or in pain. However, by the time Miss Avery drops down to the earth from the ladder in a flurry of dress, legs and flutter, the nurse in the woman Salem is systematically tickling Frank into an exquisite state of excitement, until his breathing and his sounds have so got out of phase that his body reels momentarily into a state of physical distress.

The woman Salem then switches from prodding the brother and takes hold of him, front and back, around the diaphragm. She squeezes at his lungs in a respiratory phasing and coos in, out, in, out into his ear in a professionally-adept calm tone of easy, easy.

The breathing exercises are, after all, the excuse that the woman Salem has decided upon as a reason for this visit a few hours after the operator Sloane has called upon her husband and her.

Miss Avery relaxes from the drawn-in position she has hunched herself in to repel the attack on her manchild brother. The breathing exercises. Known. She moves back to stand leaning against the kitchen wall, arms folded in a casual manner that belies the daggers she is staring at the other woman. She cannot express the intolerability of feeling, yes, jealous. Frank, though, coming back into co-ordination, slowly at first and then growing louder in tune with the rhythm of the woman squeezing about his chest:

'Get orf. Get orf. Get orf...'

This time the woman Salem lingers upon the body of Frank longer than she would normally do. She is enjoying the sheer tartishness she feels at baiting the woman Miss Avery. So she clings longer to Frank and hopes that the sister will not detect a false note in her voice.

'Thought I'd come today, instead.'

'Oh, yeah?'

'What were you doing up on the roof?'

'Fixing. Why?'

'I hear that man's still here.'

And could have bitten her own tongue. She has said it too eagerly, too soon, not teasingly enough for a Miss Avery reply other than the lugubrious:

'What man?'

It is not really a question, but a statement for a silence that is as near a command as the broodlike mothersister has ever been able to apply to any one of the invaders, ever.

Surprisingly by way of a seeming obedience, the woman Salem lets go her hold upon Frank. She is almost about to move closer to Miss Avery with a woman-to-woman confidence, when Frank seizes her in an embrace that encircles, easily, her thighs and draws her back to him so that he can nestle his head in her crutch, protected, mercifully, by *foundation*. And there he flounders at her

130

with his breath coming little by little more discernible as words:

'Get 'em down. Get 'em down.'

Jenny Salem is trapped within having an ulterior motive for being here and cannot extricate herself to leave. She can only remain where Frank has pulled her. Twists her head enquiringly towards Miss Avery, just in case something else is said. Which isn't. Again this is another frozen moment that the woman Salem will remember. It is only broken when Miss Avery suddenly straightens. She has seen something beyond the front fence. The woman Salem follows her line of sighting and sees, too, Emile Gascoigne trying not to look too obviously on watch over the Avery house from the bushes on the other side of the road. He could not, in fact, be more obvious as he stumbles backwards when he feels the sister's glare strike him. Still, he does offer the woman Salem a chance to get back on her very known tack of send-up. She winks at Miss Avery, then calls out to the hermit:

'Emile Gascoigne, man is a poor passion!'

Has to laugh, too, and does so, inviting Miss Avery into the coil of it, but only the manboy Frank responds to the invitation with a high-pitched and dry cackle that turns the woman Salem's head in case Frank, in turn, has the audacity of ridiculing her.

The lines on Miss Avery's high forehead show irritation, too, at Jenny Salem, as though she silently blames her for an anarchy enduring to happen. The hermit forgotten already, Jenny Salem finds she is caught, bumptiously, between the heavy and nose-nudging weight of Frank on her one hand and the rhadamanthine and obelisk figure of the broodlike sister on the other. It is she who is displaced suddenly. She grabs for the straw of Emile Gascoigne with a sharp thrust of her arm in the direction of the bush and:

'He's been missing for a week. We've been worried about the silly old codger.' Can only laugh. 'Codger, I haven't used that word for ages. Codger.'

A remark so unremarkable to Miss Avery that the sister continues to stare a silent disapprobation upon her unwanted guest. So that the woman, now having her whole body wiped across the itching nose of Frank in a way that might suggest her considerable figure was nothing if not wispy, can only plough on and hope to arrive at what she really means by some verbal chance:

'We didn't know what had happened to him. Lard o'mine', the patterned chuckle, 'was going to find out if he was alright when we found out it had something to do with...' Has to, this time, prod her hand in the direction of the sheds around the side in a sort of hitchhiking thumbing to indicate the man Dere and appals herself that it is so clumsy compared to the economical nod of the head only needed to indicate the hermit Gascoigne. '... with that man you've got around there.'

'What man I've got?' Replied to as though they were talking about an ant hole some kilometres off the property anyway.

'A detective, would you believe, called in on us today from the city way. He told us all about that man Dere.'

A sharpish tightening of the face muscles, a leaning forward; but the woman Avery otherwise does not react.

'Come on, Miss Avery, be a devil and ask me what about him.'

'Whatcha on about, slackhole? Eh? Eh? Eh?' Frank, in a wide-eyed, returned and near hiccoughy attention. With his finger prodding emphasis along the line of the elastic of the woman's briefs, but firming up his grip on her as she tries automatically to break away again. Besides Miss Avery is more than a handful for the woman Salem to try to urge:

'I know where he comes from, who he is. That detective, he *knew*. And told us. Just ask, be a devil.'

Miss Avery is so startled by this emphasis on herself that she almost jerks to attention. She cocks, as though the woman Salem

132

had just come to her notice and deserves the avifaunal squiz, her birdlike head on one side and stares at the other woman. There is a silence so spectacular between them that even the manchild gropes both mentally for the right words to ask why, and physically, his largelumps of hands rubbing thoughtfully up and down the far thigh of the woman Salem.

The tiny Avery body flutters in agitation, settles with a good deal of self-control, and then comes to speak in a manner of something important having just been remembered:

'We closed and locked up the front door after Dad died. I... don't suppose we should have even bothered.'

'What's that?'

'We didn't think there'd be any more visitors, you see.'

Her redbrown puttyfreckled beebitten hand thrust up, palm outward, before the countenance of the Jenny Salem woman, as though for all the world she was going to command a swamping tide to stop right there and hold high sea horses. It is a sobering gesture for a moment before the dam seems to burst in her and words gush forward to the Salem women, oh understand understand understand:

'He won't eat or drink properly. He just sits down there in the shed. He won't eat or drink enough. He shouldn't just sit there like that!' And then shut-down, her expression so angry that she would gladly turn back and bite herself.

The woman Salem almost laughs aloud at hearing what she knew she would hear one way or another. It is the comfort of people being predictable again. Funny sad little Miss Avery and poor bugger Frank, yes. And relishes knowing the answer the little mothersister will give before she asks the question:

'Alright, as a nurse, do you want me to go down and see him?'

She does not bother to look for the curt nod *yes* that she knows will answer, and is already prising off the fingers of Frank from around her buttocks. This time it is no funny business. The woman Salem is on top of it all again. Come to help, to nurse over the little sister and the poor old boy brother. She touches the woman Avery knowingly on the forearm, as women should do in such things, and leaves on her mission as the delegation for the poor Avery couple. The proprietorial Salem world in harmony again.

Down at the sheds, the woman Salem stands a distance apart and waits. The man Dere does not call her in. He does not call her in, even though she moves in by degrees. The way a real lady should when she is uninvited.

The hermit, from across the road, has watched the woman Salem move off the porch to around the side of the house. His eyes swing back to Frank there. He has observed from his imaginary hide the to-and-froings in the Avery nest for so long that he knows the manchild will follow the woman Salem. There is only a brief hiatus before Frank rolls over onto his side, halfway to pushing himself up to his feet. His head, even from across the roadway, can be seen to be pumping asking and urgent eyes after the woman Salem wait for me, wait for me. And the hermit watches the almost painfully mechanical movements of intention.

Frank reaches, finally, the edge of the porch, when Miss Avery then and only then seems to jolt awake. She turns flightily and grabs hold of the arm of her huge-formed brother, holds on with all her weight, and tries to heave him backwards. Her heels dig in comically as she tries to counter the body thrust of the man the. brother, with one of her hands seized upon one of his and the other so tugging down and backwards at the sleeves of his jumper that its neckline is stretched almost to his elbow.

'Pissorf, pissorf.'

Frank's whine at her clearly audible to Emile Gascoigne come now out into the open and staring openly, now, with open amazement at the woman, at the man-child.

The sister succeeds at least in stopping him. He tries to shake his sister off by pumping his arm up and down, but she is hanging on so fiercely that she is actually bouncing up and down at the end of it. He moves then with shuffling and loaded steps after the woman Salem and drags, despite her mute and grim determination, his sister across and down from the porch.

Emile Gascoigne hears the woman Avery shriek frustration. He sees her launch herself against the mass of her brother with a frenzy that explodes berserker. Beating at Frank's body with both arms stiff, round-arming against his back and chest as though she was pounding a bass drum. Nothing else but that one shriek comes out from her and nothing from Frank but a startled stillness, except for little vestigial movements of warding each blow off. He could be trying to catch the rhythm of a dance. Until his brain keys forth the response finally, when he flicks her off him with a backhand push that could be trying out a swinging door. The birdsister seems to take flight upon flailing arms as she is hurled back against the porch to land there thud-dish so that the hermit shudders with the sound he hears and hurries forward across the road.

Miss Avery does not move. The manchild Frank does not move. The sister, the brother remain not moving where they are. The explosion between them has been stultifying. Emile

Gascoigne, standing temerariously at the front fence of the Avery property by the gate, hears clearly Frank's unsure, fricative laugh as he stands, lodestoned, waiting for his sister, crouched and unmoving against the wall, to laugh, say, or ruffle his hair, say, and tell him it was only a game, never mind never mind. But she remains there, her head in her arms, her spindrifted body slumped pithless. And the ragged hermit out by the gate miserably and raggedly torn between going in out of taboo or staying out out of taboo. And then hearing Miss Avery say, but only once, but clearly as a bell despite the marked crack in her voice:

'You stay on that side of the fence, Emile Gascoigne.'

The voice, the sister. Frank's mansbody relaxes by taking two sideways steps that make it to a sitting down on the porch, its back against the porch post. His mind still petulantly reaches out beyond to the lost woman Salem, but quieting. The voice, the sister.

In the stillness, Miss Avery finally and wearily climbs to her feet, the wall of her house supportive for her, and causes dread in the heart of Emile Gascoigne by staggering, for the first few steps of hard and sucking breath, and then walking up the path to him. Her eyes for the first time looking for him as a one to one. He stands with no little effort and tries hard to wait for her, when all his nerves are crying for flight. But is not prepared, when she stops before him, for the sight of her eyes swollen red with tears. The skin of her face blushing rosy with freckles. She seems so red and watery and old brand *new*. And her shoulders shrugging something to do with apologetics, as if he, Emile Gascoigne, could possibly dare to interpret the gesture like that. And as he dares to look at her so sacrosanctly from so near he sees for the first time the duping unbeauty of her. Skewered suddenly on the sensual, the hermit is welled with sympathy for as much an ugly duckling as he himself has always been and actually spurts out a pity for her:

'A person's been ordered by a bloke to keep an eye on that geezer you've got in there, that's what.'

Having said that, and the world not falling in on him, he dares to detect that the woman Avery must by crying for him, and that his place in the world will surely now be with her. And so adds quickly, with a compassion that is so intimate you can only lay it down to a loved one. 'A person's not out here just looking at you.'

The woman stiffens. All her sinews seem to lift her skywards. Her whole being repulsed by being pitied by him. Her eye gone hawkish and her voice in rasp:

136

'Fool. *Fool.*'

She turns and strides away from him. The mounting fury blotting at the liquid in her eyes and drawing out her thin broodlike face from beneath the puff-made mark so restoratively that, by the time she has returned level with the bee hives there on the side of the path, the hermit has become already a memory only to be packed among a long number of lifeyears of other cringing memories best forgotten. She has already stopped there at the first of the two beehives and bends to inspect its entrance, not so much staring at the slow moving bodies of her beloved bees but scanning for the darker and fatter and pushier shape of a robber wasp, just as, behind her, the hermit groans loudly out of the deep hurt that is searing at his heart and, in front of her, Frank scans her sheepishly, but no longer remembering why he should be wanting to scan her sheepishly. Resentment rising effervescently in him for the way she has stopped there apart from him. And she, in a splurge of mutual well-being because she finds no wasp invading their hive just then, puts out the flat of the back of her hand so that her beloved bees could, and do, crawl viscously upon it, dragging their bellies and seeming to sniff.

The woman Avery stays there for a recuperative moment before she returns to stand with the head of her manchild brother cradled against her belly. At first he struggles habitually to free his head, but it is habit only and weak in gesture. Only when she knows the man Emile Gascoigne has left the front fence and has removed himself to go back across the road and into the bush does she release the near-mongoloid head of Frank. It is as though she has flicked a switch for the resumption of their usual lives. No woman Salem. No hermit Gascoigne. No man called Allan Dere. No robber wasps invading. And the time slippage in Frank's sullen voice making her smile ruefully but accustomedly, but not so he can see:

'Where yer been? Where yer been, eh?'

'Up on the roof, Frankie.'

137

'Whatcha doing up there, droopy. Eh? Watcha doing up there?'

'I was fixing the leak you know that.'

'I wanted to come, see.'

'You could have watched if you wanted Frankie.'

The slamming of his fist down upon the porch boards and his face going flushed red with frustration does not worry her. His whole hugeform bodily swinging into a danger of another tantrum does not worry her either. Squinting his eyes habitually dangerously at her:

'I wanted to come. I wanted to come, see!'

'All right Frank I'm sorry.'

'What for? C'arn what for?'

This flash of shrewdness a usual thing and so welcome, even as she sighs, knowing it.

'I'm sorry I didn't take Frankie up on the roof with me to fix the leak.'

'See? Toldyer. Toldyer, didn't I, yer dill?'

'Frankie told me yes.'

He chuckles with purring satisfaction, even as she suades him to rise to his feet with a gentle uplifting pressure on his elbow. She has never known, in moments like this, whether he has any knowledge of what he is doing. She has guessed not, is aware she probably will never know. Leads him inside and away from the path of the woman Salem still to return from the man Dere. She does not want to know. Yet, even so, she is not aware herself that her grip has tightened on the manchild's arm. Nor is the manchild. He has passed and is noticing the cat tin still there on the lip of the porch. As he is being led inside by the sister Avery, he is

138

wriggling and chuckling on the beaut image of his cat Friar. Friar to come home soon. Friar to come back to Frankie soon. Friar...

'Friar, Miss Avery. Friar. Beauty...'

The woman Salem has approached the opening of his shed with a stalking caution. Her heart has been beating fast and she has felt the flight nerves in the pit of her stomach move electrically. She has felt that surely he can hear her heart beating, can see it pulsing in the side of her neck, can see her belly jump. The sight of her belly. She has almost fainted with her inner excitement. It has been so long since she has been on the stalk that she has forgotten how difficult it is to nourish the excitement while seeming demure.

So now she has stopped and is standing there before the first of the sheds. The man Dere does not emerge to show himself.

Instead the sheds are glaucomatous and silent and that silence as bland as sheen. Only the medilocal driftings of sound from the meat works and the slight whiff in the air she has become so used to. I live, she thinks, in a torn and bloody meat world. Its smell must be like a wolf's lair. The shed before her, one of them, in which the man Dere is, *smelling* with what she has today come to know about him. The operator Sloane has baited us all, she knows. But cannot guess why he has baited, or how well his operator's 'nose' had told him to bait along the trail of the woman Salem.

The sounds, pumping the air with grunts, come, too, of Frank from the house behind her. She does not look back so see the little sister riding her whole being upon an exploded fury against Frank, her Frank. If she had, she might have tapped at the spring of emotion she was playing with. But she has not turned and does not know. Only stares in a swami holdfast at the sheds, her mind crabbing from one to the other for the telltale of the man Dere.

The woman Salem goes on now. She quietens a spasm of

139

anonymous sexual concipience and forces herself to look in the first shed. Yielding nothing but an earth smell busy composting in damp. As she then moves from the first shed to the next she could be said to be in stealth around the lair. It does not disquiet her careful steps. Her long stalking life again in gender thrill, she seems to take forever to go from the first to the second shed.

She squats on the grass. She has her dress ridden up her legs. She has worn for the occasion pantyhose and has laughed at the image of sweetly-beckoning chastity belts as she pulled them on. She is not squatting in a way that speaks volumes for her.

The man Dere, squatted in there, in against the corrugated iron wall and on the brown-pelted mattress, has quipped imperceptibly to himself that the way she is sitting in front of him does not speak volumes for her.

The woman Salem sits before the man Dere squatted in the shed, half in light and half in shadow, and does not know he could almost laugh at her. She does not know he could, too, as easily not laugh at her. They are both stirred; they both sit still.

Now she is feeling herself to be trapped in something spiking. She cannot seem to be able to close her legs. She wants to open her legs, but she does not want to open her legs like this. She sits there with all the sweet emotional tipples of her nightclubs coming back. Roots and rootings. But never a squat on grass in front of a man. She can't remember how she got down here. Not remembering, either, how she has babbled weather and Miss Avery and Frank in ludicrous splurge when she has come across him, in the second shed, squatting there, smelling highly and inert. His eyes nowhere but on her. Her eyes nowhere but on him. Both waiting there, now, in silence. Her last question — she forgets what it was — hanging in the air unanswered. He will not answer. He leans forward as much as to say to her, bitch I will not answer. And she sees the dirt upon him and smells again the shifted feral olfaction of the man Dere and then, as her eyes travel upwards, is stunned to see what doesn't look like, and then does look like, a line of dried blood across his right eye. 'Have you cut yourself?'

To see him wolfishly grin back. And she, in turn, wolfishly grins forward.

'Want me to have a look at it? I... nurse.'

The smile from the man Dere sinks back to the shadows as he lets his body sway backwards so that the woman can only barely discern him in there again. She would have gone away from there now if she has not felt his eyes working between her open legs. Aware that he will not talk, but aware that she must and remembering from her nightclub times that the tiding thing is to let the flow run:

'You don't have to explain why you were rude to me a few days ago. I'm not ashamed about my past. You shouldn't be, either. You can't go on letting the past get to you; that's what I think. Are you sitting there because they hurt you bad? Men... fighting. It's so stupid. That silly old lard o'mine gets so jealous. I know about you and Emile and I understand. You can't go on forever blaming yourself.' Pausing with the innate sense of a dancer trolling for the response; leaning forward to deliver: 'What was he like, your father?'

So that she thinks that, if he doesn't answer soon, she might spill herself evaginally there before him. The verbal touch at the very centre of her being there.

But there is only a slight leaning forward, inclining sideways towards her, by the man Dere and an almost unperceivable turning of his head to front her. The dried blood line across his eye divining the movement of his head like a line of careful makeup. She waits. The woman Jenny Salem waits for the man Dere to answer, then has to prompt, her mouth suddenly dry and her words cracking friably:

'What was he like?'

141

The man Dere, then, suddenly smiles at her insolently. Her eyes follow his hands. His hands go down to his fly and he unzips it. It is a movement of imperturbable arrogance. Then he draws his lips back as if to smile, but his teeth are clenched. It is a Luna Park grin of the mechanical papier-mâché head and his forefinger, just as mechanically, beckons her with contempt to come on in.

It takes her a stop-gap to realise what he is doing. Her legs snap shut, as if, she too, was mechanical. Jenny Salem jumps to her feet. The humiliation rises visibly into her cheeks and is all the more contusing because she has lost the knack of not letting the excitement show and that is effeminately insufferable. When she speaks, her voice has not quite, but almost rid itself of vulnerable softness. But does tremble enough in hating and furious tones:

'You...'

She leaves. The woman Salem strides back up the property of the woman Avery. She does not look to either side, but keeps her car at the front gate in focus as she would if it was the only thing she desired in all her life. She does not look to the right as she passes the kitchen porch. She does not look back to see if the man Dere has moved. Already her mind is rejecting embellishing the story of her visit she will tell her lard o'hers with hints that the man Dere should be taught another lesson. It must be, rather, an embellishment that trots the whole affair of the man Dere and the hermit and Miss Avery further along the after-dinner-mints path.

Miss Avery has stepped quickly back from the back window and has had to. The woman Salem has swung so suddenly to her feet and into stride back up towards the house that for a moment Miss Avery has felt she has been caught spying on them. Not that she has been able to see what the man Dere has been doing.

But now, stepped backwards away from the window but still in reconnaissance, she has seen the man Dere stand almost as soon as the woman Salem has strode off. She watches him as Jenny Salem

142

comes back up the track, her neck riding high and her jaw line set around thin and pursed lips, to move hemeral-optically past the house.

And she knows that, behind the woman Salem's back, Allan Dere is marching up and down his shed in mechanical agitation. Bursting into the light. Ploughing his way back into the shadows.

Miss Avery stares at him and continues to do so without blinking when her vision blurs abstractedly and he becomes a magic lantern figure strobing.

Somehow the manchild Frank has got out again and is standing suddenly in a no-man's land between the house and the sheds. Marooned and helpless to make a decision whether to follow the woman Salem back past the house or to go on to the sheds. Little boy lost. The words that had started to form on his lips as Jenny Salem came back up towards him linger on his lips as run-downs:

'Beauty. Beauty...'

'Day and night, I said, citizen.'

'A person's trying to tell you!'

'Until you drop or I say stop, citizen.'

They are standing at the sludgy end of the path that winds through the windbreak of trees that centres itself on the hermit Gascoigne's cottage. The operator Sloane has moved out from behind a pine as the hermit sallied towards the solitude of his front room with a yearning that is tearing at him.

Along his way back from the house of Avery and to here a million people have stood along his way and jeered imagined obscenities at him. He has hunched his shoulders protectively around himself and moved on through them as best he could as he has come to know how to after their tens of thousands of leering visits to him.

143

The murder of him in their millions of hearts stoning him.

Now the operator Sloane waits in the sullen silence of the hermit, hunched and head-bowed and sullen before him. He waits because he knows that the best threat to the hermit is the implied threat of the persecutions of yesterday come again today with their dark wings of possibility. He could tell the hermit that the world really is as mad beneath the surface as any of any hermit's wildest imagined horrors, that he would be no less sane than anyone else if he could realise it. But he does not tell Emile. To have him too aware of the insane probabilities of peoplefold can only do the operator good.

He has not had to threaten the hermit. He has only had to tell the old man that he knew about the north-eastern corner of that island of twenty years ago and that the man Dere has something *living* to do with that north-eastern corner of that island twenty years ago. That it is not only the man Dere, but all of the 'theys' through Dere who have returned to follow, follow him, the hermit. No escape once they're *on*. And the hermit knows yes. And the old man nods yes. He has always known, truly, that they have never really stopped following with all that murder in their hearts and the stones in their hands. And has understood the threat from the dark and city-neat operator that they have to help each other. And now, even more importantly now, with no let-up.

And, in the number of days that the operator Sloane has left to himself to live, he will keep the threat on the hermit Gascoigne to keep the vigil constant on the property of Miss Avery.

This time, however, the operator Sloane doesn't send the hermit straight back to the bush across the road from the house of Avery. But does turn the hermit around to show how the operator can skirt the property of Miss Avery and get to the bush that is nearby the sheds out at the back.

She hears the shouting from outside and starts. She has not been able to understand it, but it was human and invidiously apocalyptic and has repeated itself three times in the first short burst.

She waits breathlessly and unmoving as though, if she moved, it would resound back to be a shouting voice like a whipcrack. But, when she hears the voice muezzin again, the fear that has struck at her makes her run desperately down the passageway for Frank. She finds him in the kitchen at the table, unperturbed in sorting through a rusted chocolate tin of rusted nails and bolts and mysterious metal accretions that will stay defying description no matter how absorbingly the manchild gazes at them as they flake rubiginously between his fingers, yet adhere defiantly. Frank calmly mutters down upon each one long inarticulate expressions of patient doubt as though he was inducting merlin possibilities into each lump. And chuckling to himself with half a mind that is halfway to being able to apperceive itself at the one time and at the same time is automatically recognising the entry of his little sister on the flutter by holding up to her, without taking his eyes off the place where it has just been before his eyes, that particular accretion that he was so calmly swamping with mumbo-jumbo the moment before. And she touching it as automatically by way of possibly giving it a blessing to return to the manchild's love-absorbing eyes. It does.

The sister stands alert with the tips of her fingers resting protectively on Frank's shoulder. She listens again from there. Only faintly now can she make out the shouting and grows calmer, just as Frank comes to sense her arousal and stiffens. She pats him on the shoulder. The gesture, as usual, is enough to short circuit any of the signals of excitability in the hugeform.

Very slowly, in just as big a dread of disturbing him as she was of the voice threatening him, the woman Avery moves around the bulk of her brother and edges casually towards the kitchen door. She opens it slowly and stands poised to shut it quickly should he be frightened by her suddenly deciding to go somewhere he does not know about. But the manboy remains soothed by his discovered pile and lulled by her touch, so that he merely looks moonfully at her out of the corner of his eyes before resuming his chants over the next wonder that his hand will put before his eyes as if by sleight of someone else's mitt.

Miss Avery slips through the door and closes it behind her. She hears again the shouting and again shudders for the raw possibilities of invasion in a man shouting. All she can tell is that it is coming from around the back. With little steps that almost trip her along, she hurries to the edge of the porch. She hears again the shout, something recurring, but something coming from the bush beyond the sheds and away from the house. It stops again. The woman Avery listens again. But it has stopped this time until the next day.

Instead, in the ensuing silence, the kitchen door is flung open to thump shakily against its hinges. The manchild Frank stands there confusedly, making groping movements towards his sister but not yet with the words emerged from his fascination with the contents of the chocolate tin to cry out for the sudden loss of her, gone perhaps forever. A crooning physic'd:

'It's all right Frank.'

And has him back at the kitchen table, cocooned by the kitchen door being shut once more, before he has had time to come to the surface of the sea of fascinating things and whine at her for leaving him. With that special self-righteous tyranny of the weak.

Again she leaves him but this time returns to her honeycombs and her records of coming probabilities to be expected from her hived communities. Her mind malevolently brushing aside the thought of robber wasps upsetting the swarms and the honey flows. She has forgotten about the shouting and will do so until she will move closer to it tomorrow when it comes again.

The sister has not heard it to be a calling, over and over again, to the man Dere from the bush abutting the sheds. She has heard, but could not interpret, that the Sloane voice is repeating the call:

'Edward Louis Dere, we're coming for you now!'

Neither could she see the man Allan Dere crouched in the corner of his shed like a small boy fearfully tucking himself into as small an amount of visible space as is possible. His arms are wrapped tightly around his chest, his eyes screwed tight against the pain of what might have to be seen and admitted. And his scar across his eye a white weal as it throbs against his brain universally.

The shouting. The operator Sloane holds his head slightly away from the phone. The father the husband Mordecai Youngstein is shouting down the phone.

'Where are you, Sloane?!'

'I'm here, Mr Youngstein.'

'Smartness is just what I want like a hole in the head now, Sloane. Do me a favour.'

'I'm ringing, Mr Youngstein.' As though that is sufficient as an answer, but willing himself out of the temptation of continuing to be obdurate. 'I have got something. I don't want to raise hopes. I need time.'

'Go on.'

'It's a citizen. A poor slob joe.'

'Find his source, Sloane.'

'I want to nose in first, Mr Youngstein.'

'What the hell does that mean, schmuck?'

'Don't call me schmuck, citizen.'

'You tell me what that means.' The leader's voice gone to low, to growl, and the operator Sloane feels again the danger in the man. His is a war.

'It means I'm here and I'm here with the citizen I've tagged. I don't know if I've tagged right, but I can tell you this, Mr Youngstein, if he gets tagged and cries out no no I never, we're sunk. It's all as thin as that. He's away free and we're left with nothing.'

'You just tell me where he is.'

'Here is where I am. I want a head start in this.'

'Cut off his head and find the source.' The voice from the city of the father the husband is wolfine now. The operator Sloane fancifully envisages him motioning other ears to extensions with werewolfish swipes. He does not smile at the image.

'Mr Youngstein, listen. You've got no choice. You do it my way.'

'Where are you, or you're dead!'

The operator Sloane holds the receiver away from his ear and looks around, with old and weary eyes that feel even to himself now old and weary eyes, his hotel room in the country town. He nods to the wall as though on it was written that he has never felt so oldweary, so killingdead as he does with this case that is threatening to swamp his hold-on as a human being. And knows that the disparate horrors of the whole affair are just too waiting — whether out there beyond the country town or beyond the grasp of the woman Avery or at the other end of this line his hand is connected to — for him, Sloane, to speak oracularly. Wearyold and killingdead all of a sudden and breathing deeply within a pause before he speaks:

'Don't... don't threaten, citizen. You want the source. I don't know if there is a source.'

'Give him to me, Sloane. There must be the source. It's my daughter, Sloane!'

The present tense about the little girl Selma Youngstein hurting both of them.

'As from now, I am not paid by you, citizen. Hire another operator. Tell him to turn right at the intersection below the school. Tell him to find out about a cream station wagon at the greengrocer's by the first set of lights going into the city. Tell him to ask the cops what cars had been reported missing that day. Look up the name Rankin. Tell him about files and newspaper libraries. Find out where I am, because I'm taking that head start.'

'You're getting near to dying, Sloane.'

'You know, citizen, it's funny, but I suddenly think I am.'

The operator Sloane puts down the phone then. He has not meant to do anything but ring the father the husband and tell him where he was, precisely because he had felt suddenly so oldweary and killingdead to ask for any illusionary nonsense like head starts. But he has, irrespective.

He makes one more phone call. He rings his brother-in-law Detective Erny Roberts and is invited to dinner slightly angrily by his sister before his brother-in-law comes to the phone to, basically, invite him to dinner. The operator Sloane almost shouts into the phone a no-thanks. He wants to shout how the fuck can I, I'm down here in this died country town and I feel oldweary and killingdead and I'm dragging up ghosts that are chilling my heart and you're way up there in that great wide anonymous healthy unknowing city and you're asking me to dinner, what are you trying to do to me, I just want a sleep. But the operator Sloane finds he has not said that, finds he has only declined the invitation to dinner. Finds, yes, that he has actually asked his CID brother-in-law for a head start. And has actually told why and has actually got an okay as long as it's possible. A week at the most, Sloane. Sure a week. The CID won't exactly hinder the father the husband's inquiries, but may exactly hinder the father the husband's inquiries for, say, two days. They both laugh. The game again. Before he rang off, the operator Sloane almost laughed out aloud to his CID brother-in-law that he has never felt so tired of laughing at the game, so how come nothing.

It is the night. The woman Avery moves into her room and sighs. The end of the day. The getting-to-be intolerable sameness of the days. She has come from seeing Frank in bed and has finally entered her own bedroom for the night and has sighed, instead of screamed, for the sameness of it all. Disturbing herself.

Disturbing herself so much with such a thought that she thrashes herself into a penance by shutting her mind to how enjoyable it feels to be, finally, alone within, finally, the placenta of her own bedroom with just the bed and the shawl and the radio and the zingtingle of dozing. The little all that is so deliciously left to the day. Now she swerves herself away from the dressing table and almost blushes, not for the first time lately, at the thoughts the sight of her body in the mirror is causing.

Now the eyes outside the bedroom window of Miss Avery see her come into the room, jerk self-disgustedly with a jolt to her broodlike frame, swing around as though to back out of the room, then stop, frozen and held taut until her shoulders shrug a what-it-seems dammit.

Now the eyes outside watch her come back into the centre of the bedroom and switch on the old radio and switch on the bedside light and begin to undress. She has forgotten again to draw the blinds at night. Absorbing invasions. Perhaps all she asks is a gullibility. The eyes, the eyes. The eyes have returned. It is not because the woman Avery has this night not drawn the blinds as she has never thought to before all the invasions. It is merely because the eyes have returned, because the pieces have fallen in place for the eyes to return tonight.

They watch the tensile body of her come crazily out from under the soiled old dress, then she stands in a holed petticoat of old silken look, holed at the hip and brown from the wash, and worn, not unprovocatively, down to a sheen. Her little broodlike figure suddenly electrostatically clung to and sculpting feline curves. Materially stuck to gloss, liquidfacient. The mammae perhaps not large enough; the hips perhaps too slippery dip, but the whole Avery figure erect and unused. Brittle as a bird's.

The eyes, the eyes outside wiping themselves on the shape of her breasts come to show. She draws up her naked arms to stroke the back of her neck upward with one single caress and for a moment chalices her hair high above her, in open high worship. The eyes outside can guess how the woman inside is suddenly feeling being with nipple. Ululating.

Then she seems to come abruptly to her senses. She tears her arms back down to frame and her face switches guiltily onto the window. The eyes have not occurred to her, except in their form of an omniscient everyone-else forever watching and waiting for her to be ridiculous. That old, ugly, unwanted sister *juicing*. Quickly she crosses and pulls down the blind. Then moves to the doorway of her bedroom. Then moves back to her bed. Then cannot as yet climb into the bed. The thoughts still lingering. She turns before the mirror and thinks of a man and stretches her petticoat for a moment tightly across the front of her. She is all delta and they have called her all skinny.

The woman Avery, as, yes, brittle as a bird, whirls herself away from herself of the mirror and forces these so-familiar thoughts of her body familiarly away. Yet is at the light switch and has darkened the room and feels comfortable in undressing herself before herself in the dark, mirrorless. She doesn't want to think about what she is thinking. Only the tawny glow from the radio and bed and the usual drift.

Gradually Miss Avery returns to going snug again in the things that she knows about this bed and this radio and this time of night, when, snugged, it is alright in the all that is left of another day. And lies classically as a princess. Her face seems to be precisely divided down the centre by the light side and the dark side of the radio glow. Adumbrations.

151

The eyes outside can still just make her out.

Now the manchild lies back, his body not yet giving in to a sleep that is very near. The body of the manchild Frank, a grossly stranded object upon the bed, does not recognise the need for sleep and so the body of the manchild Frank has slowly tired itself out as the morphean urge seeps upon him. He lies there now with his arms held languidly upwards, his finger drawing lavishly slow-motioned shapes in the air. And his eyes following in heavy hypnotic tracing.

Sleep will come very soon now, well in filter and irreversible now.

He half-hears the tap on the window. He rolls his eyes towards the tapping and follows up the silverine shaft of moonlight that splashes across his bed. The eyes of the man-child set on and absorb the grotesque zoomorphic figure that now stands motionless and openly in the frame of the window there. Frank's heavy arms drop to his side, yet all the fear that has started within him is drugged by the sweet dousing of sleep.

He lies there and the figure outside his window stands there, swaying just perceptibly back and forwards and grinning its teeth phosphorescently in the moonlight.

A half an hour later, after she has limply switched off the radio, the woman Avery has to listen to at first, then has to go to investigate, the whimpering.

She does not know that her brother still lies on his back in the same position that he was in a half an hour ago. She does not know he has been looking at something in the now empty frame of the window with eyes filled with drugged fear. She does not know he has been whimpering for that half-hour's time like a little dog. She holds down the little waves of shivers that drive along his large beached body. She does so with her own body, carefully and forcibly, crooning to him and letting her known breath fan knowingly upon his face. Then closes his eyes as she would a dead man.

The manchild Frank has not moved still. He slips into sleep, his whimpering fading away. For the time and more that is necessary his little older sister sits by him. And thinks only of bad dreams.

The man is breaking in at the same time that Emile Gascoigne shuffles back across the road from the Avery property with dread of the operator's anger so real in his peopled mind that his feet stumble flatfooted against imaginary night obstacles even though the moonlight is surging, at the time, its sodalux through the splashes of clouds. That he has lost track of the man Allan Dere now conjures retribution in his mind that will threaten the whole material-turning of his material world. The point of the operator's pointing finger looms on the hermit's horizon as brontoplastic. All that that has ever squashed the stature of the hermit Emile Gascoigne in the eyes of the hermit Gascoigne. He feels discovered again and is squirming.

The hermit slips into the bush and will go to ground until the next day. What he has done is making even himself realise that he is slinking.

While the man completes his breaking in of the meat works. He sucks in the pungent miasma of living creatures, stilled biologically, opened up to the oxygen of the air, olfactive to the essence of new-laid dying, as if each death was left recorded in the air. The man thinks, but cannot recognise the transferred metaphor, of lingering farts gone rotten in a soup of bone and fat and the whitehot stinking blood and guts by the heat-heapful.

Now the man smiles and drags into his lungs great draughts of the unventilated stench. He smiles and reaches up to shut the window by which he has broken into the meat works. And listens. But nothing, only the irregular hum of the refrigeration plant at the other end of the shed. He moves that way, and moves delicately. This is with a care that is reverent. This is not a running in church, but a careful reverence towards the gods in residence.

As he goes, about halfway across the slaughter floor, the man hits his head against one of the electric saws that hang from their ceiling lines. The man does not duck, but merely stops, hurt but controlling the reaction fiercely. The gods of the slaughter watch and applaud him. He nods imperceptibly to a vast pantheon of invisible forms of meaning. Accountants that studiously watch and assess his progress. As he continues to move around, does not duck under, the pieces of machinery, the buzz of the refrigeration plant piedpipering him on.

Despite his shuffling, his feet keep slipping on the filmy floor. Gelatin seems to rise to absorb him. The blood rivers to flow up again and wash upon him and all the lowing and all the squealing and all the grunting and all the zoolatria to dying to become one bloody excoriation of the oneform that he is. Swooping upon and bringing the sweet sickly beautiful *tang* of things wretchedly bad and putrid to the each and all of his senses.

For a moment, so smothered and so smilingly indecent, the man nearly swoons and has to catch at himself to keep his balance. In his mouth he has the taste of gall and imagines he has run his pale-red pale thing of a tongue up along the walls. And lets, before going weakly on, the meat works beat at him in waves of warm sticky air that caresses a mounting nausea before he goes on to the platform, up the stairs to the platform where the hides, heaped, almost pulse his life glandularly back at him.

Now the man sits in the opened doorway of the cold room. He sits like a neophyte come to learn at the feet of a master. He sits and looks up with a tender regard. He is temporarily oblivious to the smells and the slippery tactility of the meat works around him. He is oblivious to the frost thorns that are already starting to work for the automatic reactions of his body. The man Dere sits there in the half-light tortured both mentally and physically by his fascination for the carcasses hanging from the meat hooks in there. The first one nearest him optically illuded into a whole torso of another holy man.

'Whatcha, Mr Dere. Whatcha, eh. Eh?!'

Calling out through the slacked jaw was Frank and blabbering demand for total attention.

'Don't Frank.'

'What's wrong with the goat? What's up with the drongo, Miss Avery?'

'He still needs the rest Frank I don't know I think.'

'Bloody dill. Bloody fuckin' nohoper, eh?'

'Don't listen to the men from the meat works Frankie.'

But said as automatically as the rhythm of everything else that comes from her to him. All but the soothing long given up. The most important thing left, then, anyway. And has recognised it. So awkward now to bring the manchild that is her brother into the sphere of this strangeness that is fascinating for her, having, delinquency, herself near the man Dere lodged so strangely, then, but curiously, now, in her shed. In all her years, Frank and Dad long ago excepted, she has never known where a man sleeps and how a man sleeps and what he looks like asleep. And it all tinged with the dreadful repulsion of the invasion. It has come and therefore it must hurt. The man Dere has come and therefore he must hurt. The man, men, the meat works, the man of the invasion, so she waves Frank back behind the demarcated line of her arm in a known signal of leave-this-to-me given authority by the known ply-the-game sound:

'Ssh Frankie ssh'.

155

Then is free to approach the shed of the man Dere alone. The manchild huge beside her even as she advances in front of him. The manchild stationed according to the rules of some game his sister has evoked by the gesture and the sshing; making him lumber from foot to foot in a hugeform parody of hopping from foot to foot and forcing him, with a biological incognition, to hold a huge handful of clothing and crutch tightly against the imminence of a huge micturative climax. His giggles quite painfully held peefully back.

The woman Avery now herself standing childishly created and shy before the shed of the man Allan Dere. The appalling sense of herself, however, has herself stern and rebuking enough for this aspect to be foremostly so. She holds the bowl of food leftovers that she has, again this morning, brought the man Dere for the day.

She has told her manchild brother in careful words that they can't let Mister Dere starve. The analogy has been Friar and Frank stands in piddling anticipation as she approaches the cat-form in the shed with the bowl held out by way of ritual offering truly established. The man Dere's feeding appropriative of Friar's coming back.

Then moves, when she can see him properly, into the shed to place the bowl on the ground by his sleeping form. She dare not do more. She can only place the bowl where she hopes the man Dere will come to it before the other animals in the shed. Aware, too well, of her own feelings of invasion to try to guide the alternatives. But once down there, she is caught within the unfluxing fact that she is kneeling down beside the invader rendered harmless for the moment. When does she move her hand as though it was a fragile implement to lift and manoeuvre, and places the back of it against his cheek. She could be testing for an electric shock. And he seems suddenly to fly up and to land frighteningly mentally upon her before, even so flightful as she is, she can recoil:

'Thank you.'

The man Dere has said and his eyes so largely open upon her so already. And his hand has caught hers in midflight and she cannot understand how or why it could have. Where they stay, both. She not daring for a moment to withdraw hers, feeling momentarily so *scooped* that she might well, after all the years, be an inevitability. Yet her eyes are sharp upon him, and she knows she is nuchally aroused.

Now the man Dere sits up but keeps his head turned from her. He holds her hand as a link behind him.

'Don't look at me. Miss Avery?'

'What?'

'I have a wound.'

'Oh.'

She cannot know that her answer is precise. That the man Dere who still appallingly has her hand in his is reaching up with his free hand to feel gingerly the raw and welted and weeping slash across his eye that is not at all visible or raw or welted at all. Then feels, as if he was groping behind him, the scar of the bee-sting infection on the back of her hand.

'Do you know what it's called?'

'What?'

'Stigmata. But they won't believe you.'

Having thus oracle'd, he lets go her hand but doesn't turn his head. The man Dere sits still away from her and doesn't thank her for the food she has left him.

The game is still on for Frank as his sister hurries back, birdy with colour flaming her cheeks, to him. He shouts at her but for the mananimal waiting in the shed to finally be gainsaid as the game's wanted thing:

157

'Seen me beaut cat Friar, Miss Avery?' Eh? Eh? Seen me beaut cat Friar?...'

The operator Sloane is there early today because this is the day he is going to move in. Not quite yet, though. Let the day slacken a bit first. He will see, too, first the hermit and will reapply by the implied threat of the old days returning by way of turning to his own advantage his annoyance for the vigil on the man Dere not being kept up last night. No, not quite yet. For now, the operator waits for the maddish little sparrow-hawk of a woman to move away from the shed and return to her bosscockey brother jumping up and down and shouting slur-tones about that cat again. With them, too, a coming closing in, but not just yet either.

Without his known city trappings around him the operator is allowing his wits, rather than his 'nose', to guide him to apply the pressure to a nicety of turn. So he remains out of sight behind the row of boxthorns until the sister and the manchild have returned to the house. She pulling at the brother like a beast of burden. Then, when they are out of sight, the operator Sloane edges closer to the sheds than he was yesterday before he begins to call out, with even greater insidious over-familiarity:

'Edward Louis Dere, we are coming to get you!'

He keeps ringing it into the light mid-morning air until he sees the broodlike little woman hop back around the side of the house again. He can tell how she is ruffled even from that distance. But does not only stop because of that.

There is not a sound from the man Dere in the shed.

He is at her car door and has opened it so obsequiously that she at first attends a shock before recognising the hermit Gascoigne surely come to insanity at last with such gregariousness. Thinks for a mad eclectic moment of all possible fears that she might stay in the car, petri-ordered and ignoring the openness of the door, and quite ignore an immolation surely to come from the world's order so violently and so sockedly overthrown. But the thought chaffing at the woman Salem's sense of humour so that she laughs aloud and then covers it up by getting out of the car that is again on and off, both, the Avery property with a flourish of bellicose and delighted surprise which the hermit does not have the practice to see through.

'Emile Gascoigne, what are you doing here if you're working for us?'

The person so used to not answering that he times a delay of answering to a perfection even though he is trying desperately to answer immediately:

'Eh?'

Ruminant of Frank. The inadequacy of the reply coming to them both simultaneously evidently, for, while the woman Salem raises a mockish eyebrow, the hermit Gascoigne slapsticks a raised eyebrow and eye-shot towards the Avery house, giving a clear signal that he wishes to speak about in there and only there with a crystalline clarity that, in expectancy of a visit to the Miss Avery and brother, the woman Salem finds absolutely admirable compared to his normal evasiveness. And has to ask in dubitably:

'What about Miss Avery, you naughty man you?'

'A person might know something.'

'I won't tell, Emile, my flower.'

With a clucking of his underchin that sends alarums of chaos through his nervous system that must be, and are only just, overcome if he is to deliver the import of what he has been trying to tell the world for days now:

'A person might know something, that's all I'm saying.'

159

'I see.'

'A person can't tell her what he knows. Wonder if you might tell her a person knows. Looking out. Not to worry. Keep the chin up. A person doesn't forget her and him especially, and all that.'

'What the goodness are you talking about, Emile?'

'You know. If she asks, mind. Not otherwise.'

'Oh, yes.' With a twinkle hoped for in her eye. Thinking, the really lovely thing about a visit, even another contrived visit like this one is, to Miss Avery and Frank, is that it is all and totally all a twinkle-wink and a hope anyway. There is no greater charade left to a countrified gal.

'Emile, there is no greater charade left to a countrified gal

'Only if she asks, mind.'

'Of course.'

With not a blind bit of knowing what the poor devil is talking about. But absolutely delighted that an ingredient of spiciness to her visit has been added by him. The perfect pinch. And tweaks the cheek of the miserable hermit, who has *dared* the sunlight so carefreely and desperately, before he can spring back on his arthritic heels in genuine horror of being bodily encroached upon. It shows so on his face that even the woman Salem almost, but not quite, wishes she hadn't done it. Has to, though, cover up the embarrassment of having done so by delivering a hubby-taught short left to the solar plexus of the hermit, who whoops loudly with an instinctive verbal outrage.

The woman Salem quickly turns away from him to try to scamper up the path to the house of Avery, not a little herself overawed by the pleasure she feels because of the familiarity she has wrought upon the person of the hermit. Yet when he calls after her, she cannot help but stop and look back to the hermit, miserable, possibly for perpetuity, at having failed again to congress with

160

another human being; the pleading in his voice inexpressibly sad:

'Tell her a person *knows* but can't say. Tell her a person's hands are tied, but you've seen a person around.'

'Just what I was going to say, Emile. Anything else?'

Her jokiness again against him falling short, in fact far short of both of them. She could kick herself. She would cry out to him he doesn't have to go on, but it is too late.

'Tell her... Tell her a person's willing. Tell her a person'd be in it for a few bob. Eh?'

'Who's a person?'

Akimbo, a-grinning and mockingly gracious back at him. She cannot stop herself.

'Tell her he's out here watching over her.'

Then is gone from her in a half trot that moves him across the road but at a tangent that practice of putting quick distance between himself and people who are imminently to throw stones has made perfectly fit.

For a flighty moment of mad impulse, the woman Jenny

Salem almost follows him to wherever he might lead her as an odious harridan, yes, for how she gets her emotional joltings from sipping at other people. But manages to restrain herself in this mad moment of self-analysis, and turns and swaggers down the pathway towards the house of Avery. She even feels magnificently swaggerish towards the, to her, always have been, naked-rude beehives alongside there humming a nasty come-on, it seems. Feeling, too, as she knocks at the kitchen door and receives no answer whatsoblandlyever, that she has the munificence today of being able to wait for as long as is necessary. She leaves the kitchen door and moves around the side of the house. This seems a huge time for her. She feels, as she moves, the centre of a vast

161

Outback landscape, and she herself the great sucking woman in its centre who is bloody with sexual enjoyment and is calling on discarded Aboriginal myths to spurn or support her, whichever. Fanciful. It must have been the hermit's attention. Today she feels huge with attention and it feels good.

The woman Salem finds the woman Miss Avery and Frank at the beehives down by and beyond the orchard. If she was not feeling so munificent she might have almost panicked for being so isolated there between the sheds of the man Dere and Miss Avery and the manchild or the hermit out front. And, as she waits between the calling and the secretiveness, she begins to realise how important has become the property of Miss Avery all of a sudden in her life. It is in the sway of both liking and detesting the essence of her own curiosity.

The woman Avery moves to the next beehive and will listen, as she has at the other hives, for its well-being, judged both by ear and by the vibrations of its throbbing against the palm of her good hand. It is what she plainly, and always has, knows she knows.

She has no gloves on, has never put the gloves on. She has the helmet on and has always used the hat and veil. The sun, low now, against her frock makes X-rays to her body, yet haloed. The corona dipping at her black hat as she seems to weave and duck and chirp amongst the drone, prodding with left fingertips against the hive, here, there, stethoscoping. But it is her bitten right hand that is just as noticeable from the distance, for this she is holding high, as though it was a standard that cannot ever be lowered before the fissively shooting beebodies harrying about her and it. Swollen huge and proud.

With Frank, before he notices, however myopically, the woman Salem standing by the back door, behatted and beveiled and entered into gloves and tied at the cuffs of trousers and cuffs of shirt and collar of vest, waddling in cakewalk behind her with exaggerated reverence. If not out-and-out pomposity for the ceremonial occasion. He, too, holding unsurrendered arms aloft in mimic of his buzzing sister's contaminated right hand. He is not

162

mumbling or shouting at her now; is only full of wondrous attention at the biblical nature of his sister truly at home in there. And some vestige of the Frankie of younger days causing him to prod in mimic her tiny birdlike form whenever she prods at a hive.

Miss Avery is worried and is worrying at the hives. Her swollen hand is preventing the honey collection, dishonouring her obligations to her bees even more than her promises to the brother that the collecting is to start soon, tomorrow, tomorrow. He cannot know, as he cakewalks behind her, that she is humming apologetics to her little ones as she goes. They come to the end of the row. Miss Avery drives herself on impatiently towards the second row with a cluckish apprehension surging her forward. But this interval only breaks over Frank as a boring interlude. He looks up and sees what to him is a blurred danger of a human form watching and waiting over there at the back of the house. And holds up fast between the interval of the rows, staring for a shocked moment at the unrecognised figure of the woman Jenny Salem, until reaction takes cognition and he cries out, rooted there in apprehension and fright, his breath suddenly catching and struggling for a rhythm.

Miss Avery is by his side, coxcombed, even before she herself has realised it. Her heart pounding, too, and then pounding with relief at the recognition and then annoyance that the woman Salem stands between them and the sanctuary of the house.

'It's all right Frankie you know *that.*'

From his shed, the man Dere watches and sees how bodily the little sister can drag the hugeform of the brother after her as they move towards the woman Salem. It is such an eager spurt-on and so out of character for her that the man Dere feels jealousy rise like a huge gob into his mouth. The sudden enthusiasm of the little sister he is watching seems to him the most indecent thing he has ever seen.

163

For a moment he actually hates. For a moment it is a clean and fine and crisp hatred. But now his eyelids close from all the weight of all the tiredness he has ever felt in his life. He turns his gaze from the aviflitter of Miss Avery to the cerulean sky dreamingly over there and up above him. The gums tipping the horizons of his sight beginning to gauze into fine lacings mesmeric. And sinks back into the sheer and total delight of smelling the stench that is, and that he imagines is, rising from his body and crutch.

Stunningly. Miss Avery hooks upon the arm of the woman Jenny Salem and actually releases that of Frank in order to do so. She loses not an ergon of flux as she does so, but rather docks to another form in her passing phase from the hives to the inside of her house. Stunningly, yes. Having let go of the manchild brother with an abruptness that is as stunning as the stunning keen appreciation in her aquiline eyes for the woman Salem being there. For an instant the regard is received stunnedly by the woman Salem, before Miss Avery's arm-to-arm hook-up propels, behind her, Jenny Salem towards the inside of the house with such an alarming change of historical heart that helpless panic weakens the woman Salem's knees, such that if the case actually was, after all these taunting years, the Avery woman is finally going to lead her to slaughter.

It all begins to go wrong for Jenny Salem when she begins to realise that the kitchen door is looming fast and yet there is no slackening of the broodlike sister's forcefully guiding pace. Plummeting, almost, towards the *interior* at an indecently custom-breaking rate. She feels, in a flash, part of a medieval charivari for a single moment of historic motion, with the town buffoon, huge in form as he is with oppressing presence, appareiled in beehive hat and net, like a mad monk just might befit an off-day Monday, trotting in crashingly awkward stumbles alongside the madcap float of her and the Avery woman. Blowing his rounded raspberries right into her ear through that bee-safe face net as much as to say I'm not going to shock you out of your wits, I'm just going to keep trying to shock you out of your wits. And the whole procession there one minute of the kitchen porch's time and gone the next. Rammed, all three of the people parts, inside the house of Avery.

The woman Salem, before she has been able to gather any wits from the moment of the swoop until this moment when she feels the tide ebbing fast around her, finds herself amazedly cast up on the living room interior of the house of Avery. The momentum around her has stopped as abruptly as it was abruptly forced upon her. She struggles to bring herself back to herself and to absorb the fact that, after all these years, she has been thrust bodily into the house of Avery for the actual looking, if she should so choose. And does try to so choose, pinching herself mentally to wake and look *quickly,* but cannot so *definitely* as much as she tries. Somehow her eyes refuse to leech upon anything else but the spread of old newspaper all over the luscious, otherwise, floral carpet beneath, and the breathlessly preened gaze of the eyes of the little birdwoman sister standing breathlessly across from her waiting for her to speak. She does not know, or even care, where Frank has gone to. She finds herself stunned, unable to do nothing at all to force herself into taking a good old fashioned look for chrissakes while you're there.

Nor does it help her confusion when it comes to her, zappingly, that she is not only sitting in one of the single lounge chairs there, but is in fact sitting on the lap of the brother Frank.

And he jogging her up and down on his knees and, for some reason that might not even make sense to her in a knowing state, is making heavily unmistakable choo-choo train noises in her ear with an outrageous intimacy. Even more outrageously he is holding her as fixed as a cuddly *thing* with his heavy arms weighted like chains about her belly encircled. And outrageous of even that is that her interpretation she cannot help making of the manchild's *choo-choo* is *chew-chew.* But probably the most outrageous appalling thing of all is the frozen vacuum flask quality of it all she is feeling, as though neither time nor portent nor meaning had any consequence at all. And has to talk, panicked by the sudden feeling that no one might ever again attempt to break this plane of frieze that has enwrapped her, ever. It is a cry:

'Do you think you could... ?'

Delivered smashingly at Miss Avery, but can only be finished by
her thumb jerking backwards over her shoulder at Frank, by way
of mutely begging can you get Frank to release me before
something really does happen. Which it does. For the words have
hardly drifted away before Miss Avery has pounced on the broken
silence and is suddenly calling out with a terrible anguish:

'He needs you. I must've failed him!'

And even before the woman Salem can gather up to a vocal stage
one of the thousand possible replies that might dust off this
sudden, first-ever, must be, whine of self-pity from the little sister,
Miss Avery has flown across the room and is craning face to face
with her, their noses almost meeting, her twitting eyes searching
for attention from somewhere in the wide and confused eyes of her
captured visitor before her. And her whole face thrust forward as
though its kinesis of flight has been suddenly halted just as it was
about to dash itself against that of Jenny Salem. With Frank,
thinking of frolics for three, cupping her breasts from behind and
bouncing her gleefully up and down on his lap in a pornographic
burlesque. His grip out-sized and epicene. There is not all all this,
either. For his plumigerous mothersister is now hardly whispering
right into the face of Jenny Salem what sounds like the most
shocking secret of her life:

'He's whimpering. I find my Frankie whimpering at night. I go in
there and I...'

Has to physically, of body, force a stop, by reversing herself in
flight and spinning back to the window frame where she leans
again in a cockeyed manner, as though she has never moved from
there to Jenny Salem, but has only slipped sideways. Peering,
though with an egret's eye at the other woman for an answer to
that.

Jenny Salem internally screams at herself to fend for herself. It is not a question of maintaining one's decorum now, but of rejoining oneself back to the task of being oneself before it is lost forever. She suddenly thrashes about violently with her body. Her legs and arms whirlwind and her body slithers in maelstrom. And has a moment of utter unseeing until she thankfully finds herself on the floor and out of the externally-consuming arms of Frank's *chew chew*. Miss Avery, but dully:

'Frank.'

'Pissorf. Pissorf.'

He holds still at one arm's length a bottom corner of the jumper of the woman Salem in a casual and stalemated tug-of-war with the woman. She gets to her feet now, has to stand on the lean almost directly parallel to Miss Avery's lean across the room in an exact stasis of the tug-of-war with Frank. Her jumper looking more and more like a rope at stretch.

And in that moment the woman Salem suddenly feels the unprecedented eagerness of the little woman Avery so almost obscene and exposing, and suddenly feels the bumblings of the manchild Frank no longer funny. This is not the titillation that she has, both this time and all the other times, come for. All she desperately wants now is just to get away. And still cannot *look*, but has to gouge out words she won't remember. She says:

'Come here to tell you. Watch out for him. The detective from the city told me everything. Ask that man who his father was. Only that child raper. You look out. With a childhood like that, seeing your father do all those disgusting things, must have made him funny in the head. Stands to. Stands to reason.'

And finds herself waiting. And hears herself sucking in and out her breath. But nothing out of the little sister, but the same cock-eyed look quizzing.

Her last word hangs in the air and turning to a lingering frost.

167

Reason. Reason. She waits. A silence. Only the not slight feeling of mounting chaos as she feels Frank's pull on her jumper steadily toppingly assertive once more. She swirls and rabbit-cops at the jumper noduled with his hand until his grip breaks with a sudden release that sends her toppling towards the door before she can regain her ballast. When she does so, she throws a desperate look back at Miss Avery, only to find that the little broodlike sister is nodding her bird's nod as much as to be noddingly and verbally in agreement with the direction Jenny Salem is taking:

'Don't want to detain you.'

Jenny Salem will not remember the inside of the house that she finally got into after all the years. She will not understand why she cannot recall it for any of the few days she still nearly has to live. Now she stands, having retreated hastily and in repugnance from the house of Avery, by the front of her car. She lets loathing come for the little sister inside who has so forever spoiled the enjoyment of the Frank-and-sister show.

The operator Sloane takes the phone message from the receptionist. He knows immediately that it can be from only one person and that he will have to make his move on Dere right away. He has registered this even before the receptionist has told him that it was from the city but there had been no message.

Sloane turns and walks out of the foyer again. He does not mind so much that he has to return to the property of Avery. Professional appreciation for the fact that the father the husband Youngstein has tracked him down so quickly dampens the pettish feeling of annoyance he momentarily has. It shows he is working for a professional and that adds a little something indefinable to the game of pressure he has been playing with diminishing brio. There has been no need for histrionics; a phone call has been enough.

Later the operator Sloane will make the necessary contact with the

Jewish wine maker. But for now, he will carry on with his own play, before the husband the father Youngstein can get to invade the sheds at the bottom of the Avery property with the 2nd Division of the Israeli Army. And smiles grimly at the joked thought.

This time he does not approach the sheds from the far Teachings of the property. But stops his car outside the property of Avery and strides, with urbane punchiness, to the front gate. He knows he is on parade there. Even so, he corrects the fall of both suit trousers and jacket, touches up his shoes, then turns to nod back to where he knows the hermit Gascoigne will be watching from. He does so to tell the hermit that he knows he is there, and then adds to that a wide grin of facility of entering the Avery property that he knows will tear at the hermit's cravingly timid heart. Nor does he try to hide his presence as he strolls down the path, but whistles inchoate musical sounds and tries to make as much noise of approaching the house as he can.

At the corner of the kitchen porch he stops. He does not turn towards the kitchen door of the house of Avery but insolently keeps facing the sheds. Calls a hey to the house from the side of his mouth. He hears from inside the cry of the manchild for his sister and then what is obviously a burst of stumbling against crashable things. Hears, too, the oleacious tones of the little sister, when the crashings instantly cease.

The operator Sloane waits only for a few seconds. He senses rightly that the woman Avery is not going to come to the door.

He picks up a few pieces of gravel and with a casual, sideways, underarm flick missiles them against the kitchen door. His game is going as delightfully as he would have it, when the door is angrily half-opened and she stands, hackled, with an aggressive display that the operator amusedly admires out of the corner of his eye, feudally at broach there. With Frank large as a sight-screen behind her and so caught there between fright and curiosity that physically he looks like he might at any moment topple upon and totally absorb her.

The operator does not even turn his head to look at her, but lets his tried and proven arrogant disdain take effect on the citizens. Speaks, too, out of the corner of his mouth:

'They say you're the citizens that own the cat called Friar.' Has to wait for, but quite expects, the reaction. The hugeform of the brother seems to jump with realisation and tries at the outset to break out past the rigidform of Miss Avery. Who stands against him with a fierce stolidity. He finds then, anyway, the words figured up:

'Friar? Friar?'

'Is that a yes, citizen?'

'He seen Friar, Miss Avery? He seen Friar, eh?'

'We own a cat called Friar.' Can now relax against the brother's pressure behind her gone plastic and transfer the toes dug in to her voice:

'Have you seen it?'

The operator then turns his face towards them. It is an actor's movement and an actor's smirk and he says, so that it is loaded with uncare for what happens to unhelpful citizens:

'Nope. Never heard of it.'

And passes on his way to the sheds. He knows as equally sure that the skinny little sister will keep the manchild inside out of the way just as she will undoubtedly watch him at the sheds from out of the rear window. He has never minded the audience; in fact it has always seemed to make his life feel right. He has never minded either the prospect of using the gun.

In the days that are left to him he will use it only once.

170

He begins calling for Edward Louis Dere when he is only three parts across the way to the sheds.

He stops ten metres fair and square opposite the second shed, where he knows the man Allan Dere keeps himself. Wise to the fact, too, that the man Dere will be there.

The operator Sloane looks slowly around the arboreal perimeter of the Avery property before he, again exacting theatrics for the not-quite-real effect it is in his advantage to create, turns to face the shed and gaze quite unhurriedly into the shadefield of the first shed to his right. He lets his eyesight adjust to looking at the interior of the first shed, then sectors his eyes languidly onto the second shed directly before him. And, quite as if it were a natural occasion, catches onto the man Dere sitting, yet so erect that his position seems grotesque, off to the middle left, halfway in. Sloane dwells a moment on the pleasing appreciation that it is, after all, all going to be as he expected; there might be an unexpected movement but there will not be an unexpected danger.

'Edward Louis Dere?'

There is no answer. He has not expected any until the great gush of remorse and then the processes will work automatically without any operator's help. It's how it always is:

'Edward Louis Dere...?'

To peer Magoo agog dear-me, dear-me into the face of the man Dere and tut-tutting how mistakes can be made:

'Dear me, and I was looking for Edward Louis Dere. I can see you're not Edward Louis Dere, the sex maniac and child *rooter*. I thought for a moment you might be that stupid, pathetic fucking bastard. I can see you only look the dead ringer of him. You couldn't be him, could you? No, nobody could be him, could they, citizen, not even the lowest form of animal life. Funny thing is you look just like him, citizen. You might be him, come to think of it, citizen. You're filthy and I can smell you from here, *son* citizen. They say your father defecated on little corpses he was never tried for. Now, I wouldn't know, but is that right? Me, I can understand how you just want to be alone and wallow in dirt. I can understand, *son* citizen, I truly can. Come on, you tell me now. Little girls flying up in front of you and landing down *thump*. Broken dolls still getting at the part of your daddy in you, eh? You were right to run. She was dead. She was broken all down the whole of one side, including the head. Poor little Jewish broken girl. They're after you and your mates. They know where you are, even now. Who are your mates? You tell me who your mates are. Never mind, the man will find them. He's going to break you like you broke his daughter and he'll find them. Either way, you're dead, so you might as well tell me, citizen.'

At the same time as he reaches for his gun, the operator swivels his body slightly so that what he is doing can be seen all too well by the woman Avery he knows is watching from the back window. The man Dere has not moved while the operator Sloane has been talking almost conversationally, but has had to lower his eyes from the operator's face. The gun casually brought into view, but kept held in the palm of the hand, then is turned and the front sights used to doodle in the dirt, caressingly, stroking its back.

'Your mother says you *itch* too much, citizen. I think she's right. You go around *itching* too much to be involved in anything as uninteresting as international politics, right? You've got a far more interesting thing, haven't you, citizen? You've got your own very-everything *itch*. There's your own old hermit you've got to have turn around and say I forgive you, the son, haven't you? Citizen, give it up. Come with me; I'm the only hope you've got.' And pauses to level the gun right between the starting eyes of the man Dere.

The man Dere forces himself against the fact of the gun threatening. He remembers his decision to defy that he made as he watched the operator approaching and struggles to gather himself to that same determination. It produces, instead, only a burst of fury that he cannot swallow back before it breaks over him:

'Jam it. YOU JAM IT!'

The operator Sloane smiles slowly. He straightens up and lets the gun hang down by his side. He carefully adjusts his suit's hang and then silently shakes his head sorrowfully at the man Dere sitting in there. He feels no need to do anything but amble into the shed, where he works his way round to behind Dere with an intention that is deliberately showy. And has not stopped talking to the snake as he has come on:

'You're upsetting yourself here, citizen. You're *itching* at things too much. You hit that little kid and, sure, it opens the flood gates. But don't itch at it. Don't let it build up.'

The operator Sloane is behind the citizen now and stooping for a whispering in his ear. 'Real funny things, like imagining things. Like your mother screaming at your disgusting father. Daddy of your flesh. *Selma, Selma, your father's a dirty Jew!*'

The man Dere thrashes out. He tries to twist and thrash out at the operator. Easily ready. All going as all planned. Smilingly smothering the man Dere's movements and bringing him easily to his feet with a hold that he takes right up to the point of breaking the arm. The whisper, still against the back of the ear, smutty in its familiarity, but harshly of the unimagined world: 'Come out with me, citizen. Confess. Like you want to. You do that and I might let a detective get you before a father. It's all over for you, citizen.'

He lets fall the man Dere and steps aside. The world will be quiet as he makes his way unhurriedly back to his car, across the whole length of the property of Avery. It is as the performance should have been. He has not broken his rhythm the whole time of his visit. It is best that way when he is best.

Presences in the shed and the house and the bush across the road. Almost feels like bowing as he cruises away.

'Congratulations, Mr Youngstein.'

'Sloane, don't fool with me.'

'I know, I'm just one of many thousands. You must have hired good. I thought I'd have more time.'

'Is it the man Dere?'

'Yes. No. Professionally, both, Mr Youngstein. Like I said, I need time. You move too fast and he clams up and we'll end up with nothing.'

'I don't care about him, Sloane. I want the source before it learns and diffuses.'

'What if there's no source, Mr Youngstein?'

'Are you mad?'

'No, Mr Youngstein. I remember your little girl and, yes, I want to spit. Look, I'm tired. You've discovered where I am. Alright, I'm back in the army. Give your orders, Mr Youngstein.'

'Sloane, tell me this. You close?'

'I think I am.'

'Sloane. I've been reading what's his father. He was an animal. Like father, like son. They've got him on blackmail, maybe. Either way you take such a *schmuck* apart and you mother him to cry on your shoulder because he's cracked in the head already. And *then* you squash him.'

'I'm weary tired, Mr Youngstein. Just say.'

'I say I've changed my mind about you, Sloane. I say you're doing right. I'm going to help. We're staying out of the backyard and

174

give you the time. Just remember the crying on the shoulder that has to be Sloane; that's why I'm sending you down the wife.'

The operator Sloane reacts, but the receiver in the father the husband's home has been put down. The operator knows, too, it is pointless ringing back. He lies back on the bed. He wants out, but knows he is in. For the first time in his operator's life he senses himself being suffused to an imparticularity. The wife. Joan Dere.

The night is better because this time there is the scummy cloud cover whipping across the moon in sweeping dramatic assumptions and the wind in howl. A night that is sight and sound, of too many shadows and too much swirl. It is a better night for the eyes, the eyes. The points of view.

Not even, in there, the hummy glow from the radio, nor lamplight. In the room of Miss Avery. The eyes have tried to peer in there but have not tried too hard. And have moved on around the house to the manchild's room to produce more whimpers from the child of the house. The person's footsteps sure in the dark forces of the night. The child and the eyes.

The manchild in bed is whimpering already. The night passing shadows that he has come to drowsily take as the silhouette standing outside each night intruding at him. Half-asleep he listens to the wind outside and hears the whispering-whispering of the eyes, the eyes come for him again. But is held quieter than the other nights. The whimpering, too, tonight only like a muted hive's buzz from inside his large puffed head, reduced to a simper. Sleep is catching him. The manchild is undistressed. He lies back weakly whimpering, yes, but his eyes slowly follow the shapes he is making in the air with his finger. It is almost as usual.

The person outside edges forward to the manchild's window now. He does not know why tonight he edges so cautiously. Stares hard, while the moon is mantled, into the room of the brother Frank until he discerns the second shape in there. Whips away.

175

Soon the manchild falls, quietly at first, then louder, asleep. His little sister sits at his side, as she will do for tonight and tomorrow night, but that is all for the occasional days she has left to her. She sits by her needing brother's side and listens to his whimpering, only a vestige tonight of what it has been anyway, die down. She looks down the Gulliver of him spread along the bed and she wonders at the size of him and the comparative homunculus of herself. But most of all she wonders about he and her locked together for all of this lifetime.

The man Dere, in this night of wind and howling motions, wanders like a beast, blinded but still on a swaying, swaying rampage. Between the property of Avery and the meat works he has staggered and stumbled, yet forged on before the wind as he dips in and out of sight with the skuddings of the broken clots of clouds. His direction does not seem tried for the abattoirs, but towards them he is moving. He could be caught in the flooding of the wind and only able to plough transversely against it for a while before it swings him back into the stream again and pushes him further on, drained and ineffectual, yet, to the hermit Gascoigne trying to follow him, gesticulating wildly as he goes as though he was constantly in danger of losing his balance and being sucked away. And the man Dere's voice pulsating on the gusts of wind, large and bayful, shouted and punctuated but not understandable, flagging upon the air like a doleful banner finely tracing the man Dere's progression.

The hermit Emile Gascoigne is mightily afraid. He is afraid for all things brought back into his life. He is afraid for himself, in the danger of now and in the danger of himself as his usual hermit self, for, in these past few nights, he has seen from firsthand how easy it is to stalk as he himself has been stalked, and will surely always be stalked, by *them* with the murder in their hearts and the killing words in their mouths and the stones in their hands. Detesting the man Dere who is crashing through the wild night wildly up ahead of him, and feeling pity for the man Dere up ahead of him, and seeing himself as he must be seen by others and

176

being very mightily, yes, afraid for himself in the now and the usual.

But still follows the man who is upon the night, reasonless.

Allan Dere steps back to the window. He is smothered so much with the sudden drenching of the smells of himself and the smells of the meat works and is smothered so much that he would lick himself. He steps back to the window he has entered the meat works by again but does not close it. Instead he props it open with the stick and waits.

From in there he registers for the first time how much the night is in race outside. It is good. It is as it should be. The wild drifts piling up outside the doors. The single step between the let-drift and the hold-on. He waits and sweats and registers, too, the wetness from under his arms, from between his legs from which the odours will come. Again, before him, there are only the wet, howling nights of his childhood and the wet soakened gorse island moors sogging to his young life's skin. The nights, remembered, he has had to look at in childhood and come to know as part of the worst imaginable things made present out there and raving out there, *marauding*. The spittle there was on his father's lips. The rain and the dark torment in all the eyes he has ever remembered of the great, the hugemonstrous, the perpetual night of his younglife's allhislife island life. And the dark and the gutting sounds of the word *evil* whispered in the night past the lantern light and his own bestial eyes felt like to shining it from the secret and dark cave of his secret and dark home between the sheets in his all-living, ever-there pubescent island bed. Sacked into the fetid and delicious smells of island semen.

The man Dere, sweating, waits and looks up with contusely revering eyes to the stick that props the window open and the son Dere looks across from the cliff to the tiny islet unto where the hermit has been sent packing to exile, the living image of the living evil found stealthing in the son Dere's dark and secret life. And the son Dere and the man Dere feel the dark night of the wetsoakened gorse island moors still *drooling* at their backs. So

177

that they both, the man and the son, swell and unite, never having moved from the cliff top looking down on what they have done to the living avatar, the hermit, the one crucified heaped with the sins and the guilt of the man the son the father. The son, the father of the man. Fixed in time forever, irredeemable, fashioned to form by the tegument of a reeking existence.

Such that, when the hermit carefully pushes his head through the window's opening to peek a curiosity built-up at what the man Dere has been coming these nights to the meat works for, the son and the man Dere together reach up, coiled forever together, and take hold of the hermit. Reaching easily across the isthmus to the islet off shore to pluck the living proof off and back into the main island's mainland of expiations.

Emile Gascoigne has squealed, could not jerk free of the hands that have shot out from the interior of the meat works to hold him, first, so fast and, then, to heave him into there with so little exertion. He could not know of the forces heaving from within the son and the man Dere. Nor of the screech that comes out of the son and the man as he has caught hold of, and has and is heaving, the slight and ragged person of the hermit, living proof.

The stick that is knocked aside. The window that slams down upon the form of the hermit. The cry that comes out of the form of the hermit. The explosion of breath knocked out. The wad of slaughter that hits at the nostrils of Emile Gascoigne from the shut up, now released, slaughter house.

He hears for that instant that he fulcrums upon the window frame the squealing child's voice from the son and the man Dere, the hot breath in his alarmed littleboy's face:

'Please, please'.

Before he feels himself dip in flight headlong into the fatty bowels of the meat works and the black smells of slaughter. The sweating beast in the son and the man muff him.

He will never be sure what woke him. The cold. The droning sparking of the cool room plant. The hum droning of the voice of the man Dere somewhere around. The man, there. In squat at the doorway of the cool room, face upturned to him and clearly seeable for some reason he will never equate on.

The hermit Gascoigne tries to move but his body only slews at one side as if it were, as it actually is, taut on one side and loose on the other. Swinging from one arm held hugely aloft at the end of his stretch and the point of his boots scraping only just on the floor. It is better when he comes to properly. But for now the voice of the son and the man Dere cries out in pain with such torment, when the body of the hermit moves as living proof, that the hermit dead locks himself in fear. He hangs there and crabs his mind around his body to find how it is that he is hanging, but timidly as though the very thinking would give him loudly away. To find his feet can easily reach the floor but his hung arm cannot move away from the stenchy fatness of something against him. Slowly he moves his feet to stand flat on the soles. Outerly he is aware of the sighs of the son and the man Dere over by the door. The cold of the cool room chilling at him as he edges his feet along the floor. The breath, seen through eyes opened only as much as he dare, of the son and the man Dere condensing to puffs in an arctic light and with each exhaling a catching at the breath, a little pain gripping.

Now the hermit realises that he is hung up by the sleeve of his overcoat, meat hooked with the carcass of a bullock almost folded about him. He cries out in fright, struggles rictusly upon the skewer.

Where from the doorway, the son Dere, the man Dere, both together at the foot of the crucifying hill, cry out in unison against the screaming out of the living proof.

The son and the man cry out that they will take the pain from the living proof unto themselves. That they will take the filth, the stench from the living proof unto themselves. That they will take

179

the stonings and the thorns and the spittles upon the poor bleeding uncomprehending living martyr's face unto themselves. And the persecutions and the questions and the blood tests unto themselves. The son and the man cry softly to the living proof from the foot of their island hill:

'... the hush running of the water in the harshdark moors riverlets. When they cast lots for you, I am shivering. I am with you in the sun of the desert and you turn your eyes when they have driven you beyond the saint to the beast, finally. The full circle. You see? I am just the same. Give it back to me. I'll shiver on the island shore of your nails. I hold up the cakes running out from our pores. It is me. I have done all this to you. They will break your legs. They laugh at us when the martyr's fever comes, when the knife cuts across our eyes. Yet you know it was always me. The dirt. Let me. *Please.*'

The son and the man looks sometimes to the right, sometimes to the left, sometimes back up to the living proof in crucifixion up there. He stretches out his hands towards the living proof. His fingers are trembling; his nostrils dilate. Before him he joins his hands, his manshands his childshands before him, convulsively then hopelessly drops them back into his lap.

There is no more, but the upturned face, radiant upon the living proofs countenance. There is such a sigh.

That fills the hermit with a chilling dread.

Finally he, the hermit, dares to reach up; in the stillness, dares to move. Dares to reach for the caught sleeve on the meat hook. The son and the man Dere remains motionless, his voice lowing softly but, even in this light, seen to be hugely eyeing the hermit's slightest move. The freezing air rattles at the old man and turns his breath into stoked steam as he exerts against the hook to, finally, free himself. Disbelievingly. And, too, disbelievingly, the son and the man Dere remains sitting, stationed, in rapt of all the moving flickers of the hermit in there.

Emile Gascoigne tries a step. The son and the man Dere does not go berserker because of it. He tries another. The son and the man sits only, lowly moans only, transforms eyes of adoration to follow only. As the hermit slides around the skiddish wall of the freezing room, his own eyes are on the son and the man Dere as carefully as those of a watching snake, and is shaking as he edges out towards the cold room door where the son and the man Dere sits and watches only. Now, with the hermit so close, with his eyes uplifted and adoring. Passive and devotional.

The son and the man's mouth is half open, the lower jaw slightly dropped. Neither his lips nor fingers move again. His body sits motionless as would a corpse.

There is nothing to hold back Emile Gascoigne from escaping. He finds in reality that he could have strolled away from the son and the man elegaically in stasis there. He flees then. The hermit flees with all his senses immersive to the swathing night outside. He has seen what was not imagination, something he will never speak of in all the many days he has left to him, but will be haunted by.

For Emile Gascoigne has seen, as he has edged fearfully past the son and the man Dere swivelling those eyes of adoration up to him as he passes, the blood streaming from the slash above the eye. So in cascade that, in the chill, the stigmata of the son and the man Dere steams bloodily.

It started from this day to go wrong for the operator Sloane.

He has searched for the hermit Gascoigne in the scrub across the road from the house of Avery, but has not found him. Yesterday he had gone in on the flush to the man Dere and the little redbroodlike woman and had expected the hermit to tell him if either of them had got up. But the hermit has not been found in the bush across from Miss Avery's. There is no trace of the old man having been there either, so the operator has turned, with his irritation punctuated by his tendency, anyway, towards prognathism, and made his way towards the cottage of Emile Gascoigne prognathously, tendency or no tendency.

He, the operator, has been fixed, as though skewered, on the swine-dash feeling he has had last night, when he was washed over by a wave of ineffectuality, as he lay on his hotel bed, swamped by the man Youngstein and the man Youngstein's news of sending down the man Dere's wife. He felt the beginnings of losing control of events, yes, but, more tearingly, swamped by the *wrongness* of the husband the father Youngstein.

Now even the pawn hermit is not in place when a move is to be made. And, as the operator moves towards the hermit's cottage into a deeper bushland of no regulated track, he senses how oddly out of thwack he feels himself suddenly to be. It is a sense that is made more heightened by the muddiness underfoot that keeps niggling at his priggish and picking care for his shoes, his cuffs, and his general fitness. All is somehow sudden *wrongnesses*.

The first word is a lamentation. The second is calmer. The voice has called:

'Here. Here.'

It catches the operator Sloane unexpectedly. He would not admit it frightens him, even though he has known it is the hermit calling. It is the way it is said. Again feels the tug of losing control of events and mentally thrashes at himself before he moves from the back door of the cottage around to the front. He does not move around the building openly but does so warily, against himself, against the forces trying to make him lose confidence of being in control. Where he finds the front door open, and immediately stiffens. But the hermit's voice normal low:

'Here.'

Even so, the operator moves reluctantly into the cottage. His hand is frankly on his gun; he is in display and cannot help it. The sweetly insidious smell of damp hits at him. It is the graveolence of damp decay, the sapping at a stinker earth, the suckings. And, where expected, Emile Gascoigne sits alone, on his one and singular chair, in a wanted isolation. Not in the corner of the room, seemingly crouched against discovery, like the last time the operator was there, but in plain view. Almost obscenely not as he should be.

And does not, as he should do, thrust his body protectively around his shying eyes when the operator Sloane scans slowly, imperiously, distastefully at him. Rather the old man merely seems to assume who it is standing in the doorway before him by returning an ordinary look of being very-much blasé. It does not matter which or who it is who has come. For last night, for the first time that will be ever remembered, the old hermit has seen, and remembers he has seen, the forces that can bleed a man.

So Emile Gascoigne is sitting there, openly bland, and is waiting for the forces he has seen to come on as they will surely come on. He can see from his offshore islet the white rows of the past washing against the cliffs of the main island, on which the son and the man stand looking across the sea, towards him. And the hermit is nodding *yes, yes* to him, to the son, to the man, to the son and the man of the past come back and to the operator Sloane of the now come back. It is all the same. Re-visitings.

'You're in the wrong place, citizen.'

The operator has not moved his hand from the gun. He is willfully being preposterous and not in control of his show of petulance:

'Wanted you to wait there. Day and night. Needed you this morning.'

The hermit does not wriggle to reply, needs no forcing of himself to move the words off. The operator will not, in the few days he has left to live, hear the hermit speak more sanely strong:

'You see, it's all right. You shouldn't worry. A person doesn't need to be worried about, you see. Don't worry about the past coming back. You don't have to try to worry about me.'

'Why would I worry about you, now, citizen?'

'It's come back. It's never been away. For eight months a person froze on that little island. Islet we all called it. I even got boils. A person's getting boils back now.'

'Go on, citizen. You tell me.'

'It's no good following. It's caught up. A person's seen it oozing from him. He's mad, you know. He's everywhere come, always.'

His old black finger already beckoning the operator over to him as the last word trembles vatically with it. It is a gesture that is so peremptorily out of character for the hermit and in such prophesial proportions that the operator has crossed the space between them before he himself has fully realised it. And almost jerks back with annoyance at himself for being so submerged in *wrongnesses* still. Might well have done, too, if he was not held by the lapel with surprising strength by the hermit and actually being drawn down to the old lips, the old mouth, the old, old voice old-fashioned with new superstitions:

'I feel sorry for that poor little boy. Only that woman in the house and that thing outside. That poor little Frank.'

Then pauses, then adds then, with the bunch of his hand tightening before setting Sloane loose:

'A person'll just wait here. Don't you worry about a person. A person's found it doesn't matter after all.'

He has let go of the operator's lapel. His arthritic hand drops down into his lap to rest patiently in his lap, heavy as an old dew upon the other. The operator Sloane recovers his will to recoil in repugnance. He despises the sufferance and the open doors he sees in the old man's eyes as they churn at his stomach. He will soon

184

despise with his usual professional contempt, but for now has to back step quickly away. Something about what Emile Gascoigne is seeing looking at him is chilling.

The operator Sloane does not look back. There is no use in the hermit anymore. But does stop, not turning his head, to listen, before he leaves the cottage, to the old man say:

'I see now a person has one last visit to her place.'

He comes from around the back of the sheds and his movement has him stiffly at ease. He has had to come to check up on the man Dere now that he does not have the eyes of the hermit. Without the eyes of the old man Gascoigne, the operator has to find out for himself if the game has got up, after his flushing of yesterday.

This, too, irritatingly wrong. The *wrongness* of the man Youngstein and the *wrongness* of the old man hermit. And now the wrongness in its direction in himself in having to do this. It is the sheer irredeemability of the unexpected that is most hateful to Sloane's 'nose'. He has called it noose-work. But always of others. He himself has never been out of control of things and kept in the hunt. The one, the loss freely admitted, or the other, resigning when the instinct sings.

For now, too, he steps out into the open and moves more carefully than the first time to the opening of the second shed. Where, lying on the decaying mattress, curled in a seeming desiderative foetusform and shivering, cubbied but awake, is the man Dere. He does not move, only watches, as the operator moves in to the few metres away. There is, just perceptibly, not quite the same timing in the operator's entrance. The edge gone off.

The operator does not kneel to the level of Allan Dere, but stays standing, so that he has a bearing down upon the other. The sun is at his back and his shadow blocks out the warmth that was in sap-lap on the man Dere. Remains there, his face in silhouette, playing at letting the sunlight burst off and onto Allan Dere's face by swaying smally but enough. He has straddled with careful distancing of his feet the bowl of food, covered, untouched, that has been left sometime in the early morning by the little broodlike sister. Before, again like all the other times, she has fled.

Allan Dere submissively squints against the theatrical switching on and off of the sun on his face. Then growls as a dog at the operator and finally barks as a dog at the operator, until he has to cough and has to laugh and feigns rolling over onto his back as a dog. There is nothing ridiculous about the imitation. For a moment the operator feels himself being thrown by the seriousness of the imitation and has to catch at himself for being so febrile. Instead, he holds on to what he has recognised; accusative:

'You're stinking filthy, citizen.'

'I am flea'd. I am a dog because I've got fleas. Sloane. Slobber. I have a gentleman's companion somewhere down here, Sloane. I am stinking because I smell because I'm a smeller. So ruff ruff to you.'

'You finished, citizen?'

'You're standing in the light of the bedroom window of my kennel.'

It is a response that brings the colour to the operator's cheek.

Now there is no longer pretence in Sloane's voice, but a hard falling back on himself; it is no longer a game:

'You thought about my visit yesterday, citizen? Say it right or take the consequences.'

And is waiting above the growing temerity of Allan Dere's continuing barking with a mountingly-consuming fury he is beginning to almost enjoy when the weight of Frank suddenly lobs itself upon his shoulders from behind. The manchild's arm heavily hooks around his neck in a gross over-intimacy and stays there as

186

though the operator Sloane was a comparatively small, but very familiar, bar to lean on. 'Whatcha, whatcha, whatcha...' with a panting regularity that must have surely started way back near the house when he has first sighted the operator talking to the man Dere and has recognised them as two cobbers obviously waiting for him to drop down there, without old bag Miss Avery collaring a bloke before he can get down and talk men's talk with his beaut mates from the meat works probably:

'... whatcha, eh? Eh?'

The operator Sloane is so taken by surprise that all he can do is let Frank hang there. Intolerable to be so submerged by the *wrongnesses* that even the manchild, as delicate as a drunk in mud, can come behind him without being noticed. Can only push on:

'In a few hours, citizen Dere, the father's going to send down people you're not going to like.'

'Whatcha, Mr Dere, whatcha, eh? Seen me beaut hammer?'

Waving it about as though it was a very small flag in his very large hand. The operator having to raise his voice in competition:

'Citizen, you're finished. The man's coming. He doesn't care about your dead baby in your citizen wife's womb. He's got one big frig-all for you, citizen. So your kid died, too. Selma Youngstein died, as well. You killed her, citizen.'

And has to raise his voice even higher above Frank's rhythmic *whatcha, whatcha*\ does not know he is, but can feel the irritation with the mounting hysteria in his voice:

'...I really don't give a stuff about your problems. Me, I only *represent,* citizen. I don't pass judgment on you being sick in the head. I don't pass judgment on your own childhood or your old man. I don't give a hoot about the wife you left dying inside or if the little girl Selma Youngstein was sexually assaulted before you ran her down...'

187

The man Dere reacts. He hears what the operator has said, struggles to react to what the operator has said. And at last forces:

'What did you say?'

'You heard me, citizen. Didn't they tell you they were going to sexually drive against the girl Youngstein before they got you to plough your motor-body heart against her? Tch, tch. Arabs in oversight? Or was it the other way around. You rooted and the organisation drove?'

'You *bastard liar.*'

It is taken as no insult by the operator Sloane. The man Dere has suddenly slipped back into the game that the operator has been trying to play, as he knows only how to play, ever since this morning before the *wrongnesses* began. Now the hunt again. And continues to smile. But then the man Dere still too *wrongly* reacting, for instead of directing himself to Sloane, he suddenly cries out to the manchild:

'Frank!'

Which the manchild has forever, for all of a lifetime, been waiting for. A man calling him on to help.

'Yeah? Yeah? Whatcha, Mr Dere?'

And literally tip-toes forward towards the man Dere in the shed there. Where he stands, swimmingly ready for any order and swinging his hammer underarmedly as though coyness alone prevented him from confessing he is swinging the cat back and forth by the tail. He is standing directly between the operator and the man. The operator is furious:

'Dere!'

The manchild stiffens with fright as the operator's shout hits him, seemingly, between the shoulder blades.

188

'It's all right, Frankie.'

'It's not all right, Dere. I make my last offer. You come with me or I let the man take over', fighting for, and regaining, a control that is still not *right* enough. 'To me, you're a murderer of little girls, worse than your old man. You assaulted Selma Youngstein.'

The man Dere suddenly lets his shoulders go loose and laughs and reaches up with the same movement and taps Frank with a fatherly tapping on the hand, relax, relax:

'You know, you're bluffing. He's bluffing, Frankie, isn't he?'

'Y'oughta see a bloke with them boxes, Mr Dere. Pow! Pow! Me bees need me boxes, don't they?'

The hammer swinging as his mouth moves around the 'pow! pow!' in onomatopoeic sympathy which sometimes bursts into sound and sometimes only shapes the mouth. The both, the swinging and the mouthing, drive the manchild towards the solid reality of the wall of the shed where he proceeds to demolish the tin and the wood struts with stunningly powerful blows. It is such a release of strength that it momentarily stops both the other two men, until it becomes obvious Frank's excitement is mounting itself into an equally dangerous rage.

The operator Sloane quickly crosses to Frank and grabs hold of the manchild's free hand that is swinging grotesquely in counterbalance to the smashing blows. It is the touching again. As though by clockwork, the manchild ceases at the touch and does not complain when he is led away, still held by the hand.

As they approach the house, Frank's chuckles become louder as he leans down on the shoulder of the operator, then again pants in a near perfect cadence with their married step:

'Whatcha, mate. Whatcha, eh? Seen a bloke ploughing away pow! pow! at me beaut bees, at me beaut bees boxes, what little bottlers,

189

haveyer? Haveyer? Seen a bloke's beaut cat Friar, eh?'

In repetition and fanning with an unclean breath the rigidly unturned and jaw-set profile of Sloane, the bigcity operator.

Miss Avery is already waiting for them as they turn the corner to the kitchen porch. She stands before them before the kitchen door as though it is there she has decided to position herself either to defend the house against the coming invasion or to flight herself to snatch Frank to safety, whichever must come first. And there is not a moment of welcome on her face.

Her voice a crisp cluck.

'Frank's not to talk to strangers.'

'Get orf, y'old bag. See? See, eh?'

The last parenthetically to Sloane from a tissue-paper distance from his ear and swung around by Sloane's sudden halt to be back-turned to his sister. And she only, like the last untoppled skittle, facing the right way for any confrontation, while the operator gropes mentally for the reason he has come. It is all very hard.

'How's that old slack-hole, eh, mate? Eh?'

'Shocking, Frank citizen.'

'Slack as an old yak and twice as fucken salty, eh?'

'Frank.'

Miss Avery now, too, skittled. But the manchild gone raging at her for stopping whatever imaginary fun he thought he was having with Sloane. Making overarm hammer swings at his little reddening sister as he spits out real and meant spite:

190

'Slack as a fucken yak, you. Slack as a fucken yak, see!'

The hammer seeming to project his very iron and very heavy fist. This does, however, allow the operator Sloane to break free, breathe more freely, gather stock of his operatorship, even as the little woman Avery retorts a sad rebuke, momentarily sunk back into a forever of history with the manchild, retinacular:

'Oh Frank.'

'You've got quite a handful already, citizen Avery, without harbouring a fugitive.'

'Frank's not to have visitors.'

She almost sings it aloud for all the world that seems deaf to it.

'You can go on talking country bumpkin, citizen Avery, like the farmer's wife, but the law wants that man down there in your shed. You're harbouring.'

'You're not the law, oh no.'

The woman flattens out a flat statement and clearly stands against any confirming evidence anyway, and the reply is like a slap in the face for the operator. There should be more people intimidated here.

'Hey, mug, yer seen me beaut cat Friar, haveyer? Haveyer?'

And even the manchild has somehow unwound and rewound his hugeform away and back around the person of the operator and has, now poking metally and cold-cuttedly, the cat Friar's tin biffing the operator on the nose by way of a lot of little biffs. Too much altogether.

'Shut up!'

Sloane has knocked the tin out of the manchild's hand, has chopped the arm, has flipped the hugeform of Frank around and down onto the verandah into a miserably blubbering heap — all this before the manchild can cry out to his sister and even before his sister can take the smallest step towards a rescue flurry. Now there is open fury in the operator face and a raw malice in the velated tone of his voice. He lets the little sister hurry past him to fiercely fold herself around Frank's puff-forming and whimpering head, but gives no further ground to the citizens, nor will anymore:

'You got the bitch heat, okay, you've got the bitch heat, but when that bitch heat harbours a criminal I want, there's problems. Wake up to yourself It'll be easier for you to let me take him away while he's on your property. Trespassing. Say the word, close your eyes and he's gone already, citizen bitch heat.'

'What criminal?'

'You heard it. Criminal. He takes this car and he takes this little girl, a little nine-year-old girl, and he brings the two together, citizen.'

Picks up the cat Friar's tin and smashes it against the verandah post. It cracks shockingly. The manchild squeals and huddles against Miss Avery, face averted, trying to bilocate himself. The operator settles more comfortably into voice. This is more like it:

'The little kid was flung under her mother's car. The mother couldn't get out of the car because her kid's cracked body was all over the road outside. Now you should see her mother. She's not a nice sight either. And if you're not convinced, you just ask me if that little girl had been sexually assaulted before.' But the woman Avery is to give no answer. She only looks up defiantly from Frank to the man Sloane, so that the operator begins now to realise just how much she is in battle against him, his invasion. 'Look, citizen, you don't know what this man's really like. You want me to tell about his childhood?'

'I know about him.'

'Alright, who doesn't? You want me to tell you about his wife and the dead baby she carried around and how he buggered off and left her?' and has to go on, cannot let the silence re-assume. 'You go ask him what happens around here at night. He's a pervert, a peeping tom, citizen. He's more scum than his old man was.'

Her eyes have, now, not moved from his, but rather become disconcertingly more set upon his. The operator's fury erupts within him again when he feels a maddening desire to lower his eyes from her first:

'We're not playing for patticakes, citizen bitch heat.'

'We locked up the front door when Dad died.'

The question asked, the little unroosted woman shrieks out. It is not so much to the operator Sloane or to the hermit Gascoigne or to the woman Salem or to the man Dere; it is more to the years of all the barricades put up by her thin self, torn down by the brutes; it is to the front gate being open now and the robber wasps now that the honey is rising; it is to her father, her Frank, her self; it is to the only way she can answer.

The operator Sloane does not realise he has stepped back, perhaps, for a moment of grace, to have a look at his opponent before he snorts derision at her wounding there. Turns on his heels finally, and walks back off the property of Avery and, as he does so, can capture the urbanity back into his walk. The hunt is back on and he remembers the moves, the timing. At the gate he stops and slowly scans the bush across the road. He is not looking for the hermit in there for he knows the hermit will no longer be there. What he is doing is showing the woman Avery his back. He has always made a point of showing his opponents that.

The operator Sloane does not even turn to call back about one of the last moves he has left for the days he has left, and so does not know, nor would care anyway, that the little mothersister and the manchild have already retreated inside:

'No, citizens, have not seen the cat Friar. What you've got to do, citizens, is look after your own better. That's what you've got to do.'

She has left the house, feeling tainted because she has sneaked away while the manchild hammers exhortingly at the bee boxes. He has already forgotten the violence outside with the operator, is instinctively safe beneath the umbrella presence, he thinks, of his sister and has required only a few minutes of coaxing from her and of pissorf-pissorfs from himself to immerse himself at the proper banging at the boxes. The woman Avery knows that, in this mood, he will be immersed in the hammering and in the chanting to his beaut bees for her to sneak out of the house to confront the man Dere. The words 'bitch heat' still are making her cringe and will not dampen down.

The man Dere is sitting up and seems to be waiting for her. His head rests on his arms resting on his drawn-up knees. It is the position of inurable defeat and her heart, despite herself, cries out for him.

That pity, that irreducible, allconsuming pity of herself in pity that has tyrannised her always.

'Did you bowl that little girl over?' She releases it as though she has kept it bottled up all the way from the house. Her eyes have not left off searching for his face. The words, the words *'bitch heat'*.

'No, Miss Avery. Did I hit-and-run? No.'

'Did you...'

Ask him, Miss Avery, ask the dark and violent man from the city called Sloane if the little girl was sexually assaulted and he says he might say yes and he might say no. The words *'bitch heat'*.

'No, I did not.'

194

She has asked on the battlefield and has heard on the battlefield the man Dere and the operator Sloane, both fusing together into the answer she has wanted to hear, that the little girl Selma Youngstein had not been sexually assaulted before being whipcracked. And suddenly the invasion is not all that the operator had defined it as being. And suddenly, relief has her somehow nearer the man Dere, within reach, her attention overtly on the bowl of food she has left that morning.

'You haven't eaten.'

Does not remember later whether she actually said that or not, for her hand now, her ugly and swollen hand grotesquely filled up and stretching taut, is being held by the man Dere now. She cannot know how and cannot pull it away. It suddenly has become just as fascinating for her as it is obsessive for him. Its vesicle pinpointing the centre of the back of her hand, very slightly raised, surrounded by a red ring with the blackish sunken point at its centre. Where the bee has stung. The ulosis, for all time, never to be completed. And the words, the words, at least tempering now, 'bitch heat'.

And the most alarming thing of all. The man Allan Dere has bent his head and is kissing the lesion of her hand, lightly supported in his two. Paying, lightly and reverently, accord to it.

She withdraws it from him slowly at the same time as he slowly hands it back to her side, as though it was a holy relic in itself and of itself. Already the man's face lifted up to hers and his finger tracing a line across his eye.

'See, Miss Avery, see mine as well.'

She does not know whether she has seen anything there or not and cannot know what he is talking about. She knows, though, that she feels so painful being what she is and has to escape before she becomes smothered. There is always the house and the front locked door and Frank.

She will sneak back in and complete the whole circle. It will help

195

a little that she does not remember either so weakly repeating:

'You haven't eaten.'

'She's still a sick woman, Mr Youngstein.'

'My wife's still a sick woman, Sloane.'

'I want to ask you something. I want to ask you how come they let Mrs Dere out of the hospital, Mr Youngstein.'

'She... volunteered.'

The father the husband does not need to load his voice for any particular effect. He is not accountable to the operator Sloane that is just one of his operators looking for the international connection. He knows it; Sloane knows it; the short but heavy ex-wrestler who is the husband the father Youngstein's bodyguard, and has been for years of very few words, knows it. The operator Sloane, spoiling for an out-and-out confrontation with something he can measure against, now does not nod a contentment with the reply and now antagonistically jerks his thumb at the Mordecai Youngstein's bodyguard:

'Did he make her do it? What did this muxhead do, threaten to open up the Caesarean again with his monkey fingernails?'

'Now, now, Mr Sloane.'

Youngstein. Admonishing. Includes the operator for a fraction of a moment in his distasteful survey of this hotel room of this country town.

'He didn't even bring her glasses. She's half-blind. You don't 'volunteer' and leave your glasses. I say she's still ill.'

'Then take her in and bring out the Dere animal. Tell him it's safety for her.'

'You're joking. Safety?'

'Of course I am. Sloane, get him to give the source first. Then you go home with a cheque.'

'What about the wife?'

'Take her back with you if you want her.'

'Him?'

The blank and dark regard of the complete disregard, shrugged:

'So what about the schmuck?'

The last word intoned to the rhetorical. The father Youngstein slaps the bodyguard on the sleeve with the back of his hand. It is the signal to relax; there is no danger here yet. The bodyguard does not relax. Licks his lips at Sloane and Sloane recognises the thirst, but is not worried. This is at least something he knows amongst all the wrongnesses of the amateurs.

'Mr Youngstein, I think this Dere is one-off.'

'There is the source behind him.'

'I think he's a one-off, Mr Youngstein, like I say.'

'That terrorist group, it's two faggots less. A third is talking, so don't tell me nothing from nothing! You take the woman in. You bring her out. It's your play still.'

'I do this, then I want out, Mr Youngstein.'

'Sloane, my boy, you are almost already out of it. You are thanked and you are almost out of it. I only want to hear about the source. The *schmuck* is eminently expendable. That is up to you. Whatever you think.'

It is not until they have almost reached the property of Avery that the woman Joan Dere and the operator Sloane speak.

He has got her out of her room and has treated her with a great and silent care. She has gone with him with a great and silent care, too. She has known that this changeover from the heavy and pungent company of the man Youngstein and the bodyguard is the last stage of the trip from her hospital bed to her husband Allan Dere. She will learn, too, why the father the husband is so linked to her husband that he would have used force to spirit her out of the hospital had she not very willingly come along. But tired, very tired. Her very essence seems cleaved and physically parted, and feels instinctively that there is only one gathering of strength left to her for the time being. This, she has carefully nurtured.

And, having nurtured it, now, approaching the property of Avery, she begins its release by turning to speak to the driver Sloane.

'This woman has some hold over him?'

'Yes.'

'What sort of hold? Sexual?'

'There is a hold.'

Shrugs, and has to smile at himself to find the timing still returned to him. Not the actor this time, but the stage manager. There was no need to use the words 'bitch heat'.

'Sexual? The trips he made down here? A hermit? During those?'

'You knew about them, the trips?'

'Yes.'

'But not really *about* them. His past.'

'No.'

'Any difference?'

'This woman, please.'

'There is a hold. That's all I can tell you, citizen.'

'Don't... call me that.'

She has turned away to answer that. The operator thinks it is fitness that she does so. He drives and thinks on her in mulling tones. The woman Dere could be either small and mousey as a suburban housewife or small and trim as a woman caught in circumstances that take her beyond the suburban wilt. She seems so fitful to the man Dere's experience, yet the operator Sloane finds himself even stirring with the tiny, quaking, dead-inside wife of the rapist's son sitting huddled beside him. He tells himself it is nothing but amusing for him. Dwells on her myopic helplessness without him. It is thus almost sensually that he decides to slap her with:

'That man who drove you down. His daughter, citizen. Your hubby sailed into her with your mother-in-law's car. Nine years old and broken like a doll. Her mother blown at the fuse, but don't ask for details.'

The wife of the man Dere does not answer. It all really does not really matter for the energies are just being controlledly released and there is just so much she can absorb. The operator admires the almost imperceptible way she has reacted. He decides, and enjoys performing the essential cliché in the action and the statement of the action, to shoot her an admiring glance. Thinks of Scott Fitzgerald and the glittering set. Thinks back on the wife of the man Dere beside him and stirs again.

'I'm telling you this because there's danger from the person who brought you down here, if he doesn't come out with you. There's danger for the old woman Avery. She's got a nutty brother she looks after. There's danger for him, too.'

'I see.'

199

A small and trim voice that is piping small, and catching at itself.

'No, you don't citizen. Bring your husband out. The police. It's the only way. I promise you both the police.'

'Thank you.'

'Tell me about his political affiliations.'

'I don't think any. He is too much of himself.'

'I told him and the old lady Avery that the girl Youngstein was sexually assaulted before he ran her down. It was a lie. Do you want to know why?' The woman does not answer. 'Hurry, we're almost there.'

'No, I don't want to know why.'

'Can you see?'

'Oh,' she laughed, laughing a hospitalised laugh, holding tight to the sore and physical thing of herself beyond the laugh, 'I can see as much as I need to hear.' Not meant as a clever statement, nor realised as one, except by the operator Sloane. He does not stir anymore when he glances at her, yet he is looking at a woman, and can smile to himself that that was one up for her. He can now afford to. The *wrongnesses* have receded. No *wrongness* for now.

He has pulled up at the gate of the Avery property. Leans across the wife to point the way and perceives he gets no scent from her. She still smells soaped and hospitalised. The operator Sloane is not stirring anymore, but the wife is looking at him from those close quarters as he leans across her to point the way; it is accountably that he has suddenly come into her range of seeing.

'Right down through there. Follow that path past the house. Never mind the house. The middle shed. Can you make it?'

'What's your name?'

200

As natural as if it had been the sequential answer.

'Nice of you to ask.'

But he is shaking his head. The irritation rising for the waywardness of the amateurs. All this continuing *fiddling*.

'No, I just wanted to know.'

'Sloane.'

When she does turn on him so unexpectedly frontal that the operator stiffens. She is, however, only seeking and her eyes are wide because of the asking in them. This is a need, he realises, before she can go in.

'Will you be my friend, Mr Sloane?'

'Just call me Sloane.'

He has found of himself, too, that he is now leaning across her to open the door. She takes over, their hands brushing, and leaves the car.

Sloane watches her as she has to peer myopically just to open the gate and feels pity for the woman. She really is small and mousey. And sees for the first time that here is not much of a weapon for the side to use. The danger and the weakness, both, of the husband the father Youngstein is that he is playing a game more than looking. The wrongnesses. Nothing is clear-cut professional anymore.

Feels himself snigger at the possibility of the manchild leaping out at her as she passes by the house. All she would see would be a huge and maniacal figure going for a big grab. Bowling her over and making her roll like tumbleweed.

When Frank does not, the operator opens all the car windows, turns on the car radio to a rocking sound and a volume that can both be very largely heard in the house of Avery. From the boot he

201

takes out a folding deck chair, places it cockily in plain view of the house. Gains a mawkish sun hat to his head and a newspaper to his hands. Then he sits with a wicked display of impiety for what should be, really, the niceties of the wife's invasion of the territory defended by Miss Avery, legs crossed, hat down low over brow, newspaper opened before him and settles down for a long, uncaring, ho-humming wait. Staging it there for the sole benefit of Miss Avery. And wonders, with a nice turn of possible calculation, which the little broodlike sister is most brooding over — the unasking thrust of the wife Dere into her place or himself out here insulting the very notion of her having any privacy.

He guesses that about now the little sister would just be wheeling away from the window, having made the decision to barricade. She would be taking the manchild by the hand and would be drawing him in to the room where the boxes were pretended to need fixing. And not even the chugging resistance of the hugeform little brother could prevent her storing him away in the inner keep there. She would return to the loopholes, front and back, at the watch upon him out here in the front, intending only to keep her busy, and the wife Dere out there at the sheds.

The operator Sloane is quite exactly right. At the moment he amuses himself with the speculation of the effect of their visit on the little birdlike sister inside there, the little birdlike sister has placed her brother Frank in the inner keep and is just starting to become flustered with the watch to be kept on front and back without raising the fears of Frank. But Sloane has not thought that, as she is, she keeps the manchild from knowing what is going on by using the umbilical of a repeated euphonia of words about his bees and his hammering and his beaut boxes. Delivered over her shoulder back to the box room, unctioning, even though she is so very, very frightened herself. The invasions.

As the shed comes into a focused sight, the wife Joan Dere

202

quickens her step. She is not aware that she is limping and that even the short walk down the property of Avery is starting to cause her a physical distress.

She has quickened her step unregardedly as the thought of her husband comes near to her feeling. She has carried for four months the dead child around in her body, her knowing it, he knowing. They both knowing it. She has no thought to ask him the whys of his behaviour. There is just the thought of herself and the need to say out with him according to the time she has had.

The woman Dere stops opposite the second shed, but cannot see even a blur in the darkness in there. She calls, has called, his name only once when there is a responding scuttling from in there. Waiting and calling his name again, but nothing still. No more urgent movement.

The woman Dere's thoughts go to rats and snakes. The smell of damply rotting wood and the countryside empyrean flare her nostrils. She feels the pressure of the want to suddenly run away. Whatever is in there is lurking. It is a not inconsiderable bravura that she begins talking and edging towards it:

'Allan. It's me. Please talk to me. It's left me. It... came out.'

She stops there in the sentence and there on the place. It is as though the shade line at her feet is a physical barrier of a here and there, where a state of being starts and a state of being ends. Then the breathing, her husband's breathing, leads her on and in, until she can see and she can see the man Allan Dere and can, finally then after further edging, discern.

He sits, hunched and quivering in the corner, drawn up tightly into himself. His eyes wildly nystagmic in her direction, full of fear. Her husband is cringing from her, huddled in the tiny corner of a very large desert's aesthetic's cell:

'Allan?'

Has moved with the speaking of his name the step nearer. And sees quite clearly, before he screams gutturally and she turns and flees, the side of his face and his shirt bloody with new running blood from his brow.

The operator moves from the sunning patio he has made of the roadside verge outside the front gate only twice during the visit of the woman Joan Dere to the property of Miss Avery.

The first time is when he looks up with the feeling that he is being watched. He does not move the newspaper, but gradually shifts his gaze so that he can study the bushland across the other side of the road. He is not looking for the hermit to be back on watch. He is searching at the base of the bushes over there where he has been sure he has seen a movement. To the right, yes, he catches a glimpse of something moving and immediately gets a divining feeling of what it is.

Sloane carefully folds the paper, gets up and takes a large plastic bag from the boot of the car. It will do for the purposes. He isn't gone long, has gone crooningly. When he returns, he places the plastic bag back in the boot and repairs to the stagey leisure life of the deck chair.

The second time is when Joan Dere has flighted back towards the car, towards a getting away, from the sight of her husband so in asylum down there. She has not stopped, but is tumbling back along, bumping off the corner of the house itself where the path tips at it. And now stands behind him, leaning on the front gate, not yet reacting as she will react when the realisation hits her, but still stuck there.

The operator again slowly lowers the paper with quintessential timing for a gesture of bored exasperation and asks of her humdrum:

'What are you doing?'

The woman not even seeming to be beating at herself for an answer. He whips his torso around at her and verbally slaps his venom across her face:

'Get back and see *her!*'

In a manner as if she has been motorised, the woman Dere steps back a few paces in mechanical recoil and then turns back towards the house of Avery.

The operator makes the paper crack with a flick of businesslike efficiency and settles back with a timing set to a tee.

He can only keep doing his bit nicely to a turn and hope for the right allay of the *wrongnesses.*

Miss Avery has watched and cannot believe that the woman she knows to be the wife of the man Dere has come back to the porch and has sat down on it and has not moved. There is no life in her posture, as though the soul has left the body.

She has seen the back of the wife going back out to the operator out there. And all that immense relief that the wife is not, after all, going to call in. Then to have her turned back, to have her sitting right on the porch, immobile and sedately there, doing nothing but *invading*, is not to be believed.

Now she, the woman Avery, is at the front loophole that is the kitchen window. She waits breathlessly there for the woman Dere to make her move towards, presumably, the kitchen door, but there is only her immobility there, and the battle clarion of the car radio in challenge outside. The back of the woman Dere does not move. The invader at the porch has become fixed.

She moves. Miss Avery has to move. She cannot just stand there looking out at the back of the wife, for she can hear from inside the sounds of Frank's heavier, sloppier hammering that telltale his growing disinterest to keep at the boxes. She cannot, either, keep up the soothing tones of encouragement to him any longer. It is a time for the offensive.

Miss Avery moves to the kitchen door and eases it open until it gives a splinter of seeing Joan Dere's profile. The sighting is a shock. From the back of the woman, she has not been able to see how much the shoulders are slumped or how ashen the face is. Even so, the voice of Miss Avery cockily bland:

'Can I help you?'

She might well have poked Joan Dere with an electric prod, for the woman leaps to her feet with a cry of surprise that seems to catch in her throat. Then the energy dissipates almost at once, so that the same debilitated person is there but on her feet, as if the sight of Miss Avery took back what the sound of her had given. They converse, too, in hushed voices as if the woman Dere was still in hospital and Miss Avery was marking the casualty.

'Can I help you?'

'Please... Are you Miss Avery?'

'You from the city?'

'Pardon?'

'Whereabouts in the city?'

'I'm Joan Dere.'

'I know. Would you like some water?'

Already beginning to move back into the house to get the woman a glass of water and the woman struggling to, and finally succeeding in, calling out no. Hanging on to what is there before her in case the thread is broken. Miss Avery stops but her voice suspicious for a possible unpleasantry to come:

'You look like you need a glass of water.'

206

'No.'

The woman Dere struggling, still, to form words and beginning to feel as exhausted as she looks.

'Sit down, why don't you?'

Yes, yes. Joan Dere nods gratefully a yes, yes and steps up on the porch to follow the little red and freckled woman inside. Where the shade. Where the rest. Where the chance to think and understand perhaps and to get back to coping. But the little red and freckled sister remains standing between her and the doorway to in-there with obviously not the slightest intention of inviting her in. The wife Dere cannot understand; she cannot even actually remember if words have actually passed between them or whether she has just imagined it. She cries out with such perplexity that Miss Avery is alarmed:

'*Where* '

'Lean on something, would you like?'

It is the little red and freckled woman talking, the wife sees, and talking with such solemn politeness, too. It is crazy; it is all meant as a joke. She laughs as the only thing that can be done.

The wife of the man Dere has laughed in the face of the woman Avery as the only thing that can be done. She might as well have slapped the bantamform of the little sister in the face with the one vulnerable thing. Miss Avery recoils at the woman Dere's laugh, and retreats back inside her house where the world is not, where laughs have proved not the gynandric things they are outside. And has slammed the door behind her.

Joan Dere would leave now if she has the energy to do so, but has not. She would move now because she does not comprehend a meeting or not with the woman that is said to have a hold over her husband. She is not even sure whether she has seen her husband.

What she has seen of him floats vaguely in the back of her mind; it is the same with the meeting of the woman called by the operator Sloane Miss Avery. Yet here she is, aware of herself standing on the porch of the woman Avery who she thought had just been standing in front of her. Is not now. Is alone. But cannot move, but can only wait for the something that must happen if things stand to reason. It really does not matter one way or the other. She thinks. Not now sure of that, either.

Joan Dere beings to sway, alone there on the porch of the house of Avery. She cannot know how stiffly regimented she stands there, refusing to topple, refusing to budge, refusing to take her eyes off the kitchen door as though she is willing it to re-open.

It does re-open. With a wide inevitability in tune with the surreal way Joan Dere is seeing and feeling anyway. She says before she sees who it is coming out:

'Perhaps I shouldn't have come so far so soon...'

The cool darkness seems for a moment to be moving gelatinously in bulge towards her. She is preparing for the countryside to move at her again when Miss Avery, her hair combed and pinned now to a bright little tightness, appears, struggling to manoeuvre an armchair of heavy brocade vintage out through the door and only succeeding in three parts of the task before it gets jammed on the upright skew with, at least, the front of it pointing out, even if it is dipping forward over the kitchen step. And there it stays despite the propitiative pullings of the little red woman. Who stands up and faces the woman Dere with a meekly meaningful look on her face of invitation to use the chair. Its position devotedly overlooked.

And all, really, beyond the replying resources of the wife of the man Dere. She sits, pavlovian, on the tilt forward and sideways in response to the stimulation. Even so, it is of immense relief. And to them both. Having met on the giving and the taking, their meeting suddenly takes on a spurt of verbal rapid-fire:

'I didn't mean to laugh. Did I...?'

'Frank used to bounce in that chair when he was little. Springs gone now.'

'Thank you.'

'Perhaps I should've gone over it first.'

'I didn't mean to laugh at you. I don't think I could see a chair.'

'Are you here on one long visit or is this going to be a lot of little visits? I could leave this chair out for you, if that's the case.'

They pause in confusion, yet are in the centre now where there is no operator Sloane insolent over there. Where there is no car radio, but the humminghums of the bees that will stir, and stirring, will cause stirrings. Where there is no man called Allan Dere crookedly between them. They are in interlocution, the one with the other, and neither the one nor the other knows how it has come to be. There are only the gushings between them:

'I could have had that chair out here sooner for you, but this... happened.'

And she has out extended from her, to her own disbelief too, her heavyswollen, swollenheavy bitten hand, grotesque as a giant's bent elbow. Held out to the woman Dere and taken by the woman Dere and left there by her, as much as to say I can hurt too. And there it sits, held, heavy as a club in the wife of the man Dere's hands:

'It's only a sting.'

'It's... heavy.'

Fascinated by the hand thing in her holding. That it is there, a monster, festering in her grasp. The fangs and the pincers. Under canvas or hessian. The country *thing* bred away from the light, like the colourless slugs under old lino. In the bag that they bring to take away the black, long dead flesh of the foetus. They held her dead baby for a while then shuffled it away to the incinerator, repulsed by the touch and the country-like bland looks at her suppressing their revulsion bubbling up.

The woman Dere holds the dead thing hand of the woman Avery for a while and, in order not to cry out for the horror of her baby and the revulsion of her body, drops the heavyswollen dying thing that is the hand of Miss Avery with utter repugnance, clawing at her dress to wipe the possibility of country contagion away. She has only grunted, yet Miss Avery has seen and is so sad.

'It's only a sting. Festered a bit, that's all.' Has to drive against the averment of it in case there is no time left. 'It's when you grope. Bees can't know when you... are groping.'

She has trailed off because the other woman isn't listening. This is not the thing, anyway, that is umbilical around them.

Miss Avery waits for the wife and the wife has the repulsion of it all rising in her throat as a lump to be justified, too:

'I can't help not being used to it. I don't want to run away. Even when I was young I can remember a spider clinging to the very tip of my finger and joke snakes on elastic.'

And shudders. And the woman Avery beginning to understand.

'And he looked like a spider in there. My husband. I know it looks like I'm running away.'

Miss Avery, beginning to understand the revulsion that is swelling within the other woman, is suddenly appalled by the chair she has given her to sit on and cannot now take her appalled eyes off the appalling state of it:

'We never used that chair much.'

'My husband and I were friends. What's more, I love him. He didn't even tell me he was going. Listen, the child. As far as I'm

210

concerned it... came. Not his fault. So tell him. You owe me that.'

'Why me?'

There it is; that's why she is here, on the porch, in this chair, in front of this woman who has the hold over her man. She clutches at it before it begins wavering again:

'You tell me why you. Look at you.'

Into the air. The little sister. The motherchild. The little red bird. Miss Avery. Cries out for someone who might know: 'Has someone left the front door open?'

'Give him back to me!'

'I couldn't let him starve!'

'Give him back to me!'

'*I don't know how to.*'

She has understood the revulsion, yes, and she has understood the repulsion, yes, and she does not know of how any of this has come to pass. All she knows, panting as the wife of the man Dere is panting there, is that she has something repulsive showing to the world. The invaders. To the laughers. Herself. Her funny body. Her cravingly swollen hand. The things locked away in her heart, in her house, in her sheds. Showing in the rouge-swatches of her complexion. Showing in the appalling chair that she has appallingly chosen to show as large as appalling life.

Miss Avery steps forward and stretches carefully over, truceful, to flick something off the woman Dere's dress. Picks up quickly, dispatching it from *show,* something else from the arm of the chair, even though she knows in advance that the outsider will ask and will react.

'What was that?'

She can only shrug, the little girl before the perpetual admonisher:

'Centipede. Sit still, they go around you.'

'Oh...!'

'I asked you if you wanted another chair.'

The little girl; the half-plea and the half-whine. Lost innocence showing. The form of the wife repulsed out of the chair, moving as best as she can to be away from this. The slugs, the bodies, the colourless, blackened dying and long-dead living things around and in her body. Aware, now, exactly where she is and what is happening. She spits at Miss Avery before brushing her aside:

'*Disgusting.*'

And has gone from there. It seems to be a wobbly long time before the operator can be reached. Not hearing the woman Avery in plea behind her:

'You said you didn't want another chair.'

'*Whatcha?'*

Now Frank now. Answering from the other direction with an urgency that is absolutely ready to plunge itself into sharp panic for having caught Miss Avery outside, beyond where he is. The sound of the radio, too, and other people suddenly heard going on.

As the woman Dere moves as fast as she can away from his sister towards the operator, Frank has plunged outside. The jammed armchair that held itself against Miss Avery nothing for him to push flitly forward and aside from out of the way to her, his sister. For now, so wide-eyed with the outer discovery of her, he beats a path to in-front her; but her voice comes to him as a plea to a father long ago:

'She said she didn't want another chair.'

212

Not listened to, anyway. The movement ever in his puffy eye, Frank swings himself away from her to confront the fact of the woman he does not know as the wife of the man Dere is leaving for the man Sloane he does know. *Whatcha, whatcha.* She is already at the gate and is being helped to unfathom its myopic mysteries by the operator. And the manchild now managing to wind up a bulky momentum in pursuit, his beckoning arm as he comes on giving mute mime to what his mind is thinking, c'mon here, come 'ere.

By the time the manchild has made the gate, the woman Dere has been packed away by the operator. The chair and the newspaper have been packed away by the operator. The gate has been re-earth-worked by the operator. And the operator is standing half in and half out of the driver's seat, waiting for Frank to arrive. Happily Frank does so, and all the possibilities of other people not come to take him away blazing brightly in his mind. Joying eyes.

'Whatcha. Whatcha.'

'Frank, the cat Friar, Frankie...'

'Yeah? Yeah?'

The operator waiting to say it and says it with the parting finality of the perfectly-timed exit line:

'I've seen Friar, Frank. Old Friar's come home, citizen.' 'Geez, eh. Geez...'

The sound of his asking wonder immersed in the thrum of the operator's car going off, driving off, lanceolated to the pied piper end of the cat Friar's wonder-return.

Frank has torn the gate three-parts away from its catch to catch the car. To get with Friar. His beaut cat Friar. But the car has gone and his wide eyes now follow it to where Friar has presumably been seen. Friar. Me beaut animal. Come all the way back from Darwin or from Timbucktoo or Oona-fucken-whoopwhoop. As he, the

213

manchild, trots faithfully and ever patiently after the car that has already disappeared from his view. There is no hurry. In that direction is Friar. There is only the plentitude of Friar again back home again.

He will never jog and trot and walk after so much again. And will get right to the meat works before his mind activates on the fatigue his huffing hugeform is feeling. Forgetting there how he came to be there. But not why. Friar, Friar, silly old fucken bugger.

The woman Miss Avery has answered the stern paternal eyes of Frank with her little girl's painful assertion that the woman Dere never did say she wanted another chair, did she? And has then sat, distressed and decrepit, caducous, in the chair that Frank has brushed aside from the door. She has watched, crouched small in it, the woman Dere and the operator Sloane drive off. And has watched, too, her brother Frank wrench open the gate to go off down the road after the car. She has sat and watched his beckoning arm still playing mime to his desire and his body move in a jogtrot that she would normally know is going to be bad for his asthma.

Yet the little broodlike sister cannot raise herself from the chair. And she cannot make herself want to care this time for the first time of ever.

She can only sit there and feel nothing whatsoever.

The car quickly leaves the idiot brother beyond view. The operator Sloane looks only once in his rear vision mirror and that is when they pass the meat works. Allows himself to smile at himself in that rear vision mirror. The manchild, he knows, won't get past the meat works, might make it there, will be somewhere there or thereabouts when he returns from returning the wife to the hotel in town.

They will drive, too, in silence for as long as they did when coming out to the property of Avery. The operator will not be surprised at that, but is, slightly by a purely professional eye, surprised at how drained is the face of the wife of the man Dere. He will be, however, interestedly surprised with the venom in her voice when she finally speaks; will have his eyes drawn from the glancing at her open legs to the glancing at her steady profile. The woman Dere will say, finally:

'She's... disgusting.'

'Not the best, no.'

'She's disgusting.'

'Needs taking in hand. Perhaps citizen hubby of yours is doing just that?'

'Stop it.'

He, the operator Sloane, will reappraise the wife Dere then. The rebuke is to be to him the sharp tang of an interesting woman's reaction. And in the intimacy of the rebuke that he will do well, for a diversion, again professional, to look again at the real woman wife.

In her reaction, too, there will be all that took place to her on the property of Avery; and he will need not ask but will understand:

'So I have to go in and get the citizen.'

'I want to go back to my home.'

'Minus your man.'

She will look at him. She will slowly turn her large, brown, disinterested and dispectual eyes on him, laying all sorts of ghosts anywhere near that are worth the cake:

'I said I want to go home.'

215

'Pity, a great pity.'

He will say, not really caring now, all that much, anyway. And will quietly wonder without annoyance where it all started to go wrong.

And then the woman Dere will talk a matter-of-fact thing of the cat she can hear and can know must be in the boot. She will ask about the cat cries she can hear, but she will not care at all when he does not answer. Nor will she go on to wonder, what kind of man he is, to keep a cat back there like that. But instead he will laugh very much of a self-congratulatory laugh that has in it the chess master masterfully in control of a little part of the game again:

'Just the idiot brother's cat.'

And the wife will nod and will say the last words she is to say until they reach again her hotel room:

'Her familiar, yes.'

'Familiar? Right. I'm taking the familiar cat Friar back after dropping you.'

There will be no sign of the father the husband Youngstein when they will arrive back at the wife's hotel room. The carpet on the floor there will spread a great muffness about her, will hold no possibility of the animal in lurk, in wait. Things once again of a very nice feeling nature. But she will need, from the moment he will help her from the car to the room itself, the hand of the operator to support her. He will feel her begin to shiver from the time they begin to climb the stairs. A dancing quiver tippling at the end of his fingers and he will start to become alive to it.

By the time they will have reached her room, she will not be able

216

to let go his hand. Submitting for the door to be opened. But casting him adrift with a great gathering throwing motion when she moves inside. And the operator Sloane will stand by the door and will watch the wife of the man Dere dither at many possibilities of what to do next. Then she will stop and look up at him, back there at the door, and she will speak out against a great sin mounted against her, as she will, as she does so, snap her head away from his direction:

'The sight of me was hideous to him.'

She will lie back on the bed then with her head averted so that, from the door, the operator cannot know if she is crying or not. Nor will he learn, nor does he care. He will stand there and will see the body of the wife of the quarry lying there, quite open for the quartering. The woman of the son of the rapist. The body of the wife of the rapist soft and spongy for all the whispered offers, delta'd across the dark-night island moors, omnicipient and contiguous and swelling before him.

And all the while that he will strip her lowerly and all the while that he will thrust in and at her, he will not see her face, only hear her dry rhythmic moans of being again something not hideous. And will set to. And will set on. Both. This, too, will be sweet and unspeakable. The island moors, the black and saprogenous moors. Reverberating even to the operator Sloane and the wife Joan Dere.

The operator Sloane will not afterwards stay to lie by her. He will get up immediately and will leave her there. He will say nothing to her for now and she will say nothing to him for now. And as he opens the door, leaving, the bodyguard of the father the husband Youngstein will be coming along the corridor.

The operator will not close the hotel room door after him, but will leave it widely open. It will not matter and he knows it will not matter. As he passes the bodyguard, he will half-shrug and he will half-wink, but it will be enough.

217

The bodyguard will stop opposite the open door of Joan Dere's room and will candidly gaze on her lying on the bed, clothed down to the waist but nakedly spread-eagled from there down before him. The sweat on her pubic hair will be glistening. And it will not matter if the bodyguard to the man Youngstein goes in to her or does not go in to her, the wife of the man Dere. He will not see her face.

It is her first use of getting used to the mechanical.

She sits there and gazes so leadenly after Frank, gone off many minutes ago, that she does not notice at first the man Dere come slippishly around from the side of the house. Can only swing her eyes onto him and make an uncaring register of the unkemptness of him and of the aggressive light in his eye at her. A man accusing. She has had enough of life to recognise that, but cannot move, but can only nod languidly to him, as though she was earnestly in sunsoak. His voice spurts with an annoyance that is beyond her:

'What did you do to her?'

She is about to wave a hand that would erase him from the canvas, when it occurs to her, autonomically perhaps, as the way she would see it later, that she wants to desperately, and after all, answer him. Answer him that of all the places why should he pick on her. That the purple sky. That she likes purple skies. That in the winter you can throw your breath, and would breathe here a pause before continuing to say, against purple skies. That on some mornings of your oh-so-wanting life you feel you have woken up in a bath of milky blueness, caressingful. That and in the Spring, yes, she would have the blossoms when she could tell him of how young she used to be. The blossoms and the wattles in time.

And that there has always seemed to be the humming of the queen, so lush and followful. That, when she was a girl, during the so-huge honey flows, she would crouch like a field mouse in the warm and dark folds. The warm and dark folds by the apple trees. The warm and dark folds of people then. But, instead, she hears

218

herself saying, after all that herself-time so nicely suddenly felt::

'What do you want, Mr Dere?'

He has come close, is come close. Is there before her, un-pathetic. But it does not matter, even so, to her. The little broodlike, birdformed little sister is gazing. And her hand, swollen so oddly yet factually, obeying his reaching and silent command. When, before her, stretched a long confessional way away, he holds it and strokes it and she says more to him with, now, brutishly, a great sorrow climbing upon her:

'It's only... when you grope. I told her. I told her we can all wear gloves, can't we?'

She turns it over in his hand. Flops it curiously and detached. Her own hand:

'I know it's not much to look at, is it? A man's... hand. Yes. But it's my hand. And it's sore and she held it just like you are now. Your wife, Mr Dere. Here. And, oh, it was the most dead-alive, ring-barked thing I've ever seen, lying there in her hand. Heavy and a brute. Do you know, she whipped her hands away and wiped them on her dress? I saw her do that. And I felt so sorry for her. And I know I'm ugly freckled, you see. What do you want, Mr Dere?'

Not a question and trailing off beneath one when the man Dere raises her hand, that hand, heavy and looking a brute, to his lips. And then, finally to all of the this and the that, she understands and tries to pull away. Cries out the answer to the so many reasons why and the so many reasons why not:

'Frank!'

And the man Dere, too, crying out upon her:

'Miss Avery, look around. There's thousands standing by the wall waiting to be shot. We're not the first, not by a long shot.' 'Oh, no. We can't have... strangers in here.'

219

And is on her feet, dragged up out of her lethargy, bull-roarer'd and hotflushed because she is, and making heated steps crabbishly back towards the kitchen, invaded at the gates again. But it is to Dere the anger of the rebuke. He follows her a pace or two, stands by the last verandah post, is almost by literature spluttering:

'You, this morning...'

The woman Avery on the greater momentum towards the sanctity of the kitchen and *inside,* and therefore just now with the greater flux of outcry:

'Mum died and I had to bolt up the front door. Least I thought we did. There was only Dad and Frank!'

But the man Dere is still highly *on* and is already going at her:

'You listen. You, this morning...'

The woman Avery, as much as to block off her ears because she knows what he is going to say infillingly, as he does:

'...Only you thought I was asleep. You... the smelly old woman, bends over, doesn't she? And she strokes, doesn't she?, she strokes my face with the back of her hand. Like a rat. Arching in the air to touch me.'

The woman Avery now hidden in the clovering darkness of the inside she knows so well. Retracted from the out-there, and crying:

'Why don't you leave us alone?'

Upon which the man Dere satans out a bellow of anger and frustration that has always been there, forever and the day since he was ever set on to be born. He swings a haymaker against the verandah post by him, which misses. But which carries him on and past it in a very sort of slipstream. And it seems to sweep him up and to carry him away from her as in a here-it-is, now-it-is-not fairy tale, gone now physically beyond the woman Avery, as suddenly as he came around the corner to be on her.

220

A brush to leave her. They have had a brush. A brush to sweep the kitchen porch clean. To sweep off the invader and the invaders. A brush with the man Dere, a bruising. Then feels the solidity of the old flakey kitchen chair at her behind knees, and sits. Miss Avery has sat, is sitting, will sit. Upon the kitchen chair there. She feels insufferably overwhelmed with things desirable, come to her, out of the dark and secret moors, risen to her unbiddened bidding. They stick her to the mast. Awatched.

And awashed. There is, for the days that she has left to live, no other time that she is so volunteered and volunteering as now. The change from being seated on the kitchen porch as then to being seated at the kitchen table unable to move as now is only a degree of passivity and a shift of the object from Frank to the man Dere. One state to another. For those days she has left.

Fourish. The men immoderately coming out of the meat works, their thirsts carefully contracted over the last few hours, mingled. The image of the pub in town with each one of them, promissory or nostalgically, depending on whether, whichever he is, he is going to it or not. Their bloodied clothes rancid. The day has been warmer, seasonally. The water hosed around, because of it, merely a lick. There are other, and unfettered, diversions on their seescapes than Frank. Got at last to the meat works, having now forgotten the chase after the operator's car.

Frank is scanned on. Is recognised. But is pushed past as a familiar object wan-and-chanced in the bad timing of its approach. This is knock-off time and all their eyes are as blank as Frank's as they push by him, not wanting to be delayed even by the usual bit of fun in him; it has been enough that they each have got through another day.

The manchild has trotted himself to exhaustion in the Friar wake of the car of the operator Sloane and the wife of the man Dere. That he can go no further is enough to convince him that the destination of the operator's car must surely be the meat works even though past the meat works it has patently gone. So he urges himself past the leaving men like an electron in the wrong kinetic field, punctuating, virtually, his ricocheting off of them with seemingly very particularly timed panting for the most wanted thing of his oldlife young existence:

'Friar, eh, Friar, eh, Friar, eh…?'

And for as many men, he gives out as many avid little sound explosions. His eyes are fixed on the black mouth opening of the meat works. He gets a few playful punches in his rolling gut, a few whatchas Frankie (syncopating back, with a breath, to give in return occasionally a friarwatcha and occasionally an eh-whatcha). He is seeing none of them as he goes. But arrives at the works door just as the man Kellet, having cleared the shed in that hodiurnal splash of efficiency at the end of the day, is about to bang the door locked with the finality of having a weekend firmly in sight. Frank in pant, suddenly, in his ear and has a desperate inquiry beaming from his eyes:

'Friar, eh? Friar, eh?'

Where they stand, high and hagiotypically, upon the ramp. Beached by the receding tide of the other workers. And under those massively eager and floating eyes of the manchild, Kellet finds himself almost at panic, as though, despite his own desperate haste, he is the only man left in the whole oracular and mountain-top world who can give the right answer to the riddle of existence troubling the whole of manchildkind. He feels he must, as the Apollonian chosen, gush forth with the right juice. No way known else.

Will, too, look back on it as a piece of reverie inspiration of brilliant laughing brunt when he remembers not only who the frig Friar is, but also remembers the unauthorised skinned rabbits hanging up in the cool room. And is in there and back again literally before the manchild Frank can even react himself to get in through the meat work's door to follow after. He holds out to Frank the decorticated and bloodily-striated corpse of one of the rabbits. Cradled in both his hands like a sacrificial offering to be laid very reverently upon the hands of Frank. The manboy having been brought to a standstill, torn between what he is seeing and the promise of the return of his beaut cat Friar.

'Here, Frank, old son. Been keeping the old bastard for you.'

'Geez. Geez.' With the supposed corpse of Friar there now lying stiffly across his hands and now being wheeled bodily and easily around by Kellet so that he can lock up and be off after the others.

'Geez. Geez...'

The man Kellet will make much currency out of this for the odd day to come that there is the bad taste of humour to be made out of the memory of the manchild. He will describe how the big loony half slips down to the bottom of the ramp, cradling the skinned rabbit, crooning the cat's name. Of how, down at the bottom of the ramp, the manchild did say loudly a plaintive 'Geez' and then shook the carcass as though it was a cheap watch and even then lowered his great thick head down to the corpse in his arms and seemed to listen for the ticking. Of how the poor dummy then looked up and around with a blazing helplessness. Of how he then wandered off in the direction of his crazy tightarsed sister's place, meandering towards the road and holding the rabbit deadFriar by one of its hind legs. Swinging it by his side. You would flaming read about it.

On the road for the road home. And the rabbit that is not the cat Friar, and is not a cat even, on the swing.

Seated, still, at the kitchen table in an unknown amount of time passing. Miss Avery. The little broodlike woman. Her bitten hand swelling up horrently and she will, there, let it grow until it externally consumes her.

But then she stands, suddenly alert, her neck arched and ready. It

223

is something of a coming that she doesn't know of, except that, after all these years, she knows it is finally coming. You cannot take the beating of its wings, thrillingly at your heart, sitting down. It must be warded against or received with all the warding or all the receiving that can be given. But does not, could not, look at the open doorway. But face averted. But tightly passively lifelonged waiting, until the presence shadows upon her and she looks around and up and sees and finally knows what it all has been for:

'Oh, no.'

The man Dere answers very simply. 'I'm in.'

'Oh, no.'

'Miss Avery, I'm here and that's enough.'

And the little broodlike woman cries out yes and no, but no sounds reeling out for her and only her hand going to her throat. She would, and even might, gasp. She is in shine. The man Dere goes to move in to her.

She sees and understands what he is going to do and is appalled at all of herself and flings up a wing. What she must say. Once.

'Wait:

And when he does, the little broodlike ruby freckled chippish little sister has then the space for the once time only. Not uglyfelt, not bitten and sexdearthed. Not dry and speakless. But large, yes, and full, yes, brimming and now saying to the man Dere what she has wanted to say from the very moment he arrived wanted at a wanting place at last:

'After Dad died we locked up the front door. For Frank. Oh, my Frank. But sometimes I've thought I've always wanted to say, like I'm saying now, that I've seemed to have woken up in somehow a bath of milk blue somehow and... and, oh Mr Dere, I can't ever fool around anymore.'

It is a statement and they both see that she is beautiful and dappled. The man Dere goes up and the man Dere goes down and the man Dere goes to her then.

The manchild is stopped and is holding up the skun rabbit before his eyes like an oil lantern held up to support a concentrated peer into a very black and incomprehensible darkness, when the operator Sloane pulls up just ahead of him. Does not reverse back, but waits in the car and is trying to discern what the idiot is doing so stationary back there.

Frank stares at the ribcage of the carcass dangling before his face. He is upon a rudimentary awakening that is trying to force its will on the rabbit to confess that it is not, nor ever was, the beaut cat called Friar belonging to the property of Frank Avery, not at any time in its short life. But for all of his concentration the carcass just doesn't quite manage to do so. It refuses to lay an ounce of suspected ghost.

The operator Sloane now realises what the manchild is probably doing. He gets out of the car and walks back with caution, in case the beast would bolt, to the brother. Stands there by him for a quiet and reverent moment, then taps him upon the shoulder, although he is not unkind in his elementary command:

'Put the rabbit down, Frank. It's not Friar.'

The mind and the flesh divarate, still and enough. So that the manchild turns his grateful eyes upon the operator for affirming exactly what his mind had ratiocinated. But the arm still held aloft, very still.

The operator nods into the eyes of the manchild and takes his arm. He needs only the gentle pressure of a smallish and broodlike woman to start the hugeform manchild on the way to the car. The rabbit is dropped almost peacefully onto the roadside as automatically and uncomprehendingly as if it never existed in the hand and on the mind of Frank, the manchild brother. The loss of his innocence, yes.

'Geez. Geez.'

In the car, on the road, approaching the property Avery, the operator speaks suddenly. They will have almost reached the house of Avery before the manchild comprehends this:

'I know where your beaut animal Friar is, Frank. Do you want me to get him for you?'

Sloane has to wait until they are fully stopped by the front gate before he gets an answer surging:

'Geez, eh? Friar, eh? Me beaut animal Friar?'

'Do you want him, Frank?

'Silly old fucken coot. Been all the way to China. Betcha. Yeah, betcha. Betcha Friar's been to China or ... or Darwin. Fucken Darwin, eh?' And is chuckling with a swollen delight that would, even if it is to be the sole cause, very soon anyway bring on an asthmatic attack. '... Toldya me beaut animal Friar's coming back, didn't I? Didn't I, eh?'

'You did, citizen."

'Toldya, see.'

But, somehow loosely, his heart isn't in it. He sits in the car beside the operator Sloane and nothing of any energy will come to him.

The operator moves around to open the door and heaves at Frank until the autonomic response works the lumpform into a standing position. But sedentary, rooted, nonflexed, by the side of the car by the side of the road by the side of the front gate by the cat Friar somehow been coming for too long from such an incomprehensible world away. The operator Sloane moving him away from the car door perfectly aslike he was moving a chess

226

piece that has to be dragged to the next square, shuts the door, then moves back hummingly around to his own side's door. The timing still going nice and sweet.

'Frank?'

'Whatcha, whatcha.' But in a voice residual, brecciated. 'Frank, the next time you see the beaut cat Friar, think of Mr Dere. It's all because of Mr Dere. Right, Frankie?'

'Mr Dere. Friar. Yeah.'

The manchild stands on that spot and does not move. There is a vestigial reason upon the flatness of his energy, which impresses upon him that he should not move, nor look up. He stands there waiting alone and listening alone.

And hears, long after, in the distance, what could be the report of a gun. And hears, as it comes back but long after he first hears it, the car return from back down the road. When does the man-child Frank then look up, his puffy eyes flashed up with hope and expectancy, to see and then watch the car of the operator Sloane, now not remembered as the operator Sloane but only as something or other to do with the man Dere, come back down the road, gunning and slowing, gunning and slowing.

The operator Sloane, with the blood dripping on his lap much to his later annoyance, is enjoying the stop-start teasing as he comes back past the manchild still standing there outside the property of Avery.

He slows when he gets opposite the manchild Frank, the house of Avery, the place of the broodlike little sister and the man called Dere, the son of the rapist. He slows well enough to amuse himself with a possible pinpoint accuracy of torpedoing the still warmly shot body of the cat Friar at the feet of citizen Frankie there. And is pretty well spot on but for not allowing the cat Friar to bounce so.

The operator Sloane, for the few days that he has left, will not know that his calculation wasn't too bad, not bad at all. The body of the cat Friar torpedoes to not far from the fixed person of the manchild Frank. In gape and in the loss of all innocence:

'Geez, Friar.'

The long pause that has followed while the sound of the car of the operator Sloane dies away. Frank moves three precise steps, conscious suddenly of being uninvited, over to where the cat Friar lies and stands looking down at the body with a delicacy of form of not wanting to interfere in something going on. But speaks down upon it, with the man Dere associated:

'What's up, Mr Dere? What's up, eh, Friar? Eh? Eh?'

He nudges it gently with the toe of his shoe, and looks up to span a hugely waiting horizon of the world's whole attention. It is all listening, of course. It all knows.

'Betcha Friar's just tired, see. Betcha Friar's gone all the way to China. Fucken China, geez. Toldya. Toldya, didn't I, Mr Dere? Miss Avery...?'

This is not a call to her yet. The manchild turns and walks glibly back down the path, swinging away from the house, lumbering for the old garage. Where he gropes where he knows are leaning gardening tools against the wall, amongst the cobwebs. He does not look at the pitchfork that has been the come-to-hand first and good enough. He returns up the path and out to his beaut cat Friar. Nor has he in that huge, for him, time cast a glance at the house in which there is Miss Avery. Miss Avery not at all. By Friar again now and nudging the catform once more with his toes.

'C'arn, Friar. C'arn, yer old goat...?' Will still be wanting to give the large and difficult world a moment now to give Friar the nudge get up; even chortles with the cadence of uncertainty of the practical joke or not: 'Good old Friar, eh. Eh, Mr Dere? Betcha yer've been all the way up North an' back, eh? Crocodiles up there and... and pineapples or something big as yer old lady's dingers, fair suck of the old whip.' Even calls up, a wishbone culling mimed with his little finger, Miss Avery over his shoulder: 'Miss Averyyerever beenupfuckennorth, eh?'

But it suddenly seems as though he can only stop any longer there to gather a long expanding breath, to hold it, perhaps for overlong. Then his arms, his huge hands hold the pitchfork with a new-found two-handed grip, and move it smoothly above his head. It seems to quiver in pent-up suspension for that moment.

Whenupon does the manchild explode his breath with a huge eruption and bring down, time and time again, the pitchfork to pound against the body of the cat Friar. It bounds indelicately with each smashing and the brother syncopating with screech-puffs of a huge and killing fury quite beyond control.

The manchild gone berserker. In a unitary cell, spotted by no one, alone, minusculed in a whole bush landscape. Muffling and becoming muffled. This is it, finally, but not quite finally yet, after all.

Until the body of the cat Friar is ladened with welts and the manchild redacted to his spent force. He and it, it and him, stunned to a frozen rebus.

A moment of an eternity later. And then Frank beams above the mishmash of Friar a very wide and glowing smile. He chuckles with a sheer and pure delight.

'Good old Friar, eh, Mr Dere? Told the scrawny old bag you'd be back, Friar. Didn't I?' As while he shovels the thing of the cat Friar upon the pitchfork and then bears it, with a careful horizontality of his arms, back up the path to the old garage. When there, there is no dividing point between the funereal solemnity of the manchild's stiff procession to there and the casual flick of the wrists which dispatches the bloody body of the cat Friar and the pitchfork itself to the tangles of the once garden gone to tangles. Salutes a farewell only with a verbal, 'Miss Avery? Miss Avery?...'

Frank wends his large way on to the kitchen porch and falters, but does not stop, when he finds the kitchen door closed against him. Cannot be. And goes for it still. Does knock over the driedrust pocked tin of the cat Friar. Does try to pick it up, but swingingly missing, as he goes on. Does overbalance in trying to do so and pummels his Frankbulk against the kitchen door. Which gives nothing. And holds against. Locked. How can it be?

The manchild beats at the door mightily with his hamfists. He does so at first with overlord petulance. Then comes to understand a little more. And then furies against it, against being locked out from his Miss Avery for the first time in his life. With all his might there, pounding, with all his blind panic, with all his alonesomeness, with all the lifeforce instinct of a coming attack of asthma that will soon collapse him, alone, out there. He cries and pounds. His breath claws for outlets from his body. And though the panic is full on, he can manage as softly as a bird's beat:

'Eh? Eh? Miss Avery...?'

The suffering of the lungs of the manchild finally drags him down to his knees. Frank is felled heavily against the boards of the kitchen porch there now. He drags at them and in them and his wheezing is this time a whistle and this time a savaging. And his mind screams out for his Miss Avery. That fact to life.

She with the man Dere inside. If Frank is heard, he is hardly heard at all.

Chapter 5

The son of the rapist stood in the room, a child, as he remembers he must have blinked to make one state of his father turn into another state of them having come for his father. He with them. Brought there by his mother.

The son of the rapist stood small as an eleven-year-old boy should stand in the midst of the shouting. On this side, seemingly, with him is his mother, the police. On that side, seemingly, if it possibly could be, his father. He cannot understand why there are 'sides'.

At first, the son of the now-caught rapist thought it was a woman over there. But, as the chargers and the accused came together within, oneirically, a conch-shriek from his mother, the boy saw that it was his father in the frock. Above him. Like a skyscraper coming down. And, when the mother had slashed at his father, the son of the rapist had cried out and thrown himself into his father. Burying his face and wrapping his arms in and around the belly of his father, the rapist. Smelling hugeformly above him, in frock. His father, a woman in frock.

And the boy there, even remembering being there, still cannot understand. There is the shrieking of his mother against him and the frock vertical above him sounding as pure as the sharp pain of a bee sting he might have just once had. He can't remember.

At his trial the father asserted it wasn't a dress but a tunic. He was asked the difference. Gave the singularly sole-logic answer that the fifteenth century nobleman, Gilles de Rais, Seigneur de Laval, Marshal of France, gave it always to be a tunic, not a frock. The son of the rapist did not know who his rapist father was talking about at that time. Not until much later. By then he was old enough to be hungry enough to know more.

The son of the rapist has felt the forces begin to move in him, then.

231

Chapter 6

It does happen; it has happened.

Miss Avery's mind drifts as she sinks darkly into the forever blackness. She remembers:

She was standing in the passageway almost at the doorway of the front door. Just opened. She had just unlocked the front door and the man was somewhere in the house behind her. And the manchild was also somewhere in the house behind her. And she stood in marvel at the amount of light that was again coming to pour through the front door again. Times of her father. Vaguer times of her mother. Times of her mother and father flooding back in upon her, when there was the chippy little girl of herself. Old trilahlahing voices rilling down the shaftlights, fletching through the open front door at her, re-welcomed. The lifelight, and she as if spotlit on an empty stage. She crooned softly, plaintively, ultimately, there. She crooned with a warm and sad fulfillment, stopping every now and again to listen for the man and the manchild somewhere, both, in the house behind her. They are beginning to drift so far away.

It does happen; it has happened.

The woman Miss Avery begins to sink forever darkly and her mind drifts. She remembers:

Like a tape recording, their voices sluggish as commentaries over. Her and the man Dere's entwining above the radio so loud:

'Please switch it off.'

'Let's leave it on, Miss Avery. I can't call you anything but Miss Avery.'

'Frank.'

'Frank's all right.'

'But there's Frank. He'll think...'

'How's this then?'

Laughter, laughter. She remembers, drifting, there was the laughter.

'Stubble, stubble, you ought to shave. What else? Oh, you're laughing and how you talk, sometimes light years away. And how you watch.'

'Take your finger out of my ear, madam.'

'If I open my legs, will your head fall through? Mr Dere, oh, I can't call you anything but Mr Dere, too. And all the things I've wanted to ask you. Why did you wait so silently outside my house? And when I showed you my hand, you didn't draw away, Mr Dere, and I found that so passing strange.'

'Why?'

'When I was a girl, during the honey flow, I used to crouch like a... field mouse, yes, in the warm and dark folds. The warm and dark folds by the apple trees.'

'Why?'

'In your eyes, Mr Dere, there was no further to go. And I don't think I was given any equipment to turn down that.'

'Stop tickling.'

It is happening finally as it really must and does.

Miss Avery's mind drifts as she sinks forever darkly towards the blackness forever. She remembers:

The voice waving in heterodyne down where she was drifting or up there from where she has drifted down. Little eruption sweeping towards her, spotlit, sinking darkly, on the solemn and lonely stage. The woman Salem and her in things unsaid that might have been said:

'You see, I thought I'd bolted the front door.'

'You bottle things up too much, can I still call you Miss Avery?'

'I mean, when a wife... *things* you, what's it like!'

'What, Miss Avery?'

'If she made it stand in her hands?'

Laughter, laughter; the laughter at. She remembers, drifting, the laughter at her again. There must still be time to cry out against it. She does. She might not have. But she tries to cry out against the laughing at her, for the first time mimicking her Frank not the other way round:

'Piss off!'

'Naughty, naughty, Miss Avery.'

'Please... piss off!'

'Well, poor Frank, that's all I can say if you've made up your mind with that man.'

'Have I ever starved him?'

'Never you mind, Frankie love.'

It must have been the woman Salem so far back in, now, the forever dimming past.

'Oh, Frank.'

She hears what she must have recently said forever dimming.

As her body seems to sink forever darkly, the mind of Miss Avery now drifts and remembers while it still can. It is happening as it probably must have. And she remembers where she just left off remembering:

'Oh... Frank.'

She croons in the warmlight streaming through the front door, forever fading now and beginning to chill as she moves forever after the light. The man Dere and the manchild Frank somewhere in the house behind her. She cannot cry out, only sigh with a warm and sad fulfillment. And croons again. And stiffens when, in the air, she forever remembers, the bronchial struggle and crockery being smashed.

'Oh, Frank. Please, no.'

'Yer get out of here! Mine, see. See?'

'You oughtn't go around smashing things, Frank. I know you're here.'

'Hate yer. Hate yer, see, fucken old bag.'

'Damn it, Frank.'

And seems like she is crooning forever now and sinking towards the forever blackness with such sorrow at what she is doing, had done.

'Now you're crying.'

'Not used to wine. And Frank with it.'

236

'Don't cry, Miss Avery. Sing him a song. Sing me a song. Sing us songs, my love. One of your lullabies.'

She did. She crooned again in the warmlight, again, streaming through to her from the front door she has just reopened. For the man Dere and for the manchild Frank somewhere in the dark folds of the house behind her. She heard the man Dere's sweetest thing:

'Miss Avery, listen. When I first saw you, in the morning, your hair was transparent white, blazed by the sun. No, don't cry. And when I moved I breathed in great drafts of you. And you stayed all quiet and secretive and smiling and I knew we had both come wanted to a wanting place at last. Remember?' Drifting and now forever sinking darkly towards a black hole, she remembers and remembers that she nodded.

'You shouldn't cry.'

'Don't be angry with me.'

'You shouldn't cry.'

'Frank's so unhappy!'

'No.'

She just has time to realise that her worst fears have happened at last and her mind drifts as she sinks forever darkly beneath what she cannot control.

Her voice had stopped its crooning. She could not seem to lullaby. She could not seem to nestle in the warm and dark folds of the streamlight through the opened front door moving away from her. She shivers and comes to know that there is only one way of getting into the warmlight again. Perhaps there is no way of getting into the warmlight again. She cannot croon now, yet her crooning forever seems to fill the air, to swamp upon, to immerse over the huge bellow of her little huge brother, his hunk-form, like

237

the sound perhaps, she lastly thinks, of the splintering of all the wood for all the boxes for all his bees. Then she hears the relief in her long and forever fading sigh, and finally with gratitude forever swells to surrender to it.

The whole of the operator's plans have been thrown out of kilter in a way that has stifled the few vestiges of 'nose' he hoped he had left. All the *wrongnesses* of all the too-amateur people have closed in and distorted the way it all should have been done. It is not that the operator has not foreseen the wrongnesses, but that he has been predetermined by them before he could make his *right* way work.

But the operator Sloane does not care if the man Dere is finally flushed out of his sheds or if the father the husband Youngstein unearths the holy war that he believes has made a victim of his little Selma. He does not care either whether he is paid or not paid, or attributed with the hunt or not attributed with the hunt.

The operator Sloane, however, cares very deeply that he has lost the instinctual impetus that is at the very core of his existence as an operator. And to be so brought so abruptly back to the field not so much by the bumblings of the *wrongnesses* but because of the something central that has happened that he does not know about.

The man Dere no longer mopes in the shed. The quarry has got up.

He could make the necessary two or three guesses where the man Dere might now be. But he does not want to make them, and doesn't. It is a point of honour with himself. A self rebuke. If you have lost the smell of the hunt, then, okay, stumble blindly on. The operator Sloane just cannot pretend that he even wants to think about the man Dere and the father Youngstein and the woman Avery and the manchild Frank.

He has only, now, a fury that he will vent. He will finish this. The

238

operator Sloane now has become only dangerous. And a bully.

He has returned the previous day from his second visit in two days to the sheds at the bottom of the property of Avery, where he has not found even the tracings of the food bowl of the man Dere. Whenupon he has told the wine merchant Youngstein over the phone that there will be no more pressure for any source because the man Dere has either gone from them physically or, worse, emotionally. Has not let the man Youngstein speak, but told him with a voice humming with menace that it will be ended one way or another. Then has hung up. He knows he need not hear the man Youngstein say that he is only a small fry in a sea full of friable small fry.

On the way to the hermit's cottage and to the house of Avery, the operator has dropped the wife of the man Dere at the railway station. He has not looked at the train schedule. He does not even know if the woman Dere can get back to the city from there. He has left her mechanically holding the money he has given her and driven off.

At the cottage of the hermit Emile Gascoigne, the operator has not found the hermit inside, but has tracked him down without much trouble hiding out by the boxthorn bushes behind the pines there.

He has taken the old man and has made a painful arrest of his arm, has not given any curacy that he once might have, when he had his timing in control, to the observation of how the old hermit can take the pain without making a murmur. He has led him along the path he has known is the path to the house of Avery. Nor finds it even curious that he need not push a lead after the first hundred or so metres, because the hermit Gascoigne has assumed and does direct himself to there; rather the operator applies greater pressure upon the old man's arm for presuming to know where he is being led.

And not for the first time does the operator Sloane have the submersive feeling of being on the perimeter of a revolving circle. He has to talk and it is the only thing that he does talk to the

239

hermit Emile Gascoigne before he deposits him back across the road from the house of Avery:

'Citizen, this time, I shall shoot you, citizen, if you move. I truly will. I want to know who and when and how and why and for how long.'

The hermit cannot say what he knows he could well say to the operator from the city, still dressed up suit-fine. The hermit lets the operator from the city deposit him across the road from Miss Avery's house and does not tell the other man that even he, the hermit, knows that there is the hindmost, yes, and it is full of the beast and that there are, too, always the eyes. Peeping and sniggering. Watching, waiting, prying. The eyes of the hindmost.

And as he approaches the house along the path, Sloane veers towards the front door almost before he fully appreciates that the front door is open and that it is an odd muffled sound from inside that has driven him across the wading pool of weeds to there. It seems to him at that one moment that perhaps all this has been done for the one benefit of that door being opened. That perhaps its opening, after the great eternity of struggle of his few days around here, had been hierolatrically (the word jars at him) ordained by way of audience applause for his lifelong performance. One can only try; and by that, and amazingly with that, the operator Sloane stands for a pause on the step of the front door there to adjust the cut and fall of his clothing and to almost comically polish the toes of his shoes on the back of an opposite leg.

The hermit Emile Gascoigne there watches and thinks perhaps the operator from the city has gone crazy. And it comes to him that he has the same feeling of watching as he did so many years ago, on his offshore islet looking back upon an auditorium of the main island land gone witch-huntingly insane.

Prepared, and not on his wildest dreams thought to be, the operator Sloane moves through the front door of the house of Avery and into the passageway there, mustfully and mightily so, of the house of Avery, and would not have thought, perhaps rightly, that there has been a moment passed between the time he has veered from the front path past the robber wasps at the beehives there and the now.

He takes a moment to adjust to the fauving light before he sees the movement of the two figures seemingly in struggle there. Down and in there. Bowelled within the house of Avery. His own lassitude fully on his mind, odd. Shakes his head and does see again the frocked person, perhaps, of the woman Miss Avery and does hear the cry of, perhaps, the manchild brother Frank, perhaps two women, perhaps disjointed. The one and the other for that moment perhaps fused atomically together. And then sees, at last, and hears, at last, the cry of pain from the emerging figure of the man Dere, deeper in there. His quarry where there is no fooling around anymore, brought to book, to be, without delicacy, now.

The operator Sloane, shoes polished and his suit hanging right, as is truly must dignifiedly be, goes for the man Dere then. Goes into the passageway then. Goes to reach for his gun then. And is met.

The hermit Emile Gascoigne hears the two cries that have been heard, too, by the operator Sloane. But the hermit Emile Gascoigne has not moved as the operator Sloane has moved. The hermit has stayed and waited and keeps watch there, watching a main island land go crazed and crazy.

It is the past come again. But he cannot nod that he always knew it would.

Chapter 7

The man Dere and the operator Sloane sit at the kitchen table. The breathing is solidly somnivorous in the dark, the hunnish dark of there. The curtain filters the light as late afternoon light. It could, in fact, be late afternoon, with a silence that, for this time, is vespertine.

They sit there beyond the cavernous opening of the passageway to the rooms, to the front door passageway. There is no light coming in from the passageway anymore. Not from any of the rooms. Not from the front door closed again. Only the screened rays around the kitchen curtains and those haloing the kitchen door. The two men are there as though they could be warmly in siesta.

The man Dere wakes up with a jolt. He recoils to his feet, as if springing to the alert was a direct reaction to waking up. He stands there facing the opening to the passageway, but doesn't hear what he is listening for. Looks back at Sloane by way of confirmation then moves carefully towards the passageway, where, from the side of the opening opposite the front door he tries to peer into the passageway up there.

From the other side of the passageway there is creaking. The man Dere steps back quickly, stands alert, stands defiantly until his limbs begin to tremor and until that it is not to come at him. Dares, then, to turn back to the table where he sits again, head in hands, as though he would go back to sleep.

There is no sleep, only the stillness that he has sat in for hours since it first began and since it first began to come for him. Only the ripeness of the buzzing, of the bees, of the humming, of the scratching down there in the passageway. Of knowing, like the hermit Emile Gascoigne outside, that it has finally come and of always knowing that it would.

The man Dere reaches over to the bloody towel and pads at the watery blood that seeps weakly from the wound across his right eye. He says for the first time of speaking of being there:

'Ah no. I'm not ready yet.'

Does not even have to wait against the darkness of the passageway now. He has come to know when there's a stirring. It is the towel which he looks carefully at when he takes it away from his eye. He has to tilt it towards the sepialight away from around the curtain to just make out the dark stains. Then chuckles, and feels so relieved doing so that he lets it roll into a laugh which grows indecent.

The man Dere has found that he can have the nerve to talk against it without it coming on. That it will come on when it comes on and no blowing his nose will alter that. This is, at least, something of himself, when he has never thought there would be anything left of himself when it finally caught up with him. All those waiting years.

He has never imagined it could really be cried out against. But now has laughed against it and feels the exhilaration of being himself despite it. And will talk, and will aggravate it, as it always, it seems, has aggravated him.

The son and the man together in the one person again. But not, this time, back on the black and secret night island moors where the father stealths. But in the hear-and-now, knowing that that is the here-and-now and unafraid to confront it with a son-and-a-man's voice. He extends the bloody towel, the blood of his stigmata on it, towards the darkness of the passageway:

'Here it is. You see? So, yes, you're right. It is me. You've come properly home, haven't you, Father? You see? We've leered at each other ... for how long? Skating along in front of me along the sheets of old brown lino. All those corridors of strange private places. The voices of them coming to get you whispering in the rooms, Father. In your eyes there was always those... quiet perversions. I have never had a job. I have never had a wife. I

244

never really had anything else but you, have I? I nearly had a child, but it was never a child. It was just dead and you again.'

The son and the man Dere suddenly screams at the darkness of the passageway and throws the towel towards there:

'FATHER!'

It half-shows itself then. The darkness of the passageway seems to swell like yeast, yet backs when the man Dere and the son Dere shouts at it:

'No, not yet!'

The son and the man Dere stares fiercely at the darkness until he knows that the danger has subsided for the moment. When his attention comes back to the table, there is, for the time again, only the man Dere himself and he looks across to the operator there.

'Wake up, Sloane, you lazy sod!'

Sloane seems to move in the vesperlight; it could be that he was trying to rally. The man Dere prods at him with a voice full of contempt:

'Sloane. Big man. Big operator. Here I am, Sloane, volunteering. You've got me. Here...' and has his hands chaliced for the handcuffs, 'take me in, Sloane. Shackle me.' But nothing, even though the operator seems to try to rally again. 'Sloane, Sloane, Sloane, you're all talk, Sloane. You've got a filthy, dirty tongue. I'm going to kill you, Sloane, for saying I did that... *thing* to that little girl.' And calls to the passageway again. 'Did you hear that, Father? Did you hear what he said I did? Me just as bad as you?'

The man Dere moves almost as imperceptibly as the operator Sloane across the table, but has in his hand the operator's gun. He moves it to be against the operator's skull. Where he holds it there with such a fierce grip that his hand begins to shake, and his muttered obscenities spit up incoherencies, before he lets his arm drop and his head to slump.

There is the humming quiet again. Only undefined sacred movements from inside the deep of the house of Avery.

The man Dere looks up again at the operator. There is self torment in his voice:

'Sloane, you shouldn't have said that. You lied when you said that. I never touched that little girl first.' Has stopped there, has himself to his feet and is around the table hissing sharply in the operator's ear so quickly that he is still speaking out of the same breath: 'Listen, Sloane, sometimes I think I might even have wanted to. Do you know? Ask my Father. He will know.'

Again, the operator Sloane seems to sway away from him in a revulsion against the intimacy, against what has been said in the intimacy. The man Dere straightens up as though he has been slapped in the face. The loathing he thinks he has seen filling him with a loathing for himself, for all the black hearts in him.

The operator Sloane seems to be laughing at him now.

The son and the man Dere are being laughed at now for all the black hearts in the one and the other combined again now in the one person as one. They, the son and the man, walk as one away from the jeering operator, through the streets of people shouting abuse and casting rocks outside the courthouse, outside the gaol, outside the farmhouse in which he, the son and the man, has been birthed and has been lived. There are the huge accusing crowds. There are the rightnesses of the citysuited Sloane coming in the island moors' night for the arrest and, behind, the whole crowds of the island people with their all-seeing eyes. Even the torment of the son is beneath contempt. The son wants to go towards them and say something. He does not know what he wants to say. The stones and the jeerings of abuse.

The little boy can only stop at the gate to the schoolyard, and silently cry for the man in him to come.

The son and the man Dere has not registered how long he has stood before the opening there to the passageway, to the other rooms, to the front door. The darkness only humming about his ears still.

He has stood and yet it has not come on, and he does not know why. Only that there is still only the watching of him.

He turns back to his seat at the kitchen table. As he moves there, he flips the gun that is still in his hand into a corner. It crashes to rest with an appalling loudness. He sits, then turns a disarmingly innocent smile towards the darkness of the passageway for having been so loud violating. The son is still upon him. But fading now, as the smile does. It is as though there has not been a discontinuity since he was at the operator's side, whispering of the things in his own black hearts. He can face now the seemingly-shifting form of the operator, motionless for the time:

'Yes, Sloane, you dummy, I ran over that little girl and I just kept going on and beyond. Because that was the easiest thing, you see. Sloane? You listen to me. I didn't lie to you, but I lied to Miss Avery, because that was more important, too. The easier. But, Sloane, what you did to the cat, that was the worse, Sloane. That was the cold-blooded murder, Sloane. So you can't jeer at me. And you can't jeer at me, Sloane, because...'

The man Dere reaches across the table and grabs the shoulder of the endless squirming, spitting, hating, screeching, killing, contemptuous and accusing and disheveled form of the man Sloane and does hold on for a moment, before he pushes and continues:

'... you're gone dead, Sloane.'

The, yes, body of the operator Sloane crashes muscle-bound to the floor of the kitchen of the house of Avery.

247

There are five heavy thumps upon the wall of the passageway and the man Dere has jerked alert to count each one. His breath coming in time with them and his eyes blinking in punctuation of them as he stares at the passageway to burst alive at him.

There is then the huge stentorious breathing that threatens to burst out of its horror. The man Dere waits lithically. He cannot adjust to the shock of each time. The worst is that he knows he is not ready as yet. But the breathing withdraws again and the man Dere starts to breathe more easily again. The exhilaration floods back at him, so that he has to share it aloud with the oncoming crowd:

'You all listening? The trouble is, nothing works full time, does it? But I tell you, really, I love all this. *Love* it!'

He pauses. He sweeps his arm impatiently across the weeping gash above his eye. It hurts and is sticky on the back of his wrist. There is an 'oh' of surprise from the oncoming crowd and the son quietens within it. They all would like to know what it is and how it could have got there. They wait sympathetic to the little boy, the son. He tries but there is only the puzzled sense of destination to speak for him and how he is come to be wounded. He says, with a wounded wisdom speaking amongst them all, through the man:

'Out of all of it has come this? Father, where are we? I am in the middle of... two things far away, two takings away. I am bleeding for you, Father.'

And the man Dere cries out from within the great weeping wound that the son within him has just given him. He bellows for the here-and-now:

'Miss Avery!'

Echoing, it seems. And the darkness of the passageway, exploding, it seems. Conjured and on with the coming crowd which does not believe in sympathy wounds. And the juddering presence within the passageway as he, then, shouts his filial defiance into it.

'Come on. COME ON!'

The waves rush at the hermit, the surf bucking at him again, kicking at the rocks of the low cliffs of his offshore islet. He smells again the saline of his beard; the saltwet of his beard in his mouth and the saline flurries of the wind whipping at his cold and half-clothed body there. Once again. Once again, lonely and coldshackled to his offshore islet, looking back at that main island land, the auditorium of the people there.

They have called him names with murder in their hearts, so the hermit sits again on his offshore islet and watches again what is going on with the witch-hunting crowds back on the main island land and does not interfere.

He thinks of the mussels he has yet to collect. He tastes the sea in his food again. He feels the bite of the dawn in his huddled joints again. He thinks of the old shack he huddled in. He can smell, taste, feel, touch, sense, summon again the offshore islet of his exile again. His eyes are as always on the main island cliffs across the road, across the strait. A boy is standing on those high cliffs and seems to be scanning the islet for him, the woman Jenny Salem visiting again now where the operator Sloane has visited and has not come out. The long moaning of the wind of the islet's nights; the police sirens that have come and taken him away.

It is all the same. It is the past that has come again.

The hermit Emile Gascoigne sees, and watches carefully as the woman Salem noses her car to breach the property of Miss Avery. The hermit sees the woman Salem set her shoulders back and then start in on into the property of Avery. The path, the detour around the beehives, the robber wasp perhaps, the porch.

And, as she goes to the door, the hermit watches as the woman

Jenny Salem automatically shakes out her hair with her fingers. He is merely watching, not to interfere. The tang of his offshore islet in his nostrils again as he watches the goings-on back on the main island land across the storm-water strait. Again.

The man Dere has heard the car, has heard, not seen, the approach. He does not look out past the curtains to see who it might be. There is no need for that.

The son and the man Dere has sat alerted and then moved quickly when he hears the 'yoo hoo'. He drags the body of the operator Sloane into the corner and drapes the sink curtain over the form. There in the darkness behind the cupboard of the past, the son of the rapist hides what must not be seen. Where was his father's shrine to the French nobleman mass child murderer. Where his father's rain coat semened and nail-ridged was; where his father's latex mask and gloves were. Where the semen stains and the blood groupings were. Must not be found. The son of the rapist now remembers the arrest in the sepia light of the room of his father. And the man Dere, finally, opens the door after the second knock and yoo hoo from the woman Salem outside.

While the son has been clearing, the man Dere has come to know that it is the woman Salem outside. And wants her in, for the son is hating his mother again for what she is doing, bringing the police to arrest his father.

When he opens the door and stands half-back, half-forward, the woman Jenny Salem does not show her surprise. She has become too used to the cut and thrust of men and women to be taken by surprise by any of the permutations possible. It is all potentially there somewhere. In the city or in the country. In the strip joints or Miss Avery's joint. You only have to scratch the surface. The woman Salem can smirk, and does.

Allan Dere grunts with anger at the reaction of the woman. The son and the man Dere kicks hard at her smug prejudging and lunges at her to drag her inside. In that instant she notices the bloody smear above his eye where she has seen the crust-forms those days earlier. But that is all. He has her inside and thrust against the door closed again. His breath driving at her and her eyes groping to adjust to the contused light. It has all happened so quickly. Then sees and looks at him coldly and the man Dere lets her go, as though the moment has passed when he need put any attention on her at all. Now he returns to sit at the table. Heavily at rest.

The man Dere is temporarily fatigued with the measures of the son Dere. It is just the Salem woman. What does it matter now? The people, like the figments of themselves, can come and go. The last woman was his wife, or perhaps just the figment of his wife Joan come and gone. There is Miss Avery. There was his wife. There was their own child.

The man Dere is remembering about his wife and has remembered about the dead foetus they have called his stillborn child and has remembered about Miss Avery and Frank and the pain, mostly of his own dead child never living, cleaves at him. It does not matter about the woman Salem.

Jenny Salem looks around. Even though she is in the strikingly muddled dark of this room of junk, she does not feel the panic of suffocation that she did last time she came to visit. This time is of her nurse's rounds and about the Frank's breathing exercises.

So she stands by the door, a woman apprehensive, yes, but not a woman in fright. Dark in there or not, she has the wild wasp's robbing equilibrium. You stand on your own feet and drive on in or don't go at all. She waits, however, for just a little while longer.

Outside, the self-exiled hermit, telescoping, at last safely and insulatedly, what is going on on the main island land; feels, too, that the woman Salem is moving into a situation best left alone. He knows the woman Salem will start right in.

251

Her eyes adjusted to the stricken light, the woman Salem, moral in having a valid reason for the visit, and tight-lipped, starts right in on the man Dere sitting there; feels no vibrations of a caducous situation; remains self-appointed.

'You.'

There is nothing in that to answer; even for the man Dere, not for this moment the son, there is no caring if the woman Salem comes or goes. She comes on:

'You want to draw those curtains or you'll sprout mushrooms in here.'

'Go away.'

'That's nice.' Cannot help the sarcasm. 'It's very nice, you being in here, too.'

Now she has adjusted her perspectives enough to discern the darker orifice beyond the kitchen over there, into the passageway. She can only presume afternoon naps for the little sister and the manchild and shatters the stillness by yoo-hooing to the woman Miss Avery again. There is an appalling silence to follow it. The man Dere has stiffened when she does so and fearfully searches with his eyes for any movement in the passageway and, when not overwhelmed, now turns on her. His voice in fierce threat ploughs at her.

'You call out again, before I am ready, and I'll break your neck.'

'Aren't we all cozy, then?'

'No.'

'Where is she?'

'Let me put it this way, lady. They've never poured a bucket of cold water over us, you and me, have they? Well, they've caught us finally in the position of climax. It is night on the island. Wet and *dripping.* On the moors, by the fences, when they're all asleep and you're whimpering but promising things into my ear like you are...'

And has to stop. He did not start out to say that.

Now she can see him cast about himself in confusion, his bearings lost, his thumb and forefinger on his temples in massage, the son coming back in with the man. Does think she can hear the stickiness above his eye squelching. It touches a nerve in her and she shudders:

'I'll come back.'

'I've locked the door.'

'Unlock it.'

'No.'

'I want some light in here!'

The man Dere looks up, raises an amused eyebrow at her. He cannot know the son is coming back upon him. The one, the other. The coming and going. It does not matter.

'Your palms are sweating. You've come to me in the dead of night. You know what you were looking for. Now you're worried. Did you ever think you might be wrong?'

'There's something going on in here.'

'Find it!'

Now the son and the man in the one person again is on his feet. He has a triumph in his voice. There will be as there was the first time they searched his father's room and had to go away, defeated. He can feel his father laughing at them, the fear but the triumph plinking his heart. The son and the man, too, laughs at the woman there, come and searching. Is she blind?

'Close your eyes, why don't you?'

'Not with a maniac like you around. Miss Avery?' But the call disturbs nothing that wasn't on anyway, and the son and the man Dere enjoyably brushes her voice aside like a fly he has slapped at.

'Close your eyes. One minute, that's all, and I'll unlock the door for you.'

'What for?'

His voice is low. The son's whisper in the dark. Sibilatingly:

'So we can watch you *secrete.'*

The eyes, the eyes.

'Don't you dare touch me, you… smart guy.'

'Then close your eyes and last a minute, bitch.'

Yes, smart guy she had said. She's seen them all; she's won them all. The female safaris of where she has truly come from and will never really leave. It's best to contempt at them:

'One minute, you bugger. But if you move, I'll decrutch you.'

Now the woman closes her eyes and counts aloud. Her own voice sounds obscene even to herself in the imaginaries culled up in there. The woman Salem doesn't register exactly how many seconds she has counted before she panics and has to open her eyes wide and peeling. The man Dere smiles knowingly and the son Dere giggles at her. The son and the man. She spits at them, even though she is feeling the shift of being scared:

'Cheap trick.'

'Haven't you twigged yet, bitch? You heard the breathing. It's here; oh, yes. You want to find the cupboard and my secrets? Then try to find Frank. Where's Miss Avery? You try to find me.' And has to struggle to avoid gagging on the image of it. 'It's here. Go on. Are you so dumb you can't find what you've come for?'

'Where's Miss Avery?'

'I destroyed her. Did I destroy her?'

The son now in hop scotch, confident and teasing.

'I want some light in here!'

Jenny Salem moves then from the door and towards the curtain. As she passes the son Dere he leaps at her and the man Dere holds her from behind, bending to whisper in her ear:

'You touch those curtains and I'll put your neck between my hands', before a sudden lassitude makes him let her go.

The antinodes again of dejection; the people that come and go, what does it matter? The woman Salem defiant, truly a proprietor:

'You a man. I've seen better on a stick. Bloody hell, you trot in here, knock the silly old bag silly with one big hairy look and she starts looking for the snakes in the apple trees. What are you both going to do with Frank? Put him in the fridge?'

'Frank... listen, Frank... *pumps.* '

'Poor old Frankie.'

Loudly, so that the little sister and the manchild brother in there will know she knows, and how you can reject the invasion of the man Dere. Then swings for the Christian martyr gesture she cannot control from out of the more dramatic pleasure of the strip belt world:

'Jesus, I've spat out better men than you.'

'Then do it again!'

He swings her around and forces her back upon the table. Holds her down with an unhurried surety that over-lasts her struggling and sensuates her. His body now between her legs, though she cannot remember how and his kiss, open mouth and sucking-huge, swollen in its contumescence. The woman Salem arches and submits with equal ferocity. Heaves at the man and prepares to sweetly possess him, when, shockingly, he lifts his head from hers, smirks to her as she did to him at the door, and then pushes himself off. And is crazily bowing after his performance towards the darkness of eyes in the passageway there. As though they actually existed.

The woman Salem struggles to regain her feet and hardly hesitates to slap at his face, him, the ridiculous little Miss Avery, the absurd manchild Frank, everything of this house. At least that is left to her:

'My God. You all ought to be put away in a cage!'

The man Dere cries out in fury. He grabs her and heaves her from the table; the son grabs at her, tweaks her flesh. The son and the man Dere hold and tweak and pull her up and around in front of him, when he frog marches her with dummying little jerks towards the doorway there to the passageway.

'Look there, lady. *Look.*'

The woman Salem ceases to struggle against him and makes out, at first, only a form. It seems large and phantasmagoric in the trophying light as if it was a diorama, more of the shadows. She sees then the frock form of the figure in there and cries out upon the woman Avery:

'Miss Avery!...'

Gets no further before a screwdriver is hurled by the figure at her, at them. The man Dere heaves her sideways as it hurtles past both their ears and crashes against the wall behind them. Now hears the high-pitched giggle of the son in her ear. She kicks at the son and the man Dere and screams to him and the passageway:

'You're all mad!'

Yet he will still not release her. Rather he thrusts her forward as a shield again against the mounting whispering filling the air. And the sisyphean hissing of strain from him, the son, the man in her ear:

'But this is what you came for, isn't it? To have fun with the specimens? Go on, there's Miss Avery, isn't it? *Laugh at the funny old smelly lady!'*

The woman Salem struggles, panic-stricken. She strikes out, she twists. She cannot notice that it is only making the frocked figure in the passageway more surging. But still the son and the man Dere is making huge his voice at her, around her, over her, to it:

'Laugh at the funny old dirty old stupid old lady and the funny loony brother and me! *Laugh!* And now meet my Father Miss Avery!'

Does plunge her towards and into the palpitating opening to the passageway so monstrously darkly there. She seems visible for an instant, then seems to shoot into silhouette, when she again seems to bounce bodily against the other form in there and, as strobelight, whinnies as she is struck at. Screams as she tries to ward off a blow.

The two silhouettes seem locked together for that time then seem to break apart by explosion. The woman Salem jettisons back out from the opening. She cannons against the table, but rolls around it, her right arm already hanging uselessly from its smashed shoulder. Does not register that the son and the man Dere did not lock the door as he said he had as she heaves the kitchen door open and bursts out into the largelight still left of the day.

The son and the man Dere has turned and dry-retched.

Years in deposit in his guts prove to be so dry and clawing. The son out of the man. The man out of the son. All the essences of his otherwise sweet father bursting into that heaving sadness. The make-ready.

The sonman Dere is dry-retching, is making-ready, is made ready. It can come now. It doesn't matter. The come and go of all the facts about and all the figments of and all the fantasies around. The sadnesses are not worth the cake. The pain remains lodged, cannot be spewed.

He is ready. For he has not turned to face the, now, moving shadow yeastily at his back and moving to him. Father, Mother.

The frock first. And then the grotesque arms. And then the grotesque legs. And then the grotesque arms and legs of the frock many sizes too small. And then the manchild moves out into the kitchen to stand alongside of the retching Allan Dere.

The frock of Miss Avery appallingly inadequate upon Frank and the hammer dangling lightly by his side. And he stands by the side of the man Dere as a moth gathers itself to light, warmed by the proximity which is enough, his puffy cheeks puffing immutably silent breathforms of:

'Geez, geez, geez…'

And an inchoate pain straining at his chubface.

Emile Gascoigne, in a freezing winter of watching, climbs off his salty islet rocks and, with his eyes fixed on the main island land, wades treaclishly across the strait dividing the islet and the island, across the road and up the aisle of the auditorium of the island people in such frenzied witch hunt, past the unknown boy standing on the cliffs looking back across to the self-exile islet of the hermit, towards the centre of the action where the crowds are swarming murderously around the uncovered rapist's farmhouse over there on the moors. Over there across the kitchen porch. On through the open door of the past.

He has seen the woman Salem run wounded and hysterical from the house of Miss Avery, has wondered about her uselessly swinging arm and has begun to walk towards the house almost simultaneously, certainly cosecantaneously.

Even as he steps the one step inside the kitchen of the house of Miss Avery, he sees, adjusting quickly after a lifetime of adjusting quickly to the seeing, Frank lewdly dressed in the little sister's frock standing by the man Dere, doubled over with retching, and gasps:

'Christ.'

'Fool!'

The man Allan Dere belches at him with a viciousness that will drive the hermit, finally, from the door that he has waited on for these years.

'Christ.'

Emile Gascoigne, the hermit, flees back to his ever-islet. Of himself.

'Mr Dere...?'

'What?'

'Pongs in here, Mr Dere.'

'We all pong, Frankie. Bouncing right off high heaven.'

'Mr Dere?'

'I know.'

'Ain't seen me beaut cat Friar, eh? Eh?'

'He'll be back.'

'Gotta fucken hole in me sock, Mr Dere. Miss Avery don't like me having...' The stop.

'I'm ready, Frank. Make boxes now.'

'Only bugger what can, ain't I, Mr Dere?'

'You are, Frank.'

'You ain't, see.'

'No.'

'It's my house, not yours, see.'

'Did I ever say it wasn't? I'm ready now.'

The giggle. 'Silly bugger Friar's only got one flamin' eye. See a beaut animal in Nuri-flamin'-oopta and it's me curl-a-mo Friar, betcha. Betcha. I'd go looking for bull ants and...'

The manchild sinks to his knees.

'Get up, Frank.'

The whimper. 'I ain't feeling the best, am I, Mr Dere?' The whine aloud. 'Want Miss Avery.' The outcry lacerate. *'Want Miss Avery.'*

The pause. The glass of water. The glass of water put to the brothersform hand. He drinks. Then does not drink. The stillness. The son and the man Dere bends over the manchild and the whisper above the manchild's whimper:

'So in the end, it's you, is it, Frank? I didn't hear Miss Avery cry out and that's a peculiar price to pay her for having me. I hope you didn't hurt her first.'

The manchild's fist about the glass tightens. Without perceivable effort, he crushes it in his grasp. It cracks. The son and the man prises Frank's bloody fingers apart.

'You don't have to do that, Frank.'

'Headache, Miss Avery. Headache, see.'

'We're not playing headaches, Frank.'

'Want Miss Avery!'

'She left you. She only wanted me. Miss Avery doesn't want you, but me, Frank.'

Now he is upon the manchild, Miss Avery, the Father. He is dragging them all to their feet at once. The son and the man Dere is now got in the passageway near the front door. He is holding up before him, as supplication to the manchild Frank, as a chalice of crystal grief, the bloody and hammered body of the little and broodlike sister. Has torn her from her dark forever place and is holding the little sister up before Frank, the brother, Father and beast. Chalicing her.

'You ask Miss Avery, dummy! Not you. Look, she and me...'

He pulls her close. He rocks fornications with and against her. He lewds at the manchild with the little sister. The innocents. The boys and girls. He bangs at her and bangs out:

'... Idiot, Miss Avery and me. *Rooty-roots!'*

Frank, the manchild, roars. The son and man Dere shouts to him to come on, now, come on, it's ready, it's now.

Then Frank comes on. The son and man together in the one person tries to hold for the coming. But the manchild is huge, is mountainously frightening, is the final bestiality. The son and man instinctively tries to jerk his head away from the blow of the hammer and screams.

The son and man Dere tries to run then. Blood sweeps from the gaping wound that is torn diagonally across his forehead above his eye. Exactly across the already line. Stigmata. The great wave's cleansing wash as the son of the rapist tries to run from the crowd in total surge for him now. With his now eyes of inner thrill.

The hit-and-run.

But falls in the path of the manchild before he can reach the door.

The thought. The boy, the son of the rapist's thought. They told him his father dressed in a woman's clothes. But it was his father, his father's scar. How could his father really do that?

Alone with her now, Frank stands over and whimpers down at the sparrowform of the little broodlike sister. After a while, he knows there must be something done. So nudges her at first delicately with his foot Once, twice, then with growing familiarity;

'Miss Avery? C'arn. C'arn, Miss Avery. C'arn...'

---oOo---

262